Tomorrow Doesn't Matter Tonight

by

Debra Jupe

Tomorrow Doesn't Matter Tonight

Cover Art by *Diana Carlile*

The Wild Rose Press, Inc.
PO Box 708
Adams Basin, NY 14410-0708
Visit us at www.thewildrosepress.com

Publishing History
First Crimson Rose Edition, 2014
Print ISBN 978-1-62830-487-9
Digital ISBN 978-1-62830-488-6

Published in the United States of America

"I have a dumb question." He glanced at her. "Why did you bring the knife with you tonight? What's your motive?"

Katie stopped in mid-bite. "I don't have a motive. I'm confused how to handle this. I thought you might give me some advice."

He shrugged. "Report the break in and turn it over to the police would seem the logical way to go."

"Logical? I want to stay far away from the police right now. They may somehow link this to Hazel's murder. "

"Avoiding them doesn't solve your problem. If you're so nervous about talking with them, take counsel with you."

She slammed her utensil onto the table and glared across at him. "Will you knock off the lawyer bit, legal boy? I got it. I'll get an attorney, but right now I need some reassurance from you."

Jack sat back in his chair and said through clenched teeth, "A little louder, please. The kitchen staff didn't hear the last part."

"Huh?"

He leaned forward and whispered, "You're yelling really loud. The whole place is staring at us."

Katie glanced around. She'd raised her voice too high, and the entire restaurant watched them. She smiled timidly and spoke to the crowd.

"Communication exercises. We're in couple's therapy."

"Aaahhh's" floated through the room and heads bobbed as the patrons returned to their meals.

Jack stabbed his meat. "Nice save."

Dedication

For all the laughter and joy,
I dedicate this book to my precious son, Stephen.
I'm honored God chose me to be your Mom.
Love you, baby.

Chapter 1

Jackson Pharrell jogged down a mile long driveway, zigzagging amid hundred-year-old live oaks and elms while careful to dodge the fresh pansies landscapers had planted the day before. Normally, he didn't care about flowers, but his host would be peeved if he smashed their new, expensive yard deco with his size twelve running shoe.

He continued to trek across the yard, rounded a bend, glancing at the tail ends of a shiny Bentley, Jag, and Lexus displayed in the opened three-car garage. He mentally shook his head. These people didn't know how lucky they were.

He sprinted to the end of the drive. Running in place, he pressed a button located on a squared, red-brick column located next to the drive's exit. An automatic transmitter rumbled as a wrought iron gate shook, trundling open, leading out into a neighborhood full of gorgeous, older homes with gracious, manicured lawns, but only visible from behind steel rods.

Outside the gird, he picked up his pace, his head held erect. Leaves crunched under his shoes as the crisp fall air whipped across his face. Smoke flowed from a nearby chimney, melding in the breeze.

Jack did his best to relax, glad to get a run in before his day started.

Thoughts cleared, he concentrated on exhaling

each time his right foot struck the sidewalk. He'd been skipping his regular workouts, although he still enjoyed a brisk jog every day. His mind emptied and his problems evaporated. Speed increased, his breathing deepened, perspiration flowed through his pores. He pushed his body harder, further.

Skirting the corner, he entered a less exclusive area. Nice homes, but smaller, without the privacy fences or gates guarding the entrances. He glided down the block, euphoric from the momentary freedom.

A furry, flash of gray darted in front of him. The toe of his shoe caught on a crack in the walkway. Jack briefly became airborne before he toppled flat onto his back into someone's yard.

In what seemed like slow motion, he pushed to a sitting position, shaking his head with a groan. Once the fog cleared from his brain, he twisted around, and spotted a huge, gray cat. The feline sat hunched across the lawn and glared at him, its yellow eyes taunting. Jack swore it laughed at him.

Struggling to his feet, he slid his palms over his pants and jerked. His right hand stung. He turned it over. A small spurt of blood seeped below the base of his fingers. He gagged a bit and delicately brushed the gash against his sweats when something odd on the concrete caught his eye. Tiny drops of red dotted the sidewalk.

What the—he glanced at his nick. His wound wasn't serious enough to drip this much blood. He knelt to examine the specks. Some of the spots were in the shape of a paw. His gaze lifted to the cat. It sat in the same place, now cleaning a crimson stained mitt. The animal was hurt. He straightened and took off across the grassy slope. The feline sensed him coming its way, scurried through a fence, and dashed under a bunch of shrubs.

Damn. Jack's only other recourse was to speak with the owner. He started for the front of the house when he detected more blood sprinkled over the walkway leading to the entrance. The door was left ajar. He slid to a standstill, his frame stiffened. His gaze traveled down as if drawn to the ground. Shivers prickled upon the back of his neck.

A bright pink slipper with a fuzzy ball on top rested between the door and structure. A foot was inside the shoe.

Careful not to touch anything, he crept nearer the shod foot for a closer look. His stomach coiled. A woman's body, unnaturally twisted, blood covered her upper torso and face and had splattered over the small entryway. He stumbled backward, before catching himself before he fell. After he regained his balance, he advanced forward to check on her again. She lay motionless. Her eyes were open but lifeless. Her chest was still, no signs of breathing.

This woman was dead.

****

Jack leaned a shoulder against a railed fence. Wind gusts bashed a cluster of bare limbs above him as gray clouds shrouded the early November sky and added an extra sinister touch to the already eerie setting.

Arms folded, his legs crossed at the ankles, he was careful not to glance in the direction of the grisly site again. He swallowed repeatedly in an attempt to silent his rolling stomach, but the scent of blood and death lingered, keeping his gut in a constant vortex.

It didn't help that the commotion around him had metamorphosed into total chaos. Lights flickered from the tops of emergency vehicles. Law enforcement agents, crime scene investigators, and a medical team moved about taping off the area, taking photos, and collecting evidence. Although the morning air had turned chillier, the cold didn't stop a crowd from gathering behind the yellow strip to gawk at the investigation.

Jack vaguely scanned the mass of oglers, hoping to get far away from this circus sometime in the near future. For the past several hours, a young police officer grilled him to the point that he wished he'd reported the death anonymous.

The squeal of tires halted the interview. A compact skidded to a stop on the opposite side of the street. Doors slammed. Two women emerged from the vehicle. They elbowed through the onlookers, ducked under the crime tape, and hurried up the driveway.

One was tall. Her height was enhanced by elevated shoes with heels that resembled pointed spikes and could be considered lethal. Her suit gave the impression she'd spray painted it over her perfect form. Silky, darkened tresses bounced onto her slender shoulders, cool indigo eyes surveyed the commotion as she sashayed across the concrete like a runway model. Several of the younger policeman guarding the home's perimeter, stopped what they were doing and followed her graceful strides. Jack also found it difficult to tear his gaze away. But he did. She was an attractive woman, but her demeanor reminded him too much of— he shook his head to erase the memory.

He eyed the other. A total contrast to the brunette.

Dull, blondish hair pulled back with sparkly, hair thingies, haphazardly clipped to the top of her head. Sensible flat shoes covered her feet, her eyes hid behind brown-framed square glasses. Her expression remained calm, her robust shape almost hidden behind an ankle length, khaki coat. She walked toward the frenzied spectacle in a bland manner. A corner of his mouth lifted. If Jack been a betting man, he'd guess she was the smart one.

The cop who'd been questioning him stepped away as the two woman approached. He snapped up a palm and spoke in a stern voice. "This is a crime scene. I'm going to have to ask you to leave."

Both women's mouths fell open.

Hands flew to Curvy's cheeks. "My God, what happened?"

"Is someone hurt?" Plain Lady rose onto her tiptoes and leaned sideways for a better view.

"I'm not at liberty to say," replied the officer in the same firm tone.

"We work for the woman who lives here, and we've been calling her since early this morning." Plain Lady's intonation rose to a high, nervous squeak. "We came to check on her."

The policeman motioned to the street and spoke with rigid authority. "This is an official investigation. You need to leave. Now." The ladies stole a hasty glimpse at Jack before they reluctantly turned around. The officer rotated back to him.

"You're free to go too, Mr. Pharrell." He held up a small notepad. "We have your information. We'll be in touch."

Thank God. No disrespect to the departed, but he'd

had enough of carnage for one day. Jack hitched his chin in acknowledgement toward the policeman catching an inadvertent glimpse of the marred corpse. Another icy nip of air blew through him.

Make that forever.

He pushed from the gate to follow the women off the property.

Plain Lady glanced over her shoulder. "You seem familiar. How are you involved?"

"I live a few blocks from here. I discovered the body while on a morning run."

The women came to an abrupt halt. Jack stopped too so as not to plow into them.

Curvy turned to stare at him. The color drained from her face. "Body?"

He gestured toward the house. "Someone is dead inside."

A new vehicle pulled to the curb and stopped. "Medical Examiner" printed in large letters was displayed on the side door. A sizeable, elder gentleman emerged from the sedan and pushed through the crowd. He picked up the tape and with some difficulty bent to move underneath.

The bottom of the man's shoes scraped against the concrete as he climbed the steep drive with obvious strain. He ignored Jack's group, ambled past the detectives circling the crime scene, and headed straight to where the deceased lay.

Curvy released a cry and covered her mouth with her fingers while the other looked as if someone slapped her. Neither seemed able to speak.

Curvy found her voice first. "Did they tell you who…who was killed?"

"Surprisingly, they weren't much on giving me information inasmuch as asking me a bunch of questions." He shoved his hands into his sweatpants pockets, and twisted to glance at the house before he returned to them, ready to say adios.

"Like I said, we work for the lady who lives here. I'm her assistant Tara Olifant." Plain Lady gestured at Curvy, who appeared to be in shock. "This is Vanessa King."

He raked a quick glance over Vanessa. She acted distraught, but Jack's instincts told him her distress wasn't from the possible death of her boss. Her worry seemed more personal.

"As I explained to the officer," Tara continued, "she hasn't answered her cell or her home phone this morning, which is unlike her. We've been worried, so we drove here to make sure she's okay."

Vanessa stared at Jack. "Was the person a woman?"

He nodded.

They gasped. Hugging her middle, Vanessa spun to Tara and almost whispered. "That could be Hazel."

Jack raised a brow. "Who?" His preference was to not get any more involved, though it didn't dissuade his curiosity about who the dead person might be.

"Hazel Nutt, our employer." Tara checked her watch.

He stifled a chuckle. "Hazel Nutt." he repeated, still holding in a laugh. "Are you serious? That's her real name?"

"She owns the most elegant party planning agency in the city. I'm her top consultant." Vanessa bit her bottom lip, and skimmed the area. Her eyes watered.

"Or was."

"Hazel lives alone," Tara explained. "I hate to hear anyone's dead, especially in such a brutal fashion, I'm hoping against all odds it's not her."

"Could you tell what happened?" Vanessa asked him.

"By the looks things, I'm guessing someone assisted in her demise." Their faces went blank. "She was murdered." Jack didn't know why he bothered. He was more than ready to forgo the rest of this conversation since he had a possible name of the casualty.

"I'm so not wanting this to be her." Tara turned and scowled at her partner. "But who else could it be? Hazel's not answering her phone. For years she's been estranged from the few relatives she has, and she never mixes with associates. She doesn't have real friends. No one would be at her house except consultants, and they're all accounted for."

Vanessa's eyes narrowed and frowned at Tara. "Hazel is a wonderful person. She isn't close to anybody because she puts her company first. Everyone is jealous of her success, and her family members are nothing but selfish jerks."

"Anyone who's dealt with Hazel as an employee, vender, or her competition is aware she's not a nice person. Her distance from her daughter and sister is her own doing."

Vanessa squared her shoulders. "She's taught me more about business—"

"Now isn't the best time to have this conversation." Tara interrupted. She pointed at the detectives. "The police are right over there. We don't want to draw their attention by arguing."

Both glanced in the direction of the law enforcement agents before they returned to Jack who'd taken several steps backward, ready to make his getaway.

"Wait." Tara flung out a hand. "Can you tell us anything else? Did the police give you a hint as to who might have done this?"

He shook his head. "No clue." He did a half turn. "If you will excuse me…"

Vanessa placed a palm on his arm. "Don't leave just yet." She batted her eyelashes. "You said you live around here?"

He studied this new composed air. Her concerned manner transformed into flirty. A seductive smile played at her pouty lips. This woman just performed the quickest remorse recovery Jack had ever witnessed.

"Several blocks over," he answered. "My place is on River Ridge."

She took a step closer to him. Jack swore dollar signs flashed in the woman's irises. "You haven't introduced yourself." Her voice converted to a husky tone. Full of temptation.

He almost smiled. If she only knew he stayed in the exclusive area as a guest and didn't have anything tangible of his own, she'd probably stomp on his toe with a spikey heel and leave him to asphyxiate in a veil of her stifling perfume.

Tara shook a finger at him. "Wait a minute."

A lump welled and lodged in his throat. Here it comes. This unwanted recognition had become old, fast. The horrible stares, the invasive remarks, and the rest of the humiliating shit that went with a stupid act performed in front of an entire city. He'd love to leave the state or move to someplace where he could maintain anonymity. But the luxury of disappearing escaped him.

"You're Jack Pharrell. We went—."

"I'd rather not discuss my personal issues," Jack interjected. "Let the past be."

Tara dropped her hand. "You went to Allytown High. I did too. You were ahead of me by a couple grades, but we worked on the yearbook committee together my sophomore year."

Jack leaned closer and nodded, though, he had no clue to who she was. He'd graduated fifteen years ago. He'd moved on and gotten a life. And lost it.

"Right. I remember." He lied.

Vanessa's cool palm remained on his arm. "I'm more about the present too."

Tara cleared her throat and glanced at her watch again. "Vanessa. The wedding rehearsal is in several hours, and we need to stop by the office before we head over to the chapel. We're already late. We should go now."

If he hadn't been observing her, Jack would have missed the brief guise irritation flash across Vanessa's face before her expression rapidly morphed back to normal.

She eyed Tara. "You can leave. I need to stay until they tell us who this is." She blinked and wiped away an invisible tear. "It doesn't look good that Hazel's not around."

Jack suppressed his grin from Tara's eye roll response.

"I'd like to find out if this is Hazel too, but we do have responsibilities to our client." Tara glanced at the investigation. Her skin whitened again. "This situation makes me dizzy. I can't breathe when I let myself think about what might have happened to her."

"Just a few more minutes, please. I have to know. If you need something to do, I could use a coffee to calm my nerves." Vanessa rubbed her sleeved arms. "There's a cafe a couple of blocks over. Why don't you get us one while we wait?"

"Fine." Tara voice held a hint of anger. "I'm assuming you want your usual?"

"Caffe´ Latte, of course." Vanessa turned to Jack, the corners of her lips lifted. "Would you like something?"

Jack shook his head. "Thanks, but I left my wallet at home."

"My treat?"

"I'm good. The police are through with me. I'm going to finish my run."

Soft fingertips grazed across his arm one more time before she dropped her hand, and slid her fingers into her jacket pocket to remove a business card. She flicked it at Jack. "In case you're ever in need of my services. I'm the best—wedding coordinator in the city."

A cool, hard smile touched his lips. "I don't plan on needing assistance concerning marriage any time soon."

She picked up his hand and pressed the card into his palm. "You might find you need my skills in some other capacity."

"You're kidding me," Tara groaned.

Vanessa opened her mouth, but an odd recurring squeak from behind had the trio return their attention to the investigation. The medical personal wheeled the stretcher from inside the house. A covered lump lay over the top. A body bag.

Jack didn't know the person under the tarp, but seeing the gurney guided out by a hoard of authorities was nothing short of surreal.

The police officer who'd interviewed him earlier walked to the group and addressed the women, though he centered on Vanessa. "Excuse me. Did you ladies say you worked for the owner of this house?"

They murmured a simultaneous yes.

"We need the body identified. We'd like one of you to look and tell us if this is your boss." He hesitated. "A warning though. It's a pretty gruesome sight."

"How did," Vanessa choked, "the victim die?"

"Stabbed in the back multiple times. Looks like with a smaller knife. Marks are in a six inch cluster."

Tara's expression was grim. She stared at the officer. "Do you think this might have been a robbery or—something else?"

"I can't tell you much more. Preliminaries show very little inside disturbed to be a break-in. There will be a thorough search after the coroner's office removes the deceased, but if I had to guess, I'd venture some foul play was involved." The policeman raised his brow at Vanessa and pointed toward the group. "Would you come with me to view the remains, please?"

Vanessa nodded, fluttering her eyelashes at the officer. She took the cop's arm as he escorted her up the walkway.

Her demeanor changed again. Now she appeared almost helpless. Together they walked to where the corpse lay.

The officer motioned for a medical team member to unzip the bag.

As ordered, he opened the carrier and lifted the upper side. Vanessa's exterior was poised, as if seeing dead people were the norm for her. She stepped closer. She leaned over the bloody cadaver, and then straightened with a solemn nod.

Tara gaped at Vanessa, who continued to speak with a detective. The cop seemed listen to her closely. He bobbed his head while he took notes.

Jack turned to observe some new commotion across the street. He released an internal moan. Several news vans and an animal control vehicle had shown up. Film crews crawled from the automobiles and set up to shoot the grisly scene. The animal people removed traps. The bloody pawed cat may contain DNA or give the authorities other clues.

Either way, time to disappear. He pivoted and took two steps.

"Oh, Katherine," Tara murmured.

He paused and twisted toward her. "Did you say something?"

"Katherine. Hazel's top consultant. At least she was until yesterday."

"What happened yesterday?"

"Hazel fired her. She worked for Weddings Fantastic for a long time." She indicated at Vanessa. "Those two became instant bitter enemies the second Hazel hired her on. The police will want to speak with Katherine once they're done with Vanessa."

Jack spun in Vanessa's direction. Her animated movements indicated her eagerness to give the detective an earful.

Tara brushed away a tear. "Vanessa hates Katie. She'll make sure her name is at the top of list of people to speak with."

Chapter 2

Jack rounded the corner to his friend's home and re-followed the pristine, tree lined path to the two room guesthouse where he'd resided the past week and a half.

What a day. Discovering a dead person—especially a murdered one, wasn't on his to do list—ever. The dead woman's employees kept him from making a quick getaway, and the news media bombarded him when he finally did get to leave. Reporters shoved microphones in his face, peppering him with questions from every direction. He hadn't intended on finishing his jog yelling "no comment" over his shoulder.

Nope. His entire weekend plans consisted of buying a lot of beer and drinking a lot of beer. With a case under each arm, he shouldered the door open, eager to get started.

Glad his stomach settled after the sight of way too much blood, he placed his purchases on the counter, and then strolled to the pantry. After he inserted two pastries into the toaster, he unloaded the boxes into the near-empty refrigerator.

Brunch was heating. He walked into the adjoined living area with his drink in hand, ready to get comfortable in the leather recliner. He folded his newspaper so the crossword faced outward and stretched across the coffee table for the remote. An anxious a rap came from the front. He stopped in mid-reach and whirled in the direction of the knock.

Who the hell would show up now? He squinted toward the entrance and frowned. Who'd visit him period?

A woman stood under the overhang. Although unable to make out her features, the dim light from the early afternoon sun revealed a thick, auburn mane.

He sensed her gaze on him. He tossed his hair off his forehead and lumbered to the entryway. Uneasy honey eyes peered inside, confirmed his suspicions. He wished whoever designed this place had used wood instead of the lead glass panes around the doorway. The exposure invaded his diminutive private space.

A faint snap of his toaster popped from the kitchen. The aroma of fruited pastry filled the room. He disregarded his meal and progressed in the direction of the woman. Spinning the knob, he opened the door, inviting a blast of cool air inside.

Delicate sunlight haloed her face. "Jack?" Her expression displayed astonishment.

He didn't respond. His palm rested onto the entrance's edge as he struggled to attain some recognition. She obviously knew him, though he had no idea who this lovely lady was.

She put a hand directly below her neck and double patted the top of her chest. "It me, Jack. Katherine Drapier. Aaron's sister, remember?"

Jack took two steps back, clutching the jam to keep from losing his balance.

He was sure his mouth plunged to the ground as he gawked at the tall, slender woman. She wore faded, but expensive looking jeans that tapered down her long legs. Wavy, chestnut hair flowed over her shoulders, shimmering from the sun's muted glow. The only feature that resembled the girl he once knew was the golden gaze staring back at him.

"Shit," he mumbled. Double shit. He'd said that out loud. What the hell was she doing here?

She thrust her hands into a short, suede jacket. She either ignored his blunder or she didn't hear him, as she peeked around the corner. "I thought Aaron might be here."

Jack pointed to the main residence. "Your brother lives in that monster size spread with all the luxuries." He cerebrally kicked himself for his second lack of filter within the matter of moments.

Again, she let his flippantness pass. "Aaron told me he wanted to do some renovations in the guesthouse over the weekend, so I thought he might be around."

"Change of plans." Jack's lips turned upward. "I showed up."

She returned his smile with an uneasy one and remained at the threshold.

Jack sighed softly. Though she presented a lovely picture, the death screwed his morning up, and he preferred the same thing not to happen with his afternoon. He intended to stick to his schedule. Besides, no matter how attractive she'd turn out to be, she'd forever be the annoying sibling of his closest, childhood friend.

But because he was a guest in her brother's place, he had no choice except to extend an invite. Reluctantly, he stood back and waved a hand. She hesitated for an instant, then nodded, and walked into his temporary residence.

She twirled to face him with another nervous smile.

"I'm sorry for being a bother. I need to speak with my brother." Her voice sounded cool, laced with a southern drawl, huskier than he remembered. "Do you know where he is?"

"I don't." Jack ran his palm over the back of his neck. Stiffness settled in after today's incident. Added with the crap he'd endured over the past several months, his tension gage was sky high. "You can always call him."

"I did. Dozens of times. He won't pick up." She trekked across the tiles, her boot's heels ricocheted a delicate tap against the floors as she scanned the small space.

Completed crosswords and folders littered the room, used pizza boxes, and empty beer bottles were scattered in abundance. Her tight expression tried to hide her disgust. Jack's lips twitched as he scrubbed a hand over his unshaven jaw.

Okay, he wasn't the neatest housekeeper. Must she look so appalled?

"It's been a long time," Jack said trying to divert her attention away from his living conditions. "The last we spoke was when..." She snapped a frosty glare toward him, her body visibly tensed. A tiny, buried memory churned from deep within his sub-consciousness. He mentally paused to process the recollection and perceptually recoiled. Didn't want to go there. He smiled. "Can't remember, but it's been a while."

Her frame relaxed as she wandered into the small kitchenette. She turned a pert nose in the air, and sniffed. "Smells like you're burning fruit." She glanced at the boxes sitting on the counter and raised her brows at him. "Two cases of beer? Really?"

Jack smiled lazily. "You see a lot of beer. I see a Friday night."

"What's the point? Imbibe until you forget your name?"

"Down enough to forget everything."

"Well, at least there's a goal in mind," she said dryly.

"Keep an eye on the objective. That's my motto."

Her look skated across his disheveled form without a hint of emotion. "I hear you've gone through a bad time." Her poised gaze lowered to the opened bottle in his hand. "I'm assuming your recent downfall coincides with your efforts to lose consciousness. You haven't hit rock bottom, have you, Jack?"

"Me? On the skids?" Jack released a bitter laugh. "No. I like to think of myself in a transitional phase." He lifted his shoulders in an exaggerated shrug. "So what if I'm sponging off my old school friend while I try not to drown in life."

Katie's stare dropped further, her expression uncomfortable. "Mom's kept me up to date, and of course your name's been in the media, too. Really, how've you been since—everything?"

"Couldn't be better." He smiled, though his voice sounded cynical.

Katie stole another glimpse at the string of empty beer bottles strewn around the room before returning a tawny stare to study him. Pity. Jack had seen the look before. God, he hated it when they felt sorry for him. Now she really needed to go.

"I understand things are difficult for you, Jack."

"Difficult?" His eyes narrowed as his chest rose

and fell in a rapid pace. "Difficult hardly sums up my circumstances. My reputation is damaged forever."

"Isn't what happened to you kind of your fault?" she suggested timidly.

To-fucking-uché. She had to go there. "Thank-you for reminding me how I screwed up my life."

She heaved a deep breath and softened her tone. "What happened to you is—unfortunate. Regardless, you'll find employment elsewhere."

Gulping hard, he turned away. He inhaled then exhaled. He shouldn't take his frustrations out on her. Katie had nothing to do with his situation. Like she said, his whole fucking nightmare was his doing. However, he preferred not to think about it nor did he want to draw attention to his personal shit again. What he did want was to expel her from the premises ASAP.

He rotated to her and spoke in a calmer manner, "I found another job. I'm going to work for your brother's security company. Though it's not exactly the caliber of vocation I'm accustomed to, I am grateful for the opportunity."

"Lucky for you." She folded her arms around her middle. "Finding something so quick is rare. I just lost my job too. I don't have anything at the moment."

Jack's chin dropped to his chest. He shoved his hands into his pockets.

"True, I'm fortunate. But nothing happened fast. My law firm put me on unpaid suspension, and I've been in limbo for four months now. And because of the negative publicity, no one would talk to me much less hire me. Even McDonald's wouldn't return my calls. I'm sorry for whatever you're going through, but I refuse to engage in a pissing contest to figure out which of us is in the worse shape."

What was she worried about, anyway? Her parents were loaded. They wouldn't allow their little darling to suffer financially or in any other way.

"Nothing's changed, has it?" She paced the short path between the kitchen and living room. "It's constantly you and your troubles, never any regard for anyone else's problems. Seriously, Jack, you need to grow up."

He didn't even stop to wonder about her outburst. She'd remained arrogant as ever, which is why he'd always done his best to avoid her. How this woman and his good friend came from the same parents was beyond him. Nevertheless, he refused to continue with this argument. They could go on all afternoon, but he'd preferred not to. She'd never concede defeat.

Besides, he'd scheduled his day, and damned if he'd let her ruin it.

Jack jerked his gaze away from her, no longer in any mood for her, even if she were a faux family member. "Sorry, I've yet to reach your level of maturity. On a brighter note, you grew up nicely. You're not the Katie Drapier who out-caught, out-threw, and outran every boy in the county."

She froze. "You realize I haven't gone by Katie since school, right? It's Katherine now, thank-you."

"Give me a break, Katie—excuse me, Katherine. I've been away for what, fourteen years. When I left, you were Katie Drapier, Allytown High School all-star softball pitcher, and if I remember right, you thought the name Katherine sounded proper and didn't work for a ballplayer. Too girly, is how I believe you spouted off to your mama. And so you're aware, I've been dealing with my own crap and haven't had time to sit around and worry about what name you went by nowadays."

Katie bit her bottom lip and stared at him. Her eyes dampened.

Oh shit. Tears. Crying shouldn't be an option. He wasn't good with waterworks, and he couldn't deal with any sort of weeping now. He jammed his hands in his pockets, wanting to disappear.

"I'm sorry, Katie, I mean Katherine." He lifted a shoulder. "My attitude's sucked for months."

She awarded his apology with a weak smile, swept away a tear, and sniffed.

"I'm the one who should apologize, Jack. I just barged in here, ragging on you when I had no right. This is the first time we've seen each other in a while. Please forgive me. I'm a little upset."

A little upset. Right. Jack massaged the back of his neck again. Still, he should be friendlier. For no other reason than respect for his friend, who gave him a job when no one else would and allowed him crash in his guesthouse, rent free.

She resumed roaming. "I didn't realize you were back in town."

"I avoided announcing my arrival for obvious reasons." Okay, done with the niceties. He'd already told her everything he knew, and she was disrupting his afternoon. Time for her to vacate. He inched toward the door and extended a hand to the knob. "Look, I have no clue where Aaron is, but I'll tell him to call you."

She stopped and spun to him. The calmness on her face altered into anguish, her cool disposition clearly ready to snap. Her golden eyes welled once more. "I gave the woman the best years of my professional career. My reputation is impeccable, despite her behavior. Clients seek her company out to coordinate their weddings because of me."

"What?" Jack shook his head in an effort to comprehend her explosion.

"That bitch Vanessa had her nose up Hazel's butt since day one, finally got her to do it."

He hurried to the fridge, pulled out a bottle of water, and held it up. She paused a moment before she offered a slight nod and a trembling smile.

"Do what?" He took a step toward her.

"Fire me." Her voice cracked. "My boss let me go. That bitch Vanessa's been after my job from the moment Hazel brought her on, and yesterday she succeeded. Hazel informed me my services were no longer needed."

"Hazel? The bitch Vanessa?" Jack stopped in midstride and stared at her.

"Hazel Nutt is my—was my boss." Her vocal cords vibrated. "Vanessa is another wedding consultant who works for her."

Hazel, Vanessa, Katherine, Nutt. *Oh shit.* Katie. Katherine was the fired employee of the deceased woman he found this morning, and she obviously hadn't heard the news. How would he tell someone he never cared for, her boss was dead?

Or could he just be a jerk and let her find out on her own?

He inhaled deep and motioned for her to sit. She swept a glimpse over the room and walked to the sofa, which surprisingly was void of clutter. He placed the water bottle on an end table and fell into his recliner.

She picked up the drink to take a dainty sip.

23

Jack sighed again. "Katie, um Katherine." His eyes met hers. He scooted out of his chair and relocated to the couch to sit next to her. "I have something to tell you, and it's not good."

She stiffened. "Nothing's happened to Aaron or my parents?"

He shook his head. "No, your family is fine." He leaned for his opened bottle, lifted his beer, and held it out to her. "You're going to need this."

She didn't move.

He picked up her hand, shoved the drink between her fingers, and put his hand over hers to hold the bottle in place. He positioned a palm onto her shoulder to give her a reassuring squeeze, and then let it slide to the cushion. He cleared his throat. "Hazel Nutt, your former boss, is dead." He paused. "She's been murdered."

Katie shot off the sofa, sloshing the beer onto her shirt. She ignored the wetness and choked. "What?"

"Someone killed Hazel Nutt."

She stared at him as she gradually lowered to the couch. After a long drink, she fumbled to replace the bottle on the table. "How? How did some—," her lilt quivered.

"Stabbed." He stopped. "The detective's preliminary opinion was multiple times."

Katie gasped and covered her mouth with a palm. Her gaze drifted to Jack. "How do you know this?"

"Because I'm the person who discovered the body."

Katie blinked disbelievingly, lowering her hand. She remained quiet, apparently digesting this information. "You found her...Hazel. I don't understand."

"Long story. Your former boss lives several blocks over from Aaron—."

"I know where Hazel's house is," Katie interrupted.

Jack's lips twisted.

"I'm sorry to be so short with you. I'm floored by this news." She clenched her white knuckled hands together and laid them in her lap. "It's only Friday and this whole weekend is looking to be a freaking disaster. Go on."

"I was out for my morning jog, and I accidently came upon Hazel's body. I learned her identity later."

Katie fell back against the cushions, draping a limp arm over her forehead.

"This is unbelievable."

"Your former co-workers, Tara and Vanessa showed up too. Vanessa identified the body."

She straightened, dropping her arm beside her. "Why would they be at Hazel's?"

"They were worried when they couldn't reach her." Jack glanced at her paled skin. He feared she might pass out if he told her more. "Did the police give you an idea who may have done this? Hazel didn't trust banks. She kept a lot of important documents in her home, and stored most of her cash in a safe. This had to be a burglary gone wrong."

"They're still investigating, but the detectives don't seem to believe a break in was the motive." Jack looked at her gravely. "Vanessa might have pointed you out as someone the officers should investigate."

Katie sat motionless and stared at the floor. "Of course she would."

A buzz erupted from Katie's jacket pocket. She thrust a shaking hand to retrieve her cell. She glimpsed at the caller ID. Her complexion whitened even more. "I don't think there's any wonder if Vanessa gave them my name," she muttered. "It's the police."

Jack nodded encouragingly. "Get it over with."

The conversation was quick. She hung up and released a deep sigh. "They don't waste any time, do they? They want me to come down to the station. Right now."

Chapter 3

"So this is what a full-fledged murder investigation feels like." Katie hurried across the police station's asphalt lot, her body braced against an icy wind. She tugged at her coat to bring the edges closer together, wishing she'd worn something heavier. Her thoughts reeled as she tried to downplay the detective's interrogation.

Jack lifted a shoulder. "Yep." He strolled calmly alongside her, Ray Ban aviators shielded his eyes, and at least a day old scruff coated his jawline. Hands inside his pockets, he wore a light jacket over his well-built physique. The bitter air didn't appear to affect him.

Although he only observed through a glass partition, Katie couldn't believe she allowed this man to be a part of the most humiliating experience of her life. She wouldn't have let him, except he insisted on driving her.

On one hand, she was thankful for his presence, because speaking with the authorities terrified her. Although they were on their way out, her stomach remained twisted in knots. She probably would've crumpled if she'd gone alone. On the opposite end of the plane, Jack Pharrell was with her. Even mussed and in jogging clothes, the guy was delectably gorgeous. More good-looking than in his youth.

They approached his truck. He stepped around to

27

the driver's side and popped the locks with the keypad. "I suggest you contact a legal representative ASAP. Cruz Zapata from high school is good. His firm is small, but he's helped me a lot. He can at least recommend a criminal attorney to keep on standby."

Katie nodded, absorbing his deep, smooth voice. Quiet, yet commanding.

"Sounds expensive." She slid into the passenger seat, forcing her attention away from this electrifying man, and concentrated on her real problem.

"Your dad will help."

"You honestly believe this is serious enough to get a lawyer involved? I mean, all they did was asked me questions and took down a few notes." The butterflies fluttering in the pit of her stomach converted into condors. She stared out of the window, gazing at the non-descriptive building she'd recently exited.

Jack inserted his truck key and turned the ignition. He put the vehicle in gear and backed out of the small lot. "You're wise to speak with an attorney whenever a homicide is involved. A precaution." Jack downshifted and lifted his foot off the clutch with ease. He hit the gas and sped away from the police department, smoothly changing gears.

She spun toward him and stared. "Did I hurt myself by not having counsel present? I mean, they didn't say I had a right to one or that anything I said may be held against me."

"Your Miranda rights. Only read if they arrest you. The cops are gathering information at this stage. If they call you in again, I'd seriously consider taking a lawyer with you. I wouldn't worry about it yet. You appear to be off the hook. For now, anyway."

"For now," Katie repeated in a soft voice.

"You should be fine as long as you only answered their questions and didn't give them any additional information."

"I did exactly what you told me to do."

Though not a criminal attorney, Jack did have enough knowledge to coach her on the drive over on how to speak with the detectives. He instructed her to reply to their queries, keeping her responses short but be cooperative, and not do anything to throw up red flags.

"You think I'm an actual suspect?"

Jack's jaw tightened. "No clue. Did they suggest you not leave town?"

"Only for a few days, and they instructed me in a polite manner."

"Well, if they were polite—."

"Jack. They want me to stay around until the final results of the autopsy are determined." She stopped to swallow. "You're not getting the same vibe are you?"

"I'm saying given the circumstances, they'll probably look at you pretty long before they eliminate you. Part of my training is to study body language. I watched those cops interview you. They exchanged skeptical glances throughout the entire interrogation. Not a positive sign."

"Good to know," Katie murmured. Talk about a cold punch of reality. She became squeamish when she squished bugs. No way could she murder another human. "They can scrutinize me all they want. I have nothing to hide. Besides, I gave them solid alibis. I visited my parent's after Hazel let me go, and then I went to my friend Jules place. I stayed with her until around two in the morning."

"Yes, but they haven't determined the time of death, right? If she died before two," he turned his head to her, "you're okay. What if it occurred later? Anyone who'll vouch for you then?"

"I was alone," Katie replied softly.

"Can you prove it if you need to?"

"Of course not," she snapped. She blew out a long spurt of air seeking calm before she spoke again. "How would someone verify they were by themselves if no one is with them?" she asked in a controlled, distant voice.

"No clue." Jack's tone equaled her coolness. "You'll need to find a way if they require an account of your whereabouts after two."

This entire episode was spinning out of control. Katie was a good person.

Even in the most extenuating circumstances, she couldn't kill someone in cold blood, especially somebody she knew. Now she hoped she'd persuaded the detectives and perhaps Jack. She glanced to her left and released another loud sigh.

Why did she care what he thought? He'd never seen her as anything other than Aaron's younger sister, and she was getting the sense nothing had changed in that department. Perhaps he only presented the gravest scenario, but he didn't seem to be on her side. He'd accompanied her to the police station sure…she snuck another glimpse at him, unable to understand why he'd come with her.

"I can't be the only person they're speaking with, anyway," she insisted. "Hazel has thousands of enemies."

"Had thousands of enemies. Hopefully they'll work through them all. But if they believe her killer is caught," he hesitated and threw her a warning glance, "they won't look any farther."

Katie huffed and fell against the seat, crossing her arms over her chest. "So you're saying I'll be their number one suspect."

"Stop putting words in my mouth. I'm trying to get you out of la la land."

"Excuse me. You sound like I'm about to be handcuffed and fitted for a striped jumpsuit."

"Not true. You're thinking everything is hunky-dory, and the police are questioning you in a murder investigation. You have a motive. There is a period when no one can verify your whereabouts. What I'm saying is you need legal counsel. Keep a lawyer around, just in case. Be aware, detectives check alibis. Even though the explanations should clear you, they still might want to talk to you again." He paused. "And I understand those prison uniforms are one size fits all. No fittings are necessary."

"Funny," she spouted sarcastically. "Wouldn't you like to point out how the vertical stripes widen the ass?"

"Nope. Not into butts, though I doubt if stripes vertical or otherwise are detrimental to yours."

She looked at him with raised brows, hoping he didn't detect the tremble in her hands.

"Just trying to lighten the mood." He grinned. He pressed down on the clutch and break, working the gearshift to stop at a light with ease. "I'm a leg man, by the way."

"Thanks for sharing." Katie gazed out the window.

"You're worrying for nothing. This is just the

beginning of the investigation and hopefully you'll never hear from homicide again. The buzz at the Hazel's house supported your claim. Terri, no…"

"Tara."

"Right. Tara stated Hazel alienated everyone in her life, and she wasn't a nice person, although Vanessa jumped to the woman's defense. She's quite a fan."

"She's quite an ass kisser."

Jack chuckled. "I'm curious. What did the Nutt lady do to piss off so many people?"

"Hazel always saw the dark side of situations. Actually she was the dark side. She believed the worst in everyone, and enjoyed destructive gossip. She loved to make up stuff regarding others, and was known for starting nasty rumors about the competition."

"Not uncommon. At least her maliciousness toward her competitors isn't."

"Yeah, but she hit way low, below the belt, and she's a master at putting a destructive spin on any story. My ex-employer would have made an excellent tabloid reporter," Katie stated edgily. "Her overall business tactics were questionable too."

"I didn't realize the wedding field was corrupted."

Katie waved a hand. "Oh, you wouldn't believe the dishonesty that goes on."

Jack's brows rose. "Enlighten me."

"Say we've booked two appointments. One bride gives her dream wedding details and offered a full-service package fee of four thousand dollars. The second arrives and she's dressed better than the first. Designer clothes, the diamond in her engagement ring triple the size of the earlier client, but she wants the same ceremony. Based on patron twos extra posh appearance, her rate would be jacked up to six thousand dollars or even more, depending on her affluences." She looked at him. "Understand?"

"The practice is legal, although maybe not so ethical."

"Not ethical and not good business."

"Dirty for sure. I assume you don't operate this way."

Katie stared at him. "Hazel and I constantly butted heads about this. She'd remind me the company belonged to her, and she was in business to make money whereas, I told her my reputation and integrity was on the line. I brought in the bulk of the clientele, so she left me alone most of the time. Only after Vanessa the bitch came aboard, Hazel disregarded any form of principle and basically ran the business from the gutter."

"What did Vanessa the bitch, do?"

"From day one, she worked to discredit me and the other consultants. She's a pot stirrer, loves to create drama, and always on the phone with Hazel, telling on us."

"I'd think a strong, business woman would be above petty gossip."

"I know, right? But those two were kindred. Hazel enjoyed initiating scandals about our competitors. Vanessa took things down a notch and made it internal. Hazel thought her great. She believed she hired her away from Affairs Amore, our biggest competitor, but rumors said that Vanessa included additional surcharges and fees to her costs. We also heard the procedure got her sacked from her last position. People in this industry love to talk."

"Padding the till is illegal."

"Yeah, but if your boss approves, what do you do." Katie still fumed over how Hazel indirectly required her employees to work in such a seedy method. "Not only is this behavior disreputable, exploiting specific dealer's limits variety, and after a while the weddings are the same." Katie stared out of the window. "Bottom line, Vanessa is a less than honorable planner who charges the client a flat fee, AND takes cuts from vendors through the backdoor."

"So you're saying Nutty Hazel supported this method?"

"She loved the idea. Loved Vanessa for bringing in the practice. She subtly indicated we all use her system." Katie shrugged. "I refused to comply so she fired me."

"Have you considered a lawsuit over the termination? I believe it's still doable, even though she passed away. You could file a suit against her estate."

"No lawsuit. Hazel is—was careful to keep her tracks covered. She wasn't above letting someone else take the fall, either. There's no recourse for me because Texas is a fire at will state."

"What about a plan B?"

"I've had a plan B in the works for a while. My professional standing remained at risk as long as I worked for Hazel. I was aware I'd need to make a change at some point." She smiled. "I wasn't ready to put things into action, although now I'm forced to accelerate those strategies." Katie raised her chin. "I'm going to open my own party planning agency. My goal was to knock Hazel off the peak and become the top wedding coordinator in the city."

"Ruthless. I like it."

"The last part is still in the works. The problem is I signed a confidentiality contract when Hazel hired me, and I may be bound to stay out of the industry for a certain period before I can branch out. That's why I wanted to speak with Aaron this morning. He's familiar with this sort of thing, since he owns a business. Now she's dead, the clause might be moot. At least I hope so."

Katie was ready to put the subject of Hazel, her murder, and Vanessa to rest.

"I can't believe you kept this old truck."

Jack leaned forward and patted the dashboard. "I'd never sell my baby. This is the first ride I ever bought. I worked hard on your dad's ranch, saved, and saved until I earned enough to buy it from him."

"It was a dinosaur back then. I remember when daddy brought it home, brand new. I think I was about five."

"Lots of good memories attached to this pickup. A classic."

A younger Jack driving with a cheerleader or some other popular girl snuggled close to him flickered through Katie's mind, followed by an old, familiar pang.

"Is this what you drove in your high powered attorney days?" she asked stiffly. "I bet you impressed your rich clients."

"I had a luxury automobile for work. Perk went with the job. One of many benefits I was required to relinquish after my law firm suspended me." He chuckled, though it sounded doubtful and forced. "But I always thought it pretentious to have to impress others with what I drove. Wheels are a means to get me from one place to another. Who cares if the seats heat or cool my ass? This truck is an expansion of me. Keeps me grounded, and a reminder of how I grew up, and where I came from. I don't get excited about an overpriced vehicle or an exorbitant lifestyle. Not the way I chose to live my life."

****

Jack maneuvered his pickup down a two lane blacktop, his thoughts whirled, confused as to why he'd volunteered to accompany her. Katie had been a royal pain in his ass during her adolescent years, and as she grew older, she'd become even a bigger one. Still, he'd always tried to be a nice guy. Though in the end, he'd been the asshole. He'd tucked the one sordid occurrence away in his mind for fourteen years. After seeing her today, the memory of the hurt in her eyes, grief he'd caused, haunted him. He owed her.

But now his debt was paid. He could move forward and forget about her.

He stole a side glance at her. She'd grown into a beautiful woman, although he needed to ignore that. He'd sworn off women four months ago and managed to stay clear of any temptation. He'd remained female free the entire stint. A relief to some degree, though in other ways, the celibate sorts, not so much. His "no sex until his issue was resolved" pact was beginning to waver. Even so, Katie Drapier would not be a factor if getting laid was a goal. Jack's plan was to drop her off, return to the guesthouse to his waiting beer, crossword, and football game.

"I'll check over those contracts from Hazel and see if the confidentiality clause is null," he blurted.

She twisted to him with raised brows. "What?"

Exactly. What the fuck provoked him to make such an asinine suggestion?

Did his brain and mouth not get along anymore? Get rid of her, do puzzle, and drink beer. Not search for ways to spend more time with her.

Backtrack. Claim insanity, do whatever it takes to get out of this.

"If we find out the document is void, you can start putting together a business plan. Technically, I can't dole out legal advice, though. You'd want to hire a practicing attorney before you make any serious moves. But I can give you a heads up to go forward, or point you in the right direction if you need to contest."

He sighed inwardly. So much for reverse. Apparently he'd just volunteered to help her for the long haul.

Chapter 4

Katie guided Jack to a renovated urban part of the city where she'd recently moved into a two-story loft style condo. He parked inside the building's covered lot as she directed. They took an elevator to an elegant lobby, and then she steered him down the hall, and to her front door. She inserted her key into the lock to let them in.

Jack released a low whistle. "Nice digs." He stopped and picked up a hand-painted vase on an entry table. "Wedding coordinating must pay well."

"It does all right. I was allowed to dip into my trust to pay for the rest." Katie walked further inside, shook out of her suede coat, and laid the garment across the back of an overstuffed chair. "I'm sure you lived in some nice digs when you were in Dallas. From what I understand, the job you had wasn't too shabby."

He shrugged, replaced the pot, and followed her, stepping down a stair into the open living room. "You may remember I didn't grow up with much." He released an exhale full of resignation. "The nicest place I ever lived during my youth was in the bunkhouse on your family's ranch."

"You were welcome to live in the main house, you know. You chose to stay with the hands."

"I knew I was more than an employee to your parents, but I felt comfortable where I stayed. And because of my limited access to luxury, I chose something modest by most standards when I had a chance to get a home." He aimed a mesmerizing gaze in her direction. A massive lurch punched her chest. She'd ignored the catch all afternoon, but the compression became too overwhelming. He stared right through her. Green eyes stood out, contrasting against his dark hair and the scruff spread across his chin. "Comfortable, though. A good place to chill at the end of the day. The only thing that could be considered excessive about the house was it sat on a lake." He grinned. "Total relaxation."

"You sound as if you enjoyed living there. Do you still own the home?"

Jack's gaze dropped. "Technically I do, but like my pricey car, I gave it up when I got involved with, um… too many expenses. I've rented it out."

"Sorry. I keep bringing up a sore subject, I know. I don't mean to."

"It happened. Nothing will change that, but yeah, I've talked the issue to death. Sometimes I'd rather pretend like the situation didn't exist."

"Can you do that? Act as if you're still living your old life?"

He released an awkward chuckle. "Haven't been too successful so far." He placed his hands on hips, and looked at her with a tight smile. "How 'bout you find those papers so I can take you to your car."

"I'll be back in a second."

Katie hurried upstairs and on into her bedroom. As she treaded across the carpet, she caught her reflection in a full length mirror attached to the outside of her closet door. She stopped to study her image, turning

39

from side to side, wishing she wore something more alluring than a pair of faded jeans and a comfortable sweater.

Then he may not be so quick to take her to her car. The guy might be close to the skids, but he maintained a forceful presence that overtook her entire home.

Old feelings, one-sided, youthful feelings she'd done her best to squelch over the years exploded, followed by a zing of exasperation. In a matter of hours, she'd become reabsorbed in this irresistible man.

For an instant, she forgot about her brewing troubles and traveled back in time to a more hopeful period when she believed one day Jack Pharrell would notice her. She shook her head. She shouldn't be so delusional.

Continuing through her bedroom and onto to her closet, she opened the door. The guy was never aware of her, at least as girlfriend material, throughout the entire time they'd known one another. In fact, he'd made it clear he didn't like her one bit back in the day. What happened ages ago should have been enough to stifle her dreams, since he'd smashed her heart into tiny pieces. Yet she'd managed to suppress the painful memory. She couldn't recall crying or experiencing any symptoms of grieving over his rejection. She'd acted as if the episode never happened. She may've blocked a smidgen of anger because of his careless dismissal. At some point, she'd need to deal with the disgrace, and all the other crap his slight caused. Just not now.

She wondered again about his actions today. He confused her. If he didn't care for her in the past, why did he insist on coming with her? More so, what were her motives in agreeing to accept his generosity?

Granted, if she didn't come up with a solution to her unemployment status, she'd be hard up for cash soon. She was allowed only so much of her trust. Therefore it was difficult to turn down free legal advice.

She shouldn't worry over the whys because she had other issues to focus on. Plus, he had his own stuff to deal with. She couldn't go there.

Reaching the closet's rear, she maneuvered around to a small alcove niched into the wall where her two drawer metal file cabinet sat. She squatted and opened the bottom, the place she kept her important documents, and began to flip through the papers.

"Hey, do you mind if I use your bath—whoa."

Katie flinched and did a half-spin on the tips of her toes. She tipped sideways, throwing out a hand to catch herself but was too late. She plopped unceremoniously onto her rear. Slowly, her gaze lifted.

Jack's frame filled the doorway. A T-shirt hugged the ripped muscles across his torso, the soft sweat material curved over his butt, and down the stretch of his lengthy, solid legs. Her heart assaulted her ribcage, throbbing in triple time. The heat level inside her closet shot up and passed the danger mark.

His look traveled over the small room. The dim light altered his eye color from one shade of jade to another, sparking her racing heart to jump from her chest and lodge into her throat.

"Wow, this is like a mini warehouse."

He wasn't too far off. She loved her new place, and the closet space was her pride and joy. Lined with full shelves from top to bottom, left to right on one side, the other had double bars filled with her hanging clothes, a shelf in the extreme, highest peak was for seasonal storage.

He walked farther in, opened and closed a built-in drawer, then peered across the extended length of the gap. "Damn. A window inside a closet, I've seen it all now. I can die a happy man." Jack's attention altered and fixated on her. "What are you doing down there?"

His dazzling green stare remained constant. He seemed surprised to find her on the floor, which gave her hope that he missed her buffoonish tumble.

"Um, waiting for you to check out my closet." She shoved the drawer shut and held a file out to him.

"Glad I didn't disappoint." He stepped closer, took the folder, and offered her a hand. "Need a lift?" The slight quiver of his lips indicated he was trying to hold back a smile.

She ignored the grin and stared at the strong fingers extended toward her. A fresh, angry scrape slanted across the inside his palm, making her wonder what he'd done to cause such an injury. Her speculation over the wound was brief as her concentration shifted to her immediate matter. Should she decline his offer? Or take a risk and possibly lose her ability to speak forever, and use the opportunity to discover if his hand felt the same as she'd imagined.

She ran a finger under her sweater collar before she grasped his outstretched palm. Immediately, she committed his rough, warm touch to memory. The contact lasted seconds, but still there was enough time for the fluctuation to snake through her body and deliver an earth-quaking jolt.

He hauled her to her feet, only to immediately release her, and took in the giant wardrobe again. He stared at her with raised brows. "Really?"

She gathered her wits and gave him a proud smile. "This was originally a sitting room built off the bedroom. I did the design and Pops converted it for me."

He eyed a wall of boxes. "Are those shoes?"

"Of course."

"A lot of footwear for only two feet." He dropped his gaze back to her. "Do you need them all?"

"How can anyone have too many shoes? I can't believe you even asked me that."

He grinned. "My IQ must have dropped from huffing so much leather and canvas."

"Way into a negative."

"You're talking to a man who's never had more than five pairs at once."

Katie gasped.

"I didn't realize having a low count was a problem." He gazed at the boxes again. "With shoes anyway." He opened the folder and swiftly scanned each page before he looked up. "Ready?"

They left her place and drove to Aaron's in near silence. His attorney persona took over, and their conversation about anything else ceased. The only personal interaction occurred when he asked for her number, promising to phone her once he was finished. He pulled beside of her jeep and put his truck in park. They exited from the pickup and met at the tailgate.

Katie observed him with an uncertain smile. "Thanks for helping me today."

He held her stare and spoke quietly. "Katie, I mean Katherine."

"Katie is fine."

"Katie. I know you think you're off the hook

because you didn't commit this crime, but you need to take this investigation seriously. Hazel might have been a dishonest businesswoman and a bitch too," he paused, "still she was also a prominent citizen in the community. The police are under pressure to make an arrest. Sometimes they don't fit the clues to the crime, and instead they fit a person into the evidence to satisfy the public. What I'm trying to say is innocent people are sent to prison every day, so be aware."

The corners of her trembling lips rose. "I've watched Dateline." She tried to keep the moment lighthearted, but a troublesome dread seeped within her.

"Um and..." He hesitated and cleared his throat, as he raked a hand through his hair. "About the last time we spoke. It's been years, but I wasn't exactly truthful earlier, and I wanted to say—"

"I don't know what you're talking about, Jack," she interrupted, her tone snippy.

She didn't intend to sound rude, but after the day she'd had, she couldn't handle an apology from remorse, or worse, pity. Granted, the mammoth sized, invisible mountain remained between them, but given their circumstances, she'd only be dealing with him one more time. She saw no reason to rehash the most painful disappointment during her youth. Part ways, deal with it alone, and get on with life.

"Okay, then." Jack reached for a strand of her hair and gave it a light tug.

The lock sifted through his fingers as he continued to gaze deep into her eyes. "Be careful Katie. Be very careful."

****

Vanessa King eyed the murky, isolated street. Icy

gusts lifted scatters of debris from an opened dumpster, whirling litter into the blackened sky. In the distance a train moaned off key, adding to the desolate neighborhood's eeriness.

Conscious of her surroundings, she clutched her handbag to her side and continued toward a deserted looking structure. A bleak neon sign flickered, "The Old Wagon Wheel Bar" above a near-obscure door.

She slinked passed the entrance and stopped inside, frowning as she took in the setting. The dim room was stuffy, hazed from cigarette smoke, and full of people, proving the abandoned outside appearance a ruse. Remnants of a decade old country tune sporadically rose above the noisy chatter. Every chair surrounding the center tables was filled. The booths located to the right were also occupied. Along, bar constructed from sheet-metal stood on the left. Round vinyl stools were tucked under the overhang, each contained an inhabitant as the rowdy hoards vied for a space in between the raised seats.

Looking neither left nor right, she pressed amid the packed crowd, sidestepping the throngs of mostly male patrons. She ignored their leers and suggestive comments until she reached the rear of the room. She rushed to slide into the lone empty booth. The primeval wooden table and bench seats were etched in abundant of artwork, random declarations of love, and numerous accusations of some woman named Amber something, being a bitch.

A waitress with over-processed blond hair, wearing cutoffs and a tight t-shirt covering oversized breasts, bra questionable, ambled over to her. Smacking a wad of gum, she tapped her pencil eraser against her pad.

"What'll it be?" she asked in a smoker's graveled voice with a trace of attitude.

"Diet soda."

The waitress scribbled onto her notebook. "Ain't seen you round here before."

Vanessa didn't respond to the woman's curiosity, nor did she bother to look in her direction. She kept her gaze averted, careful not to make eye contact with the many men and few women who seemed too interested in her. She wasn't afraid.

She didn't want to invite any interaction with these losers. The server shot her a seething glare and gave a haughty "humph" as she hurried away, presumably to fill Vanessa's order.

She glanced around, taking in the atmosphere. Situated in a darker area toward the rear were several pool tables. A strobe light silhouetted streaks of the player's reedy cues intermixed with shadowed longnecks tipping back.

Vanessa turned away. She detested these types of places. Tough guy wannabe's and their so-called women were nothing but a bunch of imitators. No ambition except to hang out, drink, and brag to their counterparts. Bored with low class ambiance, she stared at the scarred table, waiting for her soda to arrive. Her mind drifted to Jackson Pharrell.

What an intriguing man. Tara had relayed his history on the ride to the wedding rehearsal, plus her coworker updated her on the current troubles. Vanessa also Googled him after she left work.

Even with his problems, he was handsome enough, after he cleaned up, of course, for her to overlook his trailer park upbringing. She knew this mess he was involved in would blow over soon, and he'd return to being a respected attorney.

Then he may be a perfect addition for her future plans.

The door banged, hitting the inner wall. A blast of cold air raged throughout the bar, rushing to the far end where Vanessa waited. She jerked her chin toward the entrance, forgetting about Jack. The entire place went silent, leaving only the wail of the jukebox to fill the room.

A large bearded man, dressed in faded, denim jeans, a sleeveless vest and a bandana wrapped around head stood in the doorway. Multitudes of tattoos twisted over his exposed skin, disappearing underneath his clothing. He stepped past the entry, barreling across the hollowed plank floors, the crowd parting like the Red Sea to allow him through. His footsteps reverberated, triggering glasses sitting on the tables to rattle as he passed. He caught Vanessa's stare at once and held it as he strolled straight to her. Despite his bulky size, he glided graceful into the other side of the booth. The waitress hurried over the moment his butt cheek tapped the seat, her order-pad clutched between her hands.

"Whiskey," he commanded without a peek at her.

The woman nodded and disappeared. The crowd relaxed as everybody resumed to what they were doing. Neither he nor Vanessa spoke until she returned and placed their drinks in front of them.

"I take it you're Winston?" Vanessa lifted her soda and sipped neatly.

"Everyone calls me Winnie." He stared at her. "And you must be Vanessa."

She wiped the condensation off her glass and glimpsed around the bar again.

He smirked. "You don't need to worry about this place. People might be curious, but they mind their own beeswax."

"Do you have it?"

"Niceties out of the way and we're down to business." His grin widened. "I like that." A giant hand glided inside his frayed vest and drew out a manila envelope. He held it level with her face, but out of her reach. "Cash first."

She didn't argue, though her mouth flattened as she opened her purse and removed a thick packet. She gradually slid the money-filled container over the course tabletop. His fingertips met the package halfway and dragged the payment to him. Oblivious to the crowd, he laid his envelope in front of him and opened Vanessa's to count the bills.

"It's all there. The extra one fifty for the rush job is included."

"Gonna build that into the regular price, cuz these types of requests are always wanted fast." He flashed another toothy grin through his thick shock of whiskers and handed her the other envelope. "Your signed receipt is in the back."

She peered inside to examine the contents. "Everything looks authentic. Even the signatures appear valid."

"Take an expert to say they ain't." Winnie laughed. "And some of them won't get it right."

Vanessa smiled slyly and nodded as she resealed the top. "Good." She stuffed it into her bag, and slipped across the bench seat, prepared to leave.

"I hope whatever you're mixed up in isn't too much out of your league." He nodded at the forms she'd jammed inside her purse. "Those could get you into a shitload of trouble if you're not careful."

She stopped and skeptically surveyed him with a cool gaze. "I just paid you a large amount of money to make sure that it doesn't."

"Shouldn't." He shrugged. "But shit happens."

"You have your compensation. Consequently what occurs after our transaction isn't your concern. Though let me emphasize, after the hefty payment you require, I do not expect any shit to take place."

He howled a laugh. "You speak the truth, lady. Shit or no shit, whatever happens is none of my beeswax." He patted his coat pocket, where he'd stored his payment. "I got what I need." He raised his glass and downed the drink in one shot. "Nice doing business with you."

Chapter 5

Katie secured the door's lock, her fingers trembling. Thoughts of the day screamed in her head as her heart jumped hurdles. Jack Pharrell. Here, in her loft, driving her around town, and accompanying her to the police station.

The past fourteen plus years she'd done everything in her power to keep him out of her mind. She'd thrown her efforts into school, college, and work. The few men she dated, including the guy she was once engaged to, were exactly opposite of the tall, dark headed, young man who dominated her adolescent dreams.

It only took one encounter and fantasies of Jack began to weave into her daydreams. Reflections of him overshadowed the past and her job loss. Even in the wake of Hazel's murder, or the detective's interview didn't deter her yearnings.

She promised herself she wouldn't do this. Go crazy. She should deal with the memories, dispel old feelings, and hopefully continue with her life without looking back. Thinking in reverse made her pathetic. And her showing weakness just ticked her off.

Except for the first time ever he'd paid attention to her. Her fingertips trailed over the wisp of hair he'd stroked. Okay, the interest wasn't exactly as she'd fantasized. His eyes, greener since he'd matured, showed more concern than the wanting she'd once longed for.

Stop daydreaming and move forward. She hurried into the kitchen area and located a bottle of wine. She popped the cork and filled a goblet with the amber liquid, and then she picked up the glass and headed into the bathroom. It'd been a long, curious day. She needed to unwind.

Drink on the counter, she went to the tub, twisting the faucet knobs. Once she'd regulated the water's temperature, she lifted the handle in the middle to hold the contents inside. Hands on her hips, and stared at the rushing stream. "Salts." She swirled to a nearby cabinet and added vanilla scented crystals. "Can't have a relaxing bath without 'em."

Satisfied, she pinned her hair on top of her head, undressed, retrieved her wine, and sank into the filled tub. The warm soak was heaven. Soothing heat penetrated her skin, loosening the tension throughout her body. Lids closed, she relaxed against the porcine. Her thoughts drifted into nothingness and remained in the state for what seemed like hours. An echo of Jack's warning softly whispered... *innocent people are sent to prison every day.*

Katie shot out of the water. Chills bristled over her drenched body, only not from the cold. She didn't want to believe he was right, but she may be a viable person of interest in the death of her former employer.

How had she gone from a sought after wedding consultant to an unemployed, possible murder suspect, within the span of twenty-four hours. The premise seemed bizarre, yet as sure as she was of anything, she knew the police would want to speak with her again, and the next visit wouldn't be polite.

She dried, slipped on exercise shorts, a long sleeved t-shirt, and a pair of socks. Wineglass in hand, she returned to the kitchen, and removed a pot from the refrigerator. She placed it on the stove to let the contents simmer and went take it easy on her sofa.

Rest was far away. Hazel's murder smacked her conscious. Katie loved her job, even with the discord within the company. The women did bring her into the business, and, the association with Weddings Fantastic provided her with many contacts. Though she had little love for her former boss, she must concede the woman wasn't all bad. She wiped away a stray tear. Hazel was a part of Katie's life for countless years, and she couldn't believe her mentor was gone.

A light tap came from the front entrance. She froze. Jack? Or had the police come for her?

"Katie?" said a muffled voice from outside.

Katie released a thankful sigh and set her glass aside. She rushed to the doorway and extended an arm to unlatch the lock. She stopped.

The door was unlocked.

Hadn't she bolted it when she arrived home? She shook her head. Normally she made a habit of keeping everything secured, especially because she lived alone. Maybe this new chaos in her life caused her to be forgetful.

She threw open the door.

Jules, her closet friend since grade school, stepped inside. "Why didn't you call me?" she scolded, wiggling out of her coat. "I was worried after everything that's happened."

Katie ignored her questions and returned to her stir her food, simmering on the stove. "Soup's ready."

Jules followed her. "Your mother's, right?"

"I don't do homemade."

"I'm aware you severely lack, in comparison to your mom's kitchen's skills." She laughed. "Hard to believe you're related."

"I cook," Katie defended. "I prefer a healthier diet."

Jules wrinkled her nose. "Healthy is one thing, but this constant regime of boiled bean sprouts and kale is hardly appetizing."

"I've already had a rough day. Therefore, I'm ignoring these blatant abuses of my culinary talents and tastes in cuisine."

Jules walked to the bubbling soup and inhaled a satisfied hum. "Gosh, I wish I could convince Lila to work for me."

Katie indicated toward the pot. "I'm assuming you want a bowl?"

"Of course. And some of whatever you're drinking too." She nodded to an oversized bag she'd laid next to her jacket. "If we run out, there's another bottle from the restaurant in my purse."

"That one is yours. After today, I need a whole one to myself. Maybe more."

"I can go back and get extra after we close."

"Not necessary. I keep a couple of extras for special occasions." She looked at her friend with a wry grin. "Although this isn't anything close to a festive event."

Katie handed Jules a wineglass and returned to the stove to dip a second bowl of soup. They carried their filled dishes, goblets, and decanter into the living room to sit.

Jules spooned the broth and glanced at Katie. "I suppose this non-festive event is referring to Hazel's death?"

Katie held up her goblet and studied the clear liquid inside. "It's hitting me now," she said in a quiet voice.

"I've only heard bits and pieces." Jules picked up the decanter to fill her glass. "You must be in shock. The woman wasn't your favorite person, and I doubt you'll shed a lot of tears over her passing, still you wouldn't be human if you didn't experience some sadness."

"Hazel wasn't nice, though she did give me an opportunity to learn the business. I'll always be grateful for the chance." Katie returned her flute to the table beside her and swirled her soup with her spoon. "No matter how awful she behaved, she didn't deserve to be murdered."

"Is it for sure a murder?"

Katie nodded. "I've been inadvertently privy to some information that happened at the scene."

Jules leaned forward. "Like?"

"Like Vanessa showed up at Hazel's after they discovered her body, and she aimed the detective's in my direction."

"Figures." Jules tone was full of disgust. "Someone offs her boss and she's already causing trouble. They should be looking at her."

"I know, right?"

Her friend shook her head. "The woman has no scruples at all, does she?"

"None. There's a never ending list of people who might want Hazel dead, and yet she's made sure I'm the top suspect."

Jules gaze snapped to Katie. "You think so?"

"Hazel fired me yesterday. Supposedly that's a strong enough motive to make me the police suspicious of me."

"I guess, though you shouldn't worry too much. They'll eliminate you the moment they talk to you."

Katie hoped her friend was right. Vanessa was a liar and a conniving one. Could she be skilled enough to keep Katie in trouble for an extended period? The authorities closely watched her as they interrogated her. She had to wonder what information her adversary gave them about her that they weren't ready to reveal.

"The detectives already called me in to speak with them. I had to go right away."

"You're joking," Jules's intonation escalated. "What kind of questions did they ask you?"

"The last time I saw Hazel. My whereabouts. Can anyone vouch for me at during those times?" Katie faltered. "Why she fired me."

"So they grilled you pretty hard?"

"I'm not sure. I've never even had a speeding ticket, much less questioned in a murder investigation." She peeked at her friend. "I gave them your name as an alibi. They'll be contacting you."

"No problem. So we're on the same page, you left my place about two, right?"

"I hope they determine the time of death yesterday evening instead of this morning. That would get me off the hook."

"Told you to spend the night."

"If only I had a crystal ball." Katie took a long drink then held up her glass. "I'm going to need a lot of this before tonight's over."

Jules drained her goblet and reached for the bottle. "You were so upset last evening. We didn't talk much about why Hazel fired you. I don't understand the ol' bats reasoning. Weren't you her top consultant?"

"Yep. She released me because I refused to play by Vanessa's rules, which became Hazel's rules."

"The whole taking kickbacks from vender thing."

"Right. I suppose she made more money unethically opposed to what I brought in. Besides, my commissions were high. If Hazel thought she could cut a corner and put extra coins into her piggy bank, she didn't hesitate."

"Basically you were a sliced corner."

"Seems so. Maybe she did me a favor."

Jules looked at her surprised. "How?"

"You're aware, I've considered going on my own. This gives me that extra push. Getting fired might be a good thing." Katie gave a cynical smile. "Or would've been if someone hadn't killed Hazel the same day."

"What will happen to Weddings Fantastic now Hazel's gone?"

"No idea. I bet Vanessa is parading around the office like she's taking over." Katie laughed. "I predict a huge mutiny if she tries."

"Or a lynching."

"Yeah, and I'm going to miss it, darn it."

Jules chuckled. "Glad you're taking the high road."

"I can't think about it, right now. I have to focus on my predicament."

"Understood. Not to change the subject, but there's a rumor your old crush is back in town. With his tail between his legs."

Katie's insides turned to ice. She'd hoped Jules hadn't discovered Jack's return yet. "You're talking about Jack Pharrell?"

Jules shot her an exasperated glare. "Who else occupied your every thought growing up? Of course, I mean Jack Pharrell."

Katie tensed from the mere mention of his name. Her mind's eye seized the sight of those knee-weakening, green eyes. Memories of exchanged smiles, accidental brushes, and his fingers stroking her hair—thoughts of Jack—brought on an upsurge of hormonal electricity that bolted through her.

"Um, yeah. We've already run into each other."

Jules's brows lifted. Katie so didn't want to explain, except she couldn't lie to her friend. Realistically, today's encounter with Jack made no difference. Sure, he'd been nice, but a few ticks of politeness wouldn't take away years of unreciprocated, youthful heartache. She may as well spill.

"He was here, at the loft," Katie said uneasily.

"Jack Pharrell? Here?" Jules almost demanded. "How is that possible?"

"He's staying at Aaron's guest cottage." Katie exhaled. "I went by earlier to speak with Aaron. He wasn't home, but Jack was. He informed me about Hazel's death."

Jules stared at Katie.

"Jack discovered Hazel's body."

"Oh, well that makes sense." Jules paused, her expression vexed. "Not. How did Jack discover Hazel? And how did he know of your connection with her, and why was he at your house?"

"Still pretty upset when I got to Aaron's, I kind of

blurted out the entire story about Hazel, Vanessa, and losing my job. Reduced to tears is more like it.

Jack had been jogging and found Hazel dead. He'd met Vanessa at the scene and told me she'd indicated me as a suspect. I was nervous when the police called. He drove me to the station. Then, he volunteered to review my contracts with Hazel, we stopped by here to pick up them. That's all."

"I doubt it." Jules sat her soup bowl to the side. "You've had a thing for him since you were eight. A crush that continued until Jack went away for college. I think you still hoped for something once he left, even after the horrible things he said to you." Her friend eyed her. "How is he now?"

Katie removed the clip from the top of her head, letting her hair tumble to her shoulders. "He was...Jack. We're friends, sort of, maybe."

Jules leaned closer. "You're sure?"

"He didn't notice me any more today than he did when we were kids. I must accept that. You're correct too. He was clear on how he viewed me back then. I doubt if his opinion has changed much." She hesitated. "I think he wanted to apologize, though."

"He should. He hurt your feelings." She studied Katie. "He didn't get to, right?"

She ducked her head to conceal her warming face. "No. I stopped him. The past is better left behind."

"Not sure why you'd let him off the hook, but it's on you if he doesn't express regret." She stopped. "I assume you plan on seeing him again?"

Katie nodded. "He's reviewing my Weddings Fantastic contracts to verify if I can move forward with my business without legal complications."

"You just can't let this go, can you? You had a perfectly nice fiancé, and you blew him off. Yeah, you claimed there were issues, but I know you. I've always believed Jack was the reason you called off the wedding. You never dealt with his snub."

"Jack isn't the cause of Carter and my parting ways. Jack didn't live here when were together, heck, he hasn't been around for ages. I'm long past his brushoff. My ex and I wanted different things." Katie huffed. "What provoked this attack from you? I thought you had my back."

"Always. I'd hate for him emotionally pound you again." Jules looked dismayed. "It's been a long time. You've both grown up. I've seen photographs of him in the news, Katie. The guy may be a first class ass, but he's yummier than ever. I don't want your ancient dreams to set you up for another fail."

"He is good looking, but the attraction has disappeared." Katie assured her friend. "I need to meet with him once more and then we're done. As far as the past, I can only hold on to anger for so long before it becomes childish and spiteful."

"True. But you have unresolved feelings, and until you get the matter settled, there will always be an internal conflict."

No use arguing, Jules could read her like a book, yet she refused to concede on the subject. "May I remind you, the man's got his own problems to deal with?"

"You may, and you are correct. The guy clearly needs to get his act together." Jules made a face and wiggled. "What am I sitting on?" She lifted her bottom, and dipped a hand between the cushion. She held up a paring knife and frowned. "You keep a chef's knife in your sofa? Now I'm really going to rag on you about your kitchen skills."

"I don't know how—oh." Katie sat her empty dish aside, and stared. The sharp, silver blade gleamed in the dim light. Tremors vibrated though her, her body instantly went ice cold.

"The edge has a corroded crust over the blade." Jules examined the knife. "What in the world were you cutting?"

"I didn't use it to cut anything."

"Huh?"

"It's not mine."

"I don't understand."

Katie swallowed and gaped at the new discovery. "The knife doesn't belong to me. I don't know where it came from."

Chapter 6

Jack overlooked the pounding in his head to rise off his pillow, simultaneously lifting his lids. Yellow eyes retuned his stare. His body winced, spurring a gray streak to leap from his chest. Sharpness penetrated and sliced into his bare skin.

Jack straightened and hissed through his teeth. "Son of a bitch." A hand flew to cover the fresh slashes. He glared at the huge cat vanishing around the corner. "How the hell did you get in here?"

He moved his palm away to examine two bleeding scratches, releasing another sputter of air. For the moment he forgot about the feline and rolled out of bed. A whirlwind coiled within his head. "Oh shit, gravity works." He gripped the bedpost, and clutched his forehead with a bloodied palm until his world stopped whirling. He recovered his wound and hurried into the small bathroom.

With an elbow, he rotated the cold faucet handle while he plowed through the cabinets and drawers until he found what he was looking for. He tossed a washcloth under the rushing stream until it was soaked. He picked up the cloth, and dabbed at the streaks trailing down his middle, then held the cool wetness against the crimson gashes. His stomach rolled. He'd hoped years would pass before he had to deal with the sight of blood again, but the plasma demons obviously had different ideas.

The flow finally stopped. He flipped the stained rag onto the edge of the sink and washed his hands and forehead. Back in his room, he dug out his last clean pair of boxers, and swept up the sweats he'd dropped on the floor the night before. He snatched a T-shirt draped over a chair, sniffed the material before he pulled it on, gasping in agony. He could almost ignore the sting across his chest, but his brain was about to explode, and discounting that pain was out of the question.

Someday he would need to cut back on his alcohol intake. A glance at the opened closet full of expensive suits had him seizing a half-filled beer container from the nightstand, and finishing the warmed beverage in one swallow. But not today.

He moved into the kitchen, to a cabinet, and removed a bottle. Pain gripped his head like a boa constrictor squeezing the gray matter from his skull. He popped the lid and shook out four aspirin, dry gulped the pills.

A blast of cool air surged through the room. Jack rotated and took a step toward the front of the house and stopped short. The latch on the door didn't catch unless closed tight. The early November wind must've blown it open.

"Explains how cat the ripper got in."

He moved to the entrance to push it shut. Lock securely twisted, he stared outside. Is this the feline from the murder scene yesterday? He assumed animal control had captured the cat and would take it in for DNA testing. He stepped closer to the glass. A shadowed outline appeared on the other side.

Jack jumped away, then bent forward, and squinted. "Shit." His chest tightened, not prepared for more bad news. With a heavy sigh, he grasped the knob and twisted. "I didn't agree to pay for house calls," Jack said in a gruff voice. "This visit better be pro bono."

Cruz Zapata strolled inside, coming to a halt a step beyond the threshold. A frown played at his lips. "I like what you've done with the place." He raked a stern gaze over Jack. "You're looking well too."

"Thanks," Jack replied with an equal bite of irony.

Cruz moved further in and without an invitation took a seat on the sofa. Jack fell into an opposite chair to wait for another anvil to drop. His personal attorney wouldn't come by this early to brag about his golf game.

"I'm assuming tee time was pushed back because of the cooler weather. What do I owe this pleasure?"

"Courtesy call." Cruz sat erect with an unfamiliar glint in his eyes. "We've come across a discovery that might interest you."

"The only thing that'd grab my attention would be you telling me this nightmare is over, and my life is back to normal."

An instant vision of Jack's former existence paraded through his mind. His thriving career, the beautiful women he'd dated, the small but comfortable home overlooking the lake…golf on Saturdays.

"I'm afraid those days are on hold." Cruz almost smiled. "At least for now."

Jack released a sardonic chuckle, and fidgeted in his chair. "Nice way to put "you fucked up, dude."

"If we were out having a beer, that's exactly what I'd tell you. Since I'm calling on in a professional capacity, I'm keeping my language clean."

"Speaking of beer, you want one?"

"Did I not just say this is a professional visit?" Cruz fell against the sofa back and glanced at his wrist. "Dude, it's barely eleven."

"Don't tell me you don't drink when you schmooze clients, no matter the hour. Although I'm not practicing, I'm still in your profession. I know the drill." Jack pushed out of his seat. "Besides, time doesn't exist for the unemployed."

"Save the pity party. Don't buy it. You start to work for Aaron on Monday. You're not jobless."

"Sitting in a cubical at a computer performing background checks as opposed to advising insurance companies about the legality of transactions, and protect them from gratuitous actions? Not the same, my friend." He walked into the mini-kitchen. "While I'm grateful to Aaron for the offer of employment, I could do this job in a coma. Not even a minute challenge."

Cruz straightened and opened his mouth. He seemed about to argue then clamped his lips together. "Regardless, you look like you've had more than your share of booze, schmoozing or otherwise."

Jack chuckled as he retrieved two beers from the fridge and returned to the living area.

"Your effect on me is scary." Cruz took the bottle handed to him. "Whenever I'm around you, I revert to our partying days."

"You were the influential one back then. I owe you." Jack fell into his chair. "What's this intriguing news that motivated you to make a personal visit on a Saturday morning?" He twisted the cap off his drink. "Did I mention I'm not paying for this?"

Cruz opened his beer and took a long swallow. "Your former client has pulled this stunt before."

Jack stopped in mid-drink. His stomach constricted as he digested his old friends and counselor's words. "Say that again."

"Jenna Collin-Sheppard's insurance company sued another law firm, and the attorney representing her for malpractice. Nearly ten years ago and in different state. She won a sizeable settlement. We'll dig deeper. I bet we'll find she makes a habit of doing this kind of thing. She's a serial suer."

"Like the jargon. Should include it in the *Law Dictionary*." Jack raked his fingers hand through his too long, uncombed hair. "Damn. I knew she was calculating, but I had no clue about her shrewdness."

"Your investigators didn't do a background check on her, did they?"

"She was a client. We don't normally look into patrons credentials."

"Maybe you should start. Then the proverbial dropped ball wouldn't have smacked you in the ass."

"No reason to suspect she was playing us."

"Play you she did. She set you up to take a career ending fail." Silence fell between them, the men lost in their thoughts. Cruz finally spoke again. "Hopefully once we show her attorneys what we've discovered, we can get the lawsuits suspended against you and the firm."

"If the judge will allow you to submit the documents," Jack commented dully.

"We're anticipating we'll never see the insides of a courtroom after we present her lawyers with our findings."

"That would be a relief."

Relief was a minor description. The tightness in his chest may loosen. He might be able to inhale and not wonder if he were having a heart attack.

"No doubt, but this only gets you half off the hook," Cruz warned.

"Better half off than attached to the whole damn thing." Jack's gut squeezed and twisted, wishing life would allow do-overs. His existence had never been simple, and he fought for every step. Tough as things were, he wouldn't change one second. Until his encounter with this, this woman. He'd gladly give up everything to turn back the clock. "You clear me of malpractice, and I'll find a way to get free from the rest of this shit."

"I hope you can, brother."

"I will." Jack stated with such conviction that he almost believed it. "My representation abilities were right on. The reason we lost the case is because her company owed her former client compensation. I explained to her we stood a good chance of losing before I ever took her on."

"Yes, but winning wasn't her intention."

Obviously not. The woman attack Jack's professional behavior and, she also pounced on his personal character. She'd cried foul on so many levels, and her claims were taken seriously. Her aim was for financial gain from Jack and his law offices.

"We can expect these new discoveries to lessen her credibility. That should up the chances in the personal case too."

Jack snorted.

"You better hope so. May I remind you that your

license to practice law is suspended, along with your current attorney position?"

"No reminders required. I live with it every day."

"If your career survives this, you'll need to work your butt off to repair your reputation. It's going to take many years before people forget, and even exonerated, you won't find things easy on a personal level. You're tainted, cleared or not."

"That's fine. Nothing's been easy for me." The ever-present lump inside Jack's stomach swelled. "No matter what she says, I didn't do anything illegal. Workwise or personally. She knew the stakes."

"Right. A no strings deal."

"Strings?" Jack laughed. The woman resorted to using thick, nylon ropes, and she'd banded them around his life, coming after him at full force. He scrubbed a hand over his face. "Ah, women. Can't let 'em live, or something like that. How does the cliché go?"

"You don't need to worry about platitudes over the opposite sex. You should fixate on getting out of this crap."

"I am."

Cruz eyed him shrewdly. "So what have you been doing to keep yourself occupied? Besides keeping the stocks in your beer company sky high."

"Hmmm…found a corpse yesterday."

Cruz's brow rose.

"A murdered one."

His friend's mouth plummeted.

"I was jogging and came upon Hazel Nutt's mutilated body. I suppose you've seen the story on the news?"

Cruz nodded. "Sketchy."

"Well, if you witnessed an ass running away from the television cameras, it was mine."

Cruz laughed then his face turned serious. "Aaron's younger sister works for her."

"Worked," Jack corrected. "The Nutty lady fired her the day before she was killed. Makes Katie a viable suspect."

"Shame on many levels. She's phenomenal at her job. She coordinated mine and Daphne's wedding and reception." He looked at Jack. "How'd you find out about Katie's involvement? Aaron fill you in?"

"Aaron's been MIA for several days. Katie-or Katherine as she prefers to go by nowadays, showed up at my door yesterday looking for her brother. Somehow the conversation turned to her story, that, plus what I'd discovered at the crime scene gave me the keys to put things together. Apparently a former co-worker seems intent on making sure the authorities look at her long and hard."

"Ah, Vanessa King. She's become well-known in the area too. A huntress of sorts." Cruz leaned forward, retrieved her card that she'd insisted Jack take, and held it up. "Watch this one." He tossed it back onto the table.

Jack squinted, staring at the gold engraving etched across the cardstock. A flit of an alcohol induced memory swooped through his mind. He frowned and then he dismissed the image as an illusion.

Cruz drained his bottle and set it aside. "I can't imagine Katie Drapier killing anyone."

"Yeah, me either. The police aren't so sure."

"They'll figure it out. Its common knowledge Hazel kept valuables in her home. Bet it was a robbery."

"Doesn't appear to be, but who knows?"

"The killer, perhaps," Cruz stated, and then smiled. "Were you surprised when you saw Katie all grown up and looking so fine?"

"I didn't notice." Jack's voice was tight and cool. The last thing he wanted to think about was edgy, opinionated, shoe loving knockout.

"Are you serious?" Cruz expression converted into skepticism. "I almost fell out of my chair when I saw her. I was with my fiancé, who I'm deeply in love with. But whoa-Katie, which I can still call her." He stopped and whistled. "Grew from a cute, skinny tomboy into a real beauty."

Jack merely lifted a shoulder as a tingle below his belt reminded him of how nicely she filled out her worn jeans. Eyes of gold, auburn hair, thick and silky, the long strands grazed right below her shoulders, and though it didn't happen often, he liked the way her face lit up when she smiled.

Even so, the entire time they'd been together, he'd been either annoyed with her, or trying not to get too involved with her situation, which turned out to be laughable. Her cutting him off when he tried to apologize for his past transgression aggravated him too. Proved she remained his friend's infuriating sister. He had his own troubles to deal with, anyway. Plus, her growing quandaries could end up doubling his.

Her draw concerned the trendy area where her loft was located. Popular restaurants, movie theaters, bars, and plenty of night life surrounded the region with a lot of refurbished buildings updated into apartments or condos. If he could resolve his disputes and find a small firm to take him on, he'd definitely consider moving into her neighborhood. Had nothing to do with her.

Right. Except she'd been on his mind more than a little bit since they'd parted, and thinking of her brought the object between his legs back to life, despite his situation.

At least it did until he became too inebriated to think.

"Either you're made of stone or you're on the road to monksville." Cruz chuckled again. "The Jack Pharrell I know wouldn't let a gorgeous lady like Katie Drapier get past him without making a move."

"I discovered, the hard way, beautiful women are mere complications. Expensive too, sans her trust fund, or my present circumstances."

"Yes, but your current state is your own doing,"

"So I've been told," Jack replied dryly. "I place the blame on my material unit's nurturing skills."

"Your mommy's issues are a shrink's wet dream."

Jack swallowed hard, tasting bitter bile in his throat. "Don't need a psychiatrist to analyze my mother-son relationship." He held up his beer. "I save a lot of money on self-diagnoses."

"I bet you do." Cruz paused. "Come to think of it, Katie isn't your type at all. She's a nice lady."

"Nice? Katie Drapier was a major aggravation growing up, plus we're talking about our friend's sister," Jack reminded. "Man rule. We don't hit on our buddies relatives."

Cruz rose. "If you'd followed any rules, then you wouldn't be in the situation you're in."

"So close." Jack put his bottle to his lips and emptied the contents. "You went," he checked his watch, "almost five minutes without reminding me about my life in hell."

Cruz walked to the door. "That's what you're paying me the big bucks for."

"Ah, and remember. No bucks big or little for this particular hour. On the house."

"As much as you're going to owe me, I doubt forty minutes will affect my fee."

"Reminder. I'm not getting a paycheck at this point, and most everything I have is tied up in investments. Can't touch 'em. Hence," he spread his arms out to his sides and smiled, "the reason I'm crashing free of charge."

"We'll set you up on an easy payment plan." Cruz tapped the doorknob with his fingertips. "I'm working on getting a meeting together with Jenna's attorneys later this week. We'll discuss the particulars after. I'm sure you'll need to liquidate some of your funds, and you'll shell out a bundle to make this go away. The good news is it won't be as pricy as we once thought, and you may be able to return to being a practicing attorney sooner than we expected."

"A nice reprieve."

Cruz stepped past the threshold and outside before he turned back to Jack. "In the meantime, why don't you do something constructive other than drink or stumble upon dead people? Like get a haircut or find a razor."

Jack ran a hand over his chin stubble. "Shaved two days ago."

"You're a mess."

"You're going to miss your tee time." Jack pushed out of his chair and strolled to where his friend stood.

Cruz stuck his head around the corner. "You can't

give up, Jack."

A blast of cold air ripped across the manicured lawn, barreling through the opened door. The strong breeze lifted a folder lying on the entry table. Katie's papers scattered about the floor in a disseminated mess.

Cruz pointed to the sewn sheets. "What's all this?" He bent to pick up a page that landed at his feet. "Looks like lawyering stuff. You're not doing anything off the map, are you? Could create problems if higher powers discover you're fake practicing."

"No worries." He plucked the document from Cruz's fingers and shrugged. "Just helping out," he hesitated, "an acquaintance with legal issues. No tangibles, guidance only."

He spun away from the clutter, not wanting to view it again. He'd been excited when she'd first given him the paperwork, the thrill of sifting through clauses and phrases got his blood warmed and flowing. Once he was alone, he couldn't continue his study. His brief analysis made him realize how much he missed his work. Looking over those contracts depressed him, and he wished he'd never volunteered for several reasons even though he managed to complete the task. Now, he needed to call her, which led to an entirely different mixture of emotions he didn't want to think about.

"Good. You need to do something for someone else. Builds character."

"These past few months provided me with enough integrity development to last a lifetime. I'm ready to move forward." Jack lifted his gaze and peered out the window. "And I can't."

"Not yet."

Jack continued to stare through the glass long after

Cruz left. A gloomy haze swathed the mid-morning sky, signaling the threat of a stronger cold front blowing in. Trees quivered in the strong breeze, as several tenacious sprigs held on to the skeletal limbs for dear life. Out of the corner of his eye, a slight movement caught his attention. The gray cat sat beyond a hedge in a nest snapdragons and alyssum.

It returned his stare.

A small, beam of sunlight pierced the clouds casting an eerie radiance over the animal. They continued to look at each other. The shaft of light slowly dissipated as the sun faded into the gray swirls.

"You know," Jack whispered, staring the cat. "You know who killed Hazel Nutt."

The feline mouthed a meow, bolted, and disappeared.

Chapter 7

Katie rose in her bed, sheets snarled around her. She twirled and rolled to loosen the knotted mass. After several seconds of frantic kicking, and floundering, she finally broke free.

She pushed hair from her eyes and shook her head to drive away the wooziness. Resting upon her elbows, she stared at an exposed window trying to determine the time of day. The sun's pattern glimmered across the floor, and arced onto the wall, telling her it was early afternoon. A burr sound came from the left side. It took a moment for her to brain to adjust, and then she realized her phone laid buzzing on her nightstand. The reason she'd awakened.

She stretched diagonally over the mattress and retrieved the device. "Hello?" she mumbled, slackening into a stack of pillows with a yawn.

"Katie," came a deep voice on the other end. "Did I wake you?"

Her torso sprang upward, instantly rigid as her hand clutched the receiver. "A little."

"How can you be a little asleep?"

"Easy."

Jack chuckled. "Must be nice to snooze in the middle of the day."

"Rough night. I guess I gave out."

Lame. She should've thought of a better excuse for

her lethargic tone.

After all, Jack called her. She needed make this good. Then her memory unclogged and jiggled her back to the real world. She'd given him her number. The reason he'd phoned was because he had information for her.

"I'm assuming you're calling about the contracts."

"I am. I need to discuss them with you. In person works best so I can give you visuals. If you're finished with your snooze, can I drop by, say in an hour?"

Katie tucked her bottom lip between her teeth. Jack coming here? Nope. Would not work. Though her sensations were nothing more than an overworked imagination, an impression of his presence remained in her loft from his visit yesterday. The vibe unnerved her. She swore a hint of his scent still lingered inside her closet. Bottom line, she didn't need any more of his pheromones floating around. She had enough strangeness enter and exit her home.

Speaking of weird stuff, the strange knife lay on her coffee table. How would she explain? Plus, she and Jules left a sink full of dishes last night, and she was sure after sleeping most of the day, she looked more disastrous than her loft. An hour wasn't enough time for her to relocate the knife, clean her place, and make herself presentable.

"I plan on running errands later. How about I make a stop by the guesthouse?"

"That's a no go," he said. "Your brother and sister-in-law are going through with their renovations. The place is full of painters and designers with their drawings and swatches. They've spread shit everywhere. I'm outside braving the cold now. No privacy."

"I'm surprised Aaron and Lexie didn't invite you stay in the big house with them."

"They offered. I declined. I don't know Lexie well, and because of my circumstances, I'm uncomfortable being around people I'm not familiar with."

"Their home is large enough. You probably wouldn't run into anyone if you prefer seclusion."

"True. But I like my space. Even if I have to dodge decorators wanting to show me their samples."

"Male or female?"

"Let's not go there. Sooo, we're at an impasse on getting together, and I'd prefer to talk with you today, if possible. If you know of some place not too expensive, I'll spring for dinner." He paused. "Unless you made plans already?"

A night out with Jack. Not a real date, but still, this was the closest she'd gotten to spend an evening with him. "I do know of an eatery in the historical district downtown. The name is Broadway Bistro, located on Broadway and fourth."

"Original. Good food?"

"I've never been at night, though the lunches are delicious, and the prices are reasonable."

"See you at six."

She opened her mouth to confirm, but he'd rung off before she got the opportunity.

****

An anxious Katie climbed the trio of stairs to the renovated bistro, which was once Victorian cottage. She passed through a pair of stained glass doors to enter a small vestibule. The establishment was full of rich woods, antiques, flowering plants, and flowing fountains. The daytime patrons dined in overstuffed, leather wingback chairs, pushed up to white clothed tables. Pleasant, relaxing. A quiet place for her and Jack to discuss her contracts.

Inside, she stopped short on the top step of the entrance to the main dining area. Her gaze glided over the space, a hand covered her month. The causal lunch atmosphere had transformed into an intimate, dreamy hideaway. Lights turned low, candle flickered from every table. Soft jazz played in the background as the aroma of sizzling, mouthwatering entrée's drifted through the air. Patrons were seated in twos as the many couples enjoyed a romantic Saturday evening.

Katie took a step backward, digging into her bag. She had to call Jack and change their meeting location. A peek at this place, and he would get the wrong idea, or maybe the right one. Either way she predicted disaster brewing.

Against her better judgment, she'd talked herself out of turning around to swap her attire earlier. She'd explain away her long skirt and sparkly top as her office Christmas party outfit she wouldn't get to wear because of her termination. But overdressed combined with an amorous ambiance? Not so easy to justify.

"Katie."

Slowly she swiveled her head around and looked up. Too late.

Jack stood at a table toward the far back. He motioned at an empty chair across from him, his voice lifted above the crowd's chatters. "We're over here."

She dropped her purse to her side and sighed before she reluctantly walked to where he waited. Clad in nicer jeans, a jacket, and a button down, he'd even shaved and combed his hair. Therefore, she didn't feel as awkward dressed up.

Once they exchanged pleasantries and were in their seats, the waiter brought menus. He took their drink orders and hurried away to get their beverages.

"Nice place." Jack's mouth curved, his eyes held a mischievous twinkle. "Very, ahm," he glanced about before he returned to her. "Coupley."

Katie lifted her gaze from studying the main courses. "Jack, I'm sorry," she rushed.

He snapped up a palm. "No harm done. You said you'd only been here for lunch. You had no idea." He laid his hand next to his menu. "Smells delicious."

"The noon meals are good."

"Well, we'll enjoy." He tucked his chin, reading the selections in front of him. "We can even pretend we've always liked each other."

"That'll be fun."

The server brought their drinks, a basket of bread, and took their orders before he discreetly disappeared. Jack held her stare. He inhaled deep, reached inside his jacket pocket to retrieve a thick mound of tri-folded papers. He pushed them across the table.

"Five years."

Katie's gaze fell to documents. Her fingertips grazed the edges as she unfolded the sheets. She glanced at the highlighted clauses and gasped.

"If you leave Weddings Fantastic for any reason, you've agreed to stay out of party planning business for five years." Jack snatched a breadstick. "Unless your former employer shuts down. In other words, you can't work for the competition, which includes your own company."

She raised her eyes, her face paled. "Even though Hazel's dead?"

"From the way the clauses read, Hazel's demise has nothing to do with you staying out of the industry."

"Gotta be irony. She's burying *me* from the grave."

"Five years is a bit excessive, but from what I'm getting, this fits the Nutt's wacky M.O. A business attorney might find a possible loophole."

"Her name was Nutt for a reason." She gazed at him. "Any other options?"

"Hire a licensed lawyer and contest."

"Sounds costly."

"Yeah. If you're willing to spend some money, you might consider purchasing Hazel's company."

Her body tensed. "Seriously. Why would I?"

"I'm speculating." He gestured toward the papers. "I assume she left the business to a family member who probably isn't interested in taking over, so they may sell. Buying them may be a different angle to your plan B, or you can hope whoever inherits the company shuts them down. You might also make the acquisition to close the place, and use the loss as a tax write off, and then open your agency."

"Again, too much money. I'm trying to do this without Pop's help. I can operate a service on a shoestring budget. Run the company from my loft, and consider my home office a business expense. Besides Hazel's, Affairs Amore is the only wedding coordinators in the city who are actual corporations. The rest operate from their houses."

"Your call." He finished off his bread and reached for another. "I'd go the lawyer route. You might want to double up on legal counsel. This five year wait could be viewed as an extension of a motive to kill Hazel."

She sighed and tossed the papers aside. "Things keep getting suckier and suckier."

"You can probably get around this."

She'd debated the entire afternoon if she wanted to share the newest wrinkle in her life. Since they were pretending to be friends, she supposed she could rely on his discretion. She picked up the documents, folded them, and placed the paperwork into her bag. She went into a side pocket, captured a plastic baggie, and held it out to him. "I'm not talking about the contracts."

"What is this?" He stretched his arm until his fingers scraped the outside.

"A knife." She waited. "And it's not mine. It somehow appeared in my loft."

Jack snapped his hand back as if he'd scorched his fingertips. He stared at the bagged dagger lying in her palm. "How does something just somehow appear?"

"Good question." Katie withdrew the bag and replaced it inside her purse. "Jules found it buried in my sofa last night." She went on to explain about finding her door unlocked.

He gingerly slid a pat of butter over his breadstick. "Damn. Someone's been super busy. You're sure you latched the door?"

"I always do. I checked the locks after Jules left. Nothing inside around the edges was tampered with."

"So you're thinking someone might have broken in and hid a knife in your couch." Jack shifted in his seat. "Makes no sense."

"No," she said with a sardonic laugh in her voice. "It doesn't."

His gaze caught hers and held her stare. "What are

you going to do?" He nodded to the plastic hidden in the handbag pouch.

"Don't know. Suggestions?"

"Nope. You need to concentrate on your other issue. You called Cruz yet?"

Katie's skin heated as she shook her head.

"Promise me, you'll call. First thing tomorrow."

"It's Sunday, but I will get in touch with him on Monday."

"I have his private number. You can phone him in the morning." He took a sip of his drink, and then sat the glass down. "Contact a locksmith too. Get those locks changed."

"Good idea."

"Did you consider getting in touch the manager to your condo unit? For security reasons, most buildings install cameras in the parking garage and hallways. They usually keep the tapes for several days. Given the circumstances, they should allow you to view the video."

"I didn't think about the camera angle. But that's a wonderful idea," she said excitedly. "If those recordings show someone breaking into my loft, I could be cleared, right?"

"Be a good start. Also might confirm your whereabouts during the time of death too."

The waiter brought their food, placing an elegant meal in front of them.

Even with all of her troubles, Katie was famished. She hadn't eaten since yesterday, so she would be hungry. With the added excitement of possibly having alibis to get her off the hook, it'd take the entire kitchen to fill her up.

"I'll touch base with building management in the morning."

Jack picked up his steak knife and fork and sliced his veal. "I have a dumb question." He glanced at her. "Why did you bring the knife with you tonight? What's your motive?"

Katie stopped in mid-bite. "I don't have a motive. I'm confused how to handle this. I thought you might give me some advice."

He shrugged. "Report the break in and turn it over to the police would seem the logical way to go."

"Logical? I want to stay far away from the police right now. They may somehow link this to Hazel's murder."

"Avoiding them doesn't solve your problem. If you're so nervous about talking with them, take counsel with you."

She slammed her utensil onto the table and glared across at him. "Will you knock off the lawyer bit, legal boy? I got it. I'll get an attorney, but right now I need some reassurance from you."

Jack sat back in his chair and said through clenched teeth, "A little louder, please. The kitchen staff didn't hear the last part."

"Huh?"

He leaned forward and whispered, "You're yelling really loud. The whole place is staring at us."

Katie glanced around. She'd raised her voice too high, and the entire restaurant watched them. She smiled timidly and spoke to the crowd.

"Communication exercises. We're in couple's therapy."

"Aaahhh's" floated through the room and heads

bobbed as the patrons returned to their meals.

Jack stabbed his meat. "Nice save."

They made careful small talk throughout the rest of the meal. Jack pushed his plate away and surveyed the restaurant while Katie finished her desert. He nodded at the pair sitting several tables over. "A couple in the corner is still looking at us. Do you know them?"

Katie peeked over her shoulder and inwardly groaned. "Olga and Fredrick."

He frowned, leaning forward. "Who?"

"Vendors Weddings Fantastic used. Pretend you don't see them."

"Too late." He straightened. "They're heading our way."

Katie stiffened inside and out as the middle aged pair strolled to their table.

"Told you not to look," she said through gritted teeth, then turned to greet her former associates with a too bright smile. "Olga, Freddie, what a surprise."

"We're surprised too, Katherine." Olga tented her fingers in front of her. "Such horrible news."

"Hazel will be missed."

"Could care less about the old slug," Fredrick said. "She can corrode in hell. Your dismissal is what's devastating. A pity you're out of the business. We wanted to lend you our support."

"Thank you, you're very kind."

"We hope the situation isn't permanent." Olga glanced curiously toward Jack. "Do you have other options?"

Katie motioned in Jack's direction. "I'm discussing them with my attorney."

"Discussing," Fredrick repeated with a chuckle.

"That's where they're calling it these days."

Olga beamed at them. She patted Katie's shoulder and nodded while emitting a perceptive grin.

"Oh no. We're not..." Katie shook her head quickly and gestured between her and Jack. She glared at him for reinforcement, but he only raised his brows. "Anything."

"Of course." Fredrick's smile widened. "Don't worry." He snapped a finger to his lips. "We'll keep your little attorney client relationship a secret."

"We're praying everything works out for you, dear. Let us know when you return to the industry," Olga said as they stepped away. "We'll certainly want to work with you, no matter the circumstances."

Katie frowned. "What circumstances, Olga?"

"Hazel's murder." She and Fredrick walked toward the exit. "Hope the couple's therapy gets you back on track. You make such a lovely pair."

Katie turned to Jack, who sat quiet, his expression blank. "What do you think she was talking about?"

"An obvious fan of couple's therapy, didn't you hear? Must be working too, because we've been getting along for," he paused to check his watch, "nearly ten minutes."

"I'm meant what she said about wanting to work with me no matter the circumstances, and then referring to the whole Hazel thing."

"No clue. Sounded ominous, didn't it?" He cleared his throat. "Any chance they would have something to do with her death."

"Olga and Freddie?" Katie laughed. "Don't think so."

"Just a thought." Jack picked up his cup and took a

lingering sip.

After coffee, Jack paid the tab, then grasped her upper arm, and escorted her outside. The earlier cold front had blown through. The wind settled, and the clouds had cleared, leaving the moonless sky starry and bright. Quietly, they strolled past an array of shops. Although it was the first week of November, many were getting an early jump on Christmas. Hundreds of white, twinkly lights decorated the storefronts and landscaping, while holiday melodies danced in the light breeze, topping off the festive atmosphere.

Jack's hand remained lightly wrapped around her arm. Tiny white-hot needles pierced into her skin and tingled all the way down to her toes. Katie tried to remain calm, but her heart knocked loud enough to burst her eardrums. Exhaling was almost impossible. Forget about thinking clear.

They stopped at the front of her jeep. He released her. They turned to each other. Jack shoved his hands into his pockets, and scanned the parking lot before he rotated to face her squarely, his gaze steady, candid … staring.

Katie looked at his chin not wanting to meet his eye, yet doing her best to not linger at the unfastened top buttons of his shirt, exposing way too much chest.

"Tonight was—interesting," he commented wryly. "You understand your contracts with Weddings Fantastic now, right?"

She nodded.

"The tapes on your building's security camera should take suspicions away from you and show who broke into your place."

"I hope. If not, it's on me, I guess." Katie

moistened her lips, trying to ignore the sparkle from the fairy lights reflecting in his eyes.

"The knife…I don't know. This situation is so odd."

"Odd hardly describes it. Someone broke into my condo. Do you realize how violated I feel? A stranger was in my home. I was already afraid, but now I'm more frightened. I'm terrified to be alone in my own house. I can't sleep at night. I jump at every sound. I wonder if this person is watching me wherever I go."

Jack had the decency to appear uncomfortable. "I didn't realize what you were feeling. You shouldn't deal with this by yourself."

"I guess I am, though. I'm living in an overblown nightmare."

Jack rocked back onto his heels and exhaled loudly. "Close your eyes and pretend it's all a bad dream. That's how I've survived."

Another awkward silence settled between them. The Christmas music amplified over the roar of automobiles on the streets behind them. Katie studied him closely. He stared off into the darkness, appearing to have drifted out of the present.

"Jack?"

He abruptly returned to her. "The knife. It was a chef's knife, right?"

"Yes, a fairly sharp one." She gazed at him, confused.

"Let me have another look at it."

She retrieved the damning evidence from her purse and handed the plastic bag to Jack.

"Open your jeep door. I need some light." He turned the bag over, weighing it in his palm, seemingly stifling a gag. "This is blood on the blade." He returned the baggie to her.

"Blood?"

"Hazel was stabbed," he said in a quiet voice. "Far as I know, they haven't discovered the murder weapon." He stared directly at her. "I'm wondering if this is it."

Chapter 8

Katie stood in front of her bathroom mirror, doing her best to maintain a normal Sunday morning routine. She dipped a brush into her facial mask mixture, and then she spread the homemade goop over her forehead, ignoring little upsurges of nausea she contributed to nerves.

Her thoughts drifted. The strange knife...could it be the instrument that killed Hazel. Then the police interrogation and Jack...she sighed. No matter how she tried to keep her life in check, normal wasn't going to be possible. Sleep throughout the night barely existed.

She stirred the concoction and grazed even portions across her cheeks, wet the brush again, and raked the soft bristles gently over her chin and neck to finish off her treatment. After she was done, she picked up the bowl and put everything under the facet to rinse away the remaining ingredients.

A rap from outside interrupted her.

Her heart leaped into her throat. Visitors on Sunday morning? Perhaps it was someone from condo's main office. She'd rung them earlier to ask about viewing their videos, but because of the weekend, she'd gotten the answering machine. She left a message, and explained a condensed version as to why she needed the tapes without giving too much away. Maybe they were bringing her the cartridge now.

She rushed down the stairs and toward the knock. Skidding to a stop, she gazed at the tip of the plastic lying beneath her purse on the coffee table, leaving the blade's edges visible.

What if this was the weapon that killed Hazel? What if her intruder alerted the police? They'd gotten a warrant and were here to search her home or had come to arrest her? She didn't understand the particulars involving a search warrant. Could she refuse to allow them inside, or make them wait until she had a lawyer present? She blew out a long rush of air wishing she hadn't procrastinated on calling Cruz.

Should she hide the evidence before she answered? Then again, if they were able to legally go through her place, they'd find it hidden. There was no point in concealment.

The knock came again, this time louder.

She hurried to put an eye to the peephole and then jerked away. "You're kidding me." Katie stared at the door, fists planted on her hips, and debated whether she should open it.

"Katherine? Are you home?"

Katie heaved a sigh and reached for the knob. Vanessa sauntered past Katie, her arms stretched round a cardboard box. She stopped in the middle of the room and whipped around.

"Come in."

"I hope I'm not disturbing you. I realize it's Sunday and new jobs are posted. I assume you're searching for employment." She smiled. "Or maybe you're seeking a reasonable attorney?" Vanessa raked a gaze over her. "Or not."

"And you're here, why?"

"I've saved you a trip downtown. I packed up your belongings and am dropping them off. I'm sure under the circumstances the process would be painful for you." Vanessa paused before she moved into the dining area to sit the box down onto the table. She gave the carton an extra shove. "And inappropriate."

Katie's mouth clamped shut. She held her breath to restrain from screaming. The idea of Vanessa going through her personal things infuriated her. Why was she surprised? Of course this vile woman would clear out her large, corner space with the window, facing a nearby park. She'd probably already moved in, on the road to force her way into Hazel's private office.

"How kind of you, Vanessa." Her tone dripped with sarcasm.

"I do what I can to help. You're holding up—." She glanced around the loft, before she faced Katie, and flashed another fake smile. "Well, your place is nice. I hope you'll be able to afford it now that you're out of work."

Katie returned Vanessa's phony smirk with one of her own. She gulped back the bile as her stomach rolled. "Thank-you for the concern, but I made a good income throughout my time at Weddings Fantastic. I'll be comfortable for quite a while."

The money jab evidently hit home, the smug expression on Vanessa's face soured, though for only a moment. "Hmm, isn't everyone in your family wealthy—except you?" Vanessa let go a tinkling laugh. "It must be wonderful to depend on others for financial support during leaner times. Wish we all had such an easy life."

Katie's blood simmered. "My family's finances are

none of your business." She grasped the opened door and yanked it to widen the gap. "Thank you for bringing my stuff."

Vanessa sneered as she walked toward the exit. She halted near the doorway and spun to face Katie "I didn't bring everything."

"What did you want to keep a souvenir to remind you how you've helped wreck a company and several careers? Mine in particular?"

A gleam flashed in her eyes. "The police went through the entire building. They took the spare suit you'd left. And your shoes. I'm thinking they're checking for DNA."

Ah, the real reason for this unwelcomed visit. Vanessa hadn't just dropped by to goad Katie over her job loss, or a need for a lawyer, but she came to gloat.

Since day one, the woman had done her best to bring Katie down, and now she reveled in her impending collapse.

"I'm sure you were helpful in directing them to my office," she stopped. "You showed them where my personal items were located? This also means you knew where I kept my things. You've snooped through my stuff."

"I do my best to cooperate. Of course, I researched for information to keep the authorities informed. It's the law, Katherine. I not only want Hazel's killer caught, I expect her to be punished for this horrible crime."

"Yes, and we all know you—wait they took my Bruno Magli pumps? Those cost me an entire commission. They're returning them, right?"

Vanessa lifted a slim shoulder. "I would imagine they'll be considered evidence. Besides, you're going to need to get over your silly shoe addiction. They won't allow you to wear anything but generic sneakers in prison."

"While I think it's wonderful you've convicted me without a shred of evidence, let me inform you I've never killed anyone," Katie grinned, "yet."

"Huh. That sounds like a threat."

"More like a promise." She pulled at the door again. "Now that you've polluted my home with your antagonism, will you please leave?"

"You must admit you have a powerful motive." Her gaze drifted toward her coffee table and settled on her purse.

Katie's heart pounded. She should've put the damn knife somewhere out of sight. Anxiety gripped her tighter. Katie turned away from her uninvited guest and released a long, internal shudder. Once again, she wondered how the chef's knife mysteriously got inside her home and if it was the murder weapon. Someone put it there. Someone as in the real killer? She swung toward Vanessa. Was she the culprit? Suspicions churned as memories wafted to the unlocked door.

Katie gulped hard. "People get fired from their jobs all the time," she said, doing her best to keep the tremble out of her voice. "Few kill their former bosses over termination, unless their mentally off balance. I definitely don't fall into that category."

Vanessa's eyes narrowed. "Don't play coy, Katherine." She stepped closer and pointed a finger close to Katie's face, who resisted the urge to slap it away. "It wasn't only the job you lost, but you stood to lose the entire company. You knew Hazel was going to make some major changes and that's why you killed her," Vanessa hissed. "Let me tell you, you were too late. She rearranged everything before she died, and you're out. No más. I made sure the police is aware your animosity over this, too."

Katie's brow puckered. "What are you talking about?"

"Katie?"

She swirled around. Her heart tightened. Jack stood in the opened doorway of her loft, his emerald eyes darting. His dark hair looked like he'd jammed his fingers through it repeatedly.

She didn't even stop to wonder why he showed up this morning, she was glad he was here. He stepped through the entrance his surprised gaze bounced from her to Vanessa. The sight brought a thin frown to his lips, his features appeared worried.

"Jack?" Vanessa's brief stunned guise evolved into a flirty smile. "I didn't realize you knew Katherine."

Jack glanced at the woman and then stared at the floor. "We go way back," he mumbled.

"Tara mentioned she went to school with you, and Katherine attended your high school too, didn't she?" She displayed a spiteful glimpse at Katie. "I can't imagine the two of you even being acquaintances."

Katie spoke through gritted teeth. "Jack is friends with my brother."

"That explains the connection. I seem to recall Tara saying something about you being an athlete, Katherine. I'm guessing a guy like Jack wouldn't run in the same circles with a "female" jock."

Jack looked up, a serious gaze fixated on Vanessa. "We didn't have a lot in common. Katie comes from a normal loving family. I didn't grow up in the best of circumstances. My mother deserted me when I was twelve, and I've never met my father. The Drapiers took me in instead of allowing me to go into foster care. I'll always be grateful."

"Hmm, how fortunate for you that Katherine has such wonderful parents."

"Vanessa, I appreciate all you're efforts, but Jack and I must attend to some business. I'm sure you have a list of others to terrorize this morning, and I'd hate for you to get behind."

Vanessa ignored Katie, flipping a lock of hair over her shoulder. She strolled to Jack. "I'm glad you called the other night," she said to him in a whispery voice. "I had a great time at the pub."

Katie's mouth dropped, her arm collapsed and smacked her outer thigh. Jack had phoned Vanessa. He'd asked her out and she's obviously accepted. Like she wouldn't.

Katie glared at him. He fidgeted nervously.

"Well, I'll leave you two to your—," Vanessa self-assured grin widened as she ambled into the hallway. She twirled to face them, "meeting. Let's get together again, Jack. Soon. And Katherine…"

Katie slammed the door. She swirled round to Jack, who now appeared to have gathered his faculties. She glared at him. Her arms folded across her middle, her mouth formed a straight line. Jack and Vanessa had met the other night. As in a date?

Jack's lips slightly curved, but his gaze darkened with concern. "I'm not going to even ask what that was about." He walked to the counter and gestured toward the empty wine bottle. His brows rose. "She drove you to drink?"

Katie dropped her arms and shook her head, her throat thick from agitation. "You see an empty bottle, I see a Saturday night."

A side of Jack's mouth lifted. "Touché."

She struggled to keep her emotions in check. Speaking with Jack always unnerved her. No matter how hard she tried not to, they ultimately ended up in a fight, and she wanted to avoid that. Needing something to do, she stepped to the bar and snatched the empty wine bottle, prepared to throw it in the trash. Her fingers curled around the neck of the decanter. A large, warm hand covered hers.

"Katie," he said softly. "Calm down. She's gone."

She raised her eye to meet a penetrating gaze. Neither spoke. A burst of white-hot shudders ignited in the pit of her stomach. The tension upped a hundred degrees. The spark in Jack's stare generated Katie's heart to give a steadfast thud, as an ocean of water formed inside her mouth. His solid, muscled chest moved up and down slowly, demanding her attention.

As always, his presence captivated her, forcing her to overlook her anger, and forget about everything except for the man holding her hand. The essence of what his touch implied roasted her insides to the point she shook with desire. Anything and everything else happening in her life escaped her. Fearing she was about to pass out, she broke eye contact, catching a glimpse of the box sitting on the table.

He squeezed her hand. "Katie?"

There gazes met again. A blast of reality cerebrally smacked her in the head.

He'd been with Vanessa. And knowing her, the situation wasn't innocent. Instant agitation had Katie ready to explode. To the point of kicking him out of her loft. Except she wanted to know the reason for this surprise visit.

She released the bottle and broke free of his grip. "I'm calm."

"I can tell." His gaze remained on her, his mouth slowly turned up. "So I'm too curious not to ask. What was the purpose of Vanessa's visit?"

Katie sighed. He wasn't going to give her the explanation she wanted, but she had to let this go. Their relationship went slightly beyond professional. Realistically she didn't own Jack. He was allowed to date whomever he chose. Besides Vanessa, there was a little matter in their past that kept jabbing her.

She motioned at the box, sitting on the table. "She cleaned out my desk."

"Ouch."

"I know, right. The police were at the office. They took my extra suit I kept there and this great pair of pumps I'd only worn, like twice."

"Oh no. They took your shoes. That leaves you with what, nine thousand other pairs." He folded his arms over his chest and nodded. "Shoe stores better stock up."

She opened her mouth to retort, but the words jammed inside her throat. A palm flew to her to her abdomen. A rapid wave of nausea rolled through her gut.

The other hand gripped the back edge of a chair. She could almost feel her skin turn green. Poised to run to the bathroom, she took a step and then came to an abrupt halt. Sweat dotted her forehead. She swallowed, forcing a sudden surge of queasiness away as she deeply inhaled several times. Thankfully, the sickness faded.

"A little hung over are we?" Jack observed her. His intense look was blatant reminder of her ratty shorts and an old t-shirt she'd put on first thing this morning.

"Jules stopped by after I got home the other evening. We shared a couple of bottles of wine, and I finished off what we didn't drink last night. I'm not a drinker. I guess those last few glasses did me in."

"Best to not become a pro, no matter how bad the situation."

"Are you speaking from experience?" Katie asked sharply.

"I've recently developed an expertise in professional drinking."

"You know booze never solved any problems."

"Neither does milk." Jack stepped into the kitchen. "Do you have tomato juice?" He didn't wait for her to answer, but opened the refrigerator and bent to peer inside.

"Bottom shelf, side door." She watched him warily. "That's an odd question. Did you come over here to borrow juice?"

"No, I came over because I forgot to give you Cruz's phone number. We kind of drifted into some uncharted waters last night when discussing the knife, and ignored any solutions." He turned to her. "Glasses?"

"Top cabinet left of the sink."

He went to the indicated cupboard and removed a tall glass. "I also wanted to let you know the police called me this morning. They're collecting evidence from everyone who worked with Hazel and witnesses from the crime scene."

"Why?"

"They want the clothes we wore that day for DNA testing. Either to omit that person, or," he stopped and shrugged. "That's the reason they wanted your things. Vanessa wasn't giving you the whole story."

"Bitch"

Jack laughed and rotated to face her, his palm resting on the counter. "Now go wash, and I'll make you my hangover cure. Guaranteed you'll feel good as new in no time."

"Wash?"

"You've got—," he circled his face with a forefinger, "stuff. I can't have a serious conversation with someone who has blue crap spread over their face. I prefer to see someone's expression."

"Oh, my mask." How could she forget her facial was still in progress? Heat grew under the thick pack as she hurried upstairs toward her bathroom."

"Katie?"

Katie froze, her entire body tensed.

Jack gazed at her with a sharp look. "We need to talk."

Chapter 9

He didn't want to get involved. If he stayed another second, he would end up regretting it. Jack should say, "see ya", walk away, and let Katie figure things out.

Yet here he was, in her kitchen, preparing a hangover cure.

Adding pepper to the brew, he searched the drawers until he found a spoon. He stirred the concoction until the mixture blended. Utensil in the sink, he carried the glass into the main area, and sat the drink on a coaster before he relaxed onto the couch. Since he didn't get much of an opportunity yesterday, he took advantage of his alone time, and studied her living space. The place, painted in various shades of green, came off warm and open, the furniture was overstuffed, comfortable. Better than what those overpriced designers were doing at the guesthouse, even if Katie's décor seemed a little too feminine for his taste. Still everything was neat. Tidy.

Elbows resting on his knees, he swiped a palm across his face. He used to be well-organized. Until his life plummeted to the proverbial rock bottom. Then he ceased to care anymore. Jack dropped his hand and slouched into the cushion. *Don't think about the past.*

He inhaled deeply and straightened. He turned his nose upward, sniffing again. A sweetness lingered. Pleasant. Dangerous. Coming from—he swung his gaze to the floating staircase. Katie quietly descended, clean, and fresh faced.

Then it hit him. Like a thousand pound piece of steel collided into his head. The wonderful fragrance belonged to her.

Golden eyes captured and held his as she gently stepped over the tiled floor. She sat across from him, dressed in running shorts and a tight fitting t-shirt, a pair of bright, lime green socks covered her unshod feet. Her skin gleamed from scrubbing. She'd pulled her thick, auburn mane into a loose ponytail, and she let it cascade down a shoulder.

Jack swallowed hard and did his best to disregard the lovely vision as he gulped for air. He may suffocate from the growing friction between them. This tension wasn't like the hostility from the past. No, this conflict was totally different. Sexual.

Your best friend's sister. Don't go there.

He picked up the glass and extended his mixture to her. "Bottoms up."

She took the drink, and raised the beverage for a timid sip as he confined his attention on her mouth.

She made a face from the taste. "This is a real surprise."

He blinked to reorganize his focus.

"I mean, you." Katie cleared her throat and skimmed the room. "Here."

"I'm thinking I arrive just in time by the way you two were going at it. Rub you both with oil and throw you into a vat of Jell-O, and this would be an enjoyable morning for me."

"Can gelatin be used as a weapon?" She lifted the glass to him then sat it onto the table without drinking.

"Seriously, if that woman stayed any longer I might be a suspect in two killings. Only this one would be valid."

"She does seem to antagonize you."

"Because she's hell bent on having me arrested, convicted, and spend the rest of my life in prison for Hazel's death."

Jack didn't think so. No doubt Vanessa had a conniving streak, but he couldn't believe she would sink low enough to railroad an innocent person to jail. Yes, she did point the police in Katie's direction, but because of her circumstances with Weddings Fantastic, they would've investigated her anyway, no matter who delivered the information. Vanessa wasn't determined to hang her out to dry. She just enjoyed pushing Katie's buttons.

"You're overreacting." His tone reflected his doubt. "You don't like each other, so you've both blown the situation out of proportion."

Katie stared at him like he'd dropped in from outer space. "Keep hanging around her." She shrugged and returned to her drink. "You'll see."

Jack remained silent. He had enough experience with Katie to know when not to argue.

"I can't believe you're interested in her," she blurted. Her pale skin altered to crimson. She quickly looked down, her expression scrunched as if she wished she could take back her outburst.

Jack interested in Vanessa. At one point he thought their evening was a dream, and he barely remembered spending time with her. He should explain. But if he clarified, it'd mean he had feelings for Katie, and he wouldn't allow that to happen.

He cleared his throat. "What did Vanessa say that

makes you think she's implicating you in the murder?"

"To start with, she did give the police my name."

"You were the latest terminated employee. They would've zoned in on you anyway. What else you got?"

"Several things. Most I can dismiss as idle. But she did say something about changes Hazel made which would affect me and make me kill her. That bothers me."

"Well, she did fire you. That is a huge change."

"Yeah, but that's not it. This was somehow, different."

She leaned back and propped her legs onto the table in front of her, crossing her ankles. The pit of his stomach stirred, and spiraled downward. Jack did his best not to stare. Her ass was great, but those legs were spectacular.

Control, Jack. Remain in control. Stop the crazy thoughts.

He lowered his chin and focused on the tile pattern between his feet. He hoped he wasn't drooling. This monk-like existence he'd been living was beginning take its toll.

He cleared his throat, again redirecting his concentration on their conversation. "Different, how?"

"I can't put my finger on any one thing."

"Maybe something classified?"

"You obviously didn't know Hazel Nutt. She never spilled her business secrets."

"Nope. I'm glad I missed the pleasure." He certainly was happy he hadn't met the conniver from rumors circulating. He especially disliked the woman over her treatment of Katie.

"So you said earlier we needed to talk about

something. I'm sure you didn't come all the way over here to defend Vanessa."

He ignored her adverse remark and glanced at the plastic covered handle sticking out of her handbag. Chills peppered down his neck. His initial instinct was rush the evidence to the detectives right away. Except deep inside, he understood the repercussions. Katie didn't kill Hazel. She deserved a fighting chance.

He bobbed his head toward her purse. "Do you think it's wise to leave that so accessible? Even if it wasn't the murder weapon, if Vanessa happened to glimpse underneath, you'd be sunk."

"She didn't see anything." She frowned at her pocketbook. "I can't decide what to do with it."

"You know what needs to be done."

She leaned forward and set the glass down hard enough for the contents to slosh over the side. Falling back into the sofa, she fingered the strands from her ponytail and stared at the tip of the baggie. "Turn it over to the police." She sighed. "After I call a lawyer."

"Legal boy taught you something."

"I'm scared, Jack," she almost whispered. "I'm afraid the authorities won't believe me."

"You're taking a bigger risk if Vanessa or the person who planted that alerts them that you're in possession of the possible evidence used in a killing. What's more, you've got a stranger, maybe a murderer, going in and out of your home at will. The other reason I dropped by was to suggest you consider staying with your folks until this is over and the guy is locked away."

Her mouth flattened. "I don't think so. I contacted the complex about getting a video tape, and I plan on changing the locks. That should be enough."

"I disagree."

"Disagree all you want. I'm not going to let whoever this is manipulate me, Jack. I'm won't play their game."

"Game? Games have rules. This guy works according to his own guidelines."

She turned to face him, staring him directly in the eye. "If he's aware he's getting to me, I let him control me."

He released a sarcastic laugh. "This person's already proven he can get to you whenever he wants. That makes him all the more dangerous, Katie. You need either some physical protection or to go into hiding until whoever this is, is behind bars. Whoever broke into your place is probably Hazel's killer. Don't assume they will stop at one murder if their plan doesn't work out." Jack hated being so gloomy, but the idea of anything happening to her, especially something as irreversible at death, troubled him. More than unjust to another human. "Forgive me if I sound like a parrot, but let me stress again—find an attorney, and let's get you some protection."

"I will. At least on the lawyer part. I'm supposed to meet my parents for brunch in a couple of hours. I'll ask Pops to call Cruz."

Jack eyed her suspiciously. "Are you going to let them in on everything?"

Katie's dad was always overprotective of his little girl, and she was close to her mother. Her family wouldn't allow her to stay alone if they were aware of the circumstances.

Her skin flushed as she picked up the glass rolled it

between her palms. "I'm not sure how much I'll tell them."

She planned on handling this by herself, but he refused to let anything happen to her. Best let her think she was getting her way.

Jack glanced at the beaker sandwiched by her hands. "Stomach better?"

She brought her drink to her mouth to finish off the liquid then licked away the excess moisture.

Jack focused on her tongue, swiping across her lips, moving in slow motion. He scooted to the edge of the sofa and rose to his feet, needing to go before he did something stupid.

She held up the empty glass. "This must be good stuff. My stomach was double knotted. This relieved my pain."

"Glad I could help. I'm repeating myself, but be careful, Katie. If you insist on being stubborn, then at least be aware of your surroundings. Don't go anywhere alone, and keep all doors and windows doubled and tripled latched." He laid a card on the coffee table. "Cruz's home number is on the back. Call him."

****

Katie strolled into the elegant restaurant's vestibule where she was scheduled to meet her parents for brunch. Jules met her at the front entrance, her arms full of menus.

She looked at her friend in mock surprise. "Double duty today? Maître d' and restaurant owner?"

"I'm filling in until Maurice's replacement gets here. He called in." Jules rolled her eyes. "Again."

"He seems to be doing that a lot lately."

"He's got an emergency at least once a week. I'd fire him except he's been with me forever, and my customers love him so much they may abandon me if I let him go."

Jules guided her through the luxurious entryway of her pride and joy, and halted at the vast entrance leading into the dining area. "I've already seated your parents." She pointed to the handsome couple sitting next to an arched window reflecting the mid-morning sun. She leaned closer to Katie and lowered her voice. "Are you going to tell them about finding that knife?"

"Not sure."

"Your mother will freak, and expect your dad to insist you move home if they believe someone is going inside your place without your knowledge."

"Probably. It'll be a fight to keep my space, and I'm not up for another battle today."

Jules frowned. "Another battle?"

Katie laughed sarcastically. "Let me tell you about my morning visitor."

"I can't believe Vanessa actually came to your apartment, and she's done more to indicate you," Jules exclaimed after Katie finished explaining Vanessa's uninvited visit. "There's no level of low the woman won't stoop. I wouldn't be surprised if she hid the knife in your couch, though I can't imagine why she would."

"How about if the knife was used to kill Hazel?"

Jules stared at her.

"Hazel was stabbed. They haven't found the murder weapon. It's covered in something, and it might be blood."

"And you think Vanessa did this?"

"She's determined for me to be arrested, and spend

the rest of my life in prison to get me out of the party planning business. Though the jury's still out if she's clever enough to break into my apartment."

Jules fingers tightened around the leather bound menus and clutched them to her chest. "Sounds like her methods goes way beyond getting you out her line of profession. She's acting certifiable."

"She always was. Her true colors are becoming more vibrant to the naked eye."

A new group of customers arrived. Jules put on her professional smile and nodded. She kept her attention focused on the waiter replacing her while she and Katie talked. Once assured the party was cared for, she returned to Katie. "Did Jack get back to you on those contracts?"

"We, ahm, had dinner last night to discuss them."

Jules looked surprise. "Whose idea was that?"

"His." Katie debated in sharing the events of their evening now, or wait and deliberate the specifics later. After Jack's suggestion the knife was the possible murder weapon, she and her friend would want to spend a lengthy amount of time dissecting the premise. Right now, she needed to get inside and speak with her parents. "He dropped by this morning too."

Jules' lips turned up. "He's coming around a lot. Sounds as if he's changing his opinion where you're concerned. How about an apology?"

"Not yet. And don't get any ideas. He also went out with Vanessa."

Jules' expression fell as she shook her head. "He's got major taste issues when it comes to women, present company excluded."

"Thanks. There's other stuff I want to talk over

with you too. But we'll postpone that conversation until we have an entire evening."

"We'll need more vino. Good thing I got in a new shipment. I ordered a lovely Rosa´ I want you to try."

"Can't wait."

"What did Jack say about the contracts?"

"I have to hold off for five years before I can start my party planning business."

Jules gasped and gave her a hard look. "Katie, that's crazy. Jack's help is limited, I hope you plan on getting some professional legal advi—"

"Hey girls."

The women jumped.

"Tara." Jules glanced at Katie.

Katie returned her friend's worried gaze. They'd known Tara since school and through Weddings Fantastic, though they weren't close friends. On the surface, Tara appeared to be a straight shooter, but privately Katie was never certain of her former co-worker's alliances. Katie didn't trust her. She wondered how much of their conversation Tara overheard.

Jules smiled too bright at Tara. "Table for one? Follow me and I'll seat you. Andre´ is the best. He'll be taking care of you."

"No need." She waved at Jules. "I'm here for a meeting, and I'm early. I'll go to the bar and have a Bloody Mary while I wait." Tara rotated toward Katie and held out her arms. "I'm so sorry about you losing your job. Then this whole sorted mess with Hazel," she choked.

Katie hugged her in return. "I'm at a loss as to what to say too."

The women separated. Tara pushed her glasses up

her nose and sniffed. "It's still fresh. Hazel wasn't the best example of the human race, and she made a lot of enemies." She fanned a hand in front of her face to fight off the tears. "I can't believe someone killed her."

"I'm having a difficult time wrapping my mind around that too." Katie fumbled, straightening the strap on her bag.

"I'm glad you're out and about," Tara told her. "After everything you've been though, it'd be easy to hole up."

"I'm meeting my parents for brunch." Katie gave her a strained smile. "Sunday ritual."

Tara nodded and scanned the room. "You're extremely courageous to brave such exposure, given the circumstances."

Katie glanced nervously at Jules, who shook her head.

"What circumstances?"

"The rumors, Katie. The gossip circulating around town about you."

"Gossip?" Jules hackles rose. "This restaurant is located main hub of the city. I hear everything, and I haven't heard a word concerning Katie."

Tara turned to Jules. "People probably wouldn't say anything to you because you're her friend. Believe me they're talking. A lot."

Katie gulped loud and stared at her former co-worker who gave her a sharp look in return. She steeled herself, preparing for what was about to come. "What are they saying, Tara?"

Tara blinked repeatedly, her expression innocent. "Your imminent arrest for Hazel's death." A hand flew to her chest. "Please don't take this as my personal opinion, because I know better. But the whole town believes you killed her. They think you're a murderer."

Chapter 10

"This is quite a pickle, Katie." Cruz placed the phone's receiver into the cradle. He stood behind a polished mahogany desk, tapping a pen on a legal pad. The handsome attorney studied Katie with a cool, dark gaze, who returned his stern stare with a seething glare of her own.

Teeth clenched, she dug her nails into the leather chair she occupied. "You think, Cruz?" She straightened and tightened her grip. "I'm in a pickle?" Grasp slackened, she fidgeted restlessly in her seat. "The whole town believes I killed Hazel."

Her mother, Lila sat next to her, wringing a wadded tissue between both hands. Seated on the other side of Katie, ankle crossed over his leg, his cowboy hat hitched onto his protruding knee, was her father, Jed.

Forced to come clean over brunch, thanks to Jack for contacting them, both were ready to jump into action before Katie had a chance to explain. Her dad had already done what she'd postponed doing, and called Cruz. They drove here straight from the restaurant. This was how she found herself in his office late Sunday afternoon.

Katie's mother leaned over and patted her daughter's arm. "Easy, darling. Cruz is going to help you." She looked at the younger man across from her, her expression pleading. "You can make this go away,

111

right?"

"He damn sure better," growled her father. He plowed his fingers through thick, graying hair. "I pay your firm a lot of money for personal and business dealings. I expect you or someone in this office to get my baby girl out of this—" He squinted. "What did you call it? Pickle?"

"I'll do whatever I can, Jed. This is a small firm. There isn't a criminal defense attorney on staff," Cruz clarified patiently. "Therefore, murder cases aren't our specialty. We're acquainted with quite a few lawyers who do handle this type of situation. We'll find someone to step up for her."

"I don't want just anyone, Cruz. I expect the best, and by best I mean get my daughter out of this mess." Jed nodded at the phone on Cruz's desk. "What exactly did your police friend say?"

"They received an anonymous tip Katie is in possession of an item connected to the victim's death. The detectives working the assignment will speak with the court about issuing a warrant to search her place. If they discover the knife and determine it to be the murder weapon there's a good chance they'll arrest her. The only positive is it's difficult to find a judge available on Sunday, so they probably won't make a move until tomorrow. Lucky this is a smaller city or they could obtain authorization with a phone call."

Katie's head spun. She clutched her stomach. Her "hangover" nausea returned.

"That easy?" Her father gave Cruz a doubtful look. "What's our options?"

"None really. There's a good chance the judge will deny the request since the source is an unknown individual. No real substance to support the claim."

"They'll let this go?" Jed asked.

Cruz shrugged. "Anything's possible, but again we're dealing with a smaller town with a "bubba" mentality. Which means, sometimes they bend the rules and don't require a named informant." He gazed at Katie. "Be prepared. Though the warrant must be specific, authorities can go through an entire home. They make a huge mess, and they don't do clean up."

"That just makes my day," Katie mumbled.

"Sorry I can't give you better news. You should've brought me the knife the moment you discovered it. We could've started damage control earlier. Actually calling me before they interviewed you would've helped more. Either way, we still need to turn the blade over to homicide so it can be analyzed. This situation might be over if your condo units cameras worked," Cruz stated. "I find it strange someone accidently turned them off. I wonder if the person who broke in managed to disengage the equipment before they entered Katie's loft."

"That is a huge blow," Lila said quietly. "We appreciate you taking the time out of your weekend, you've helped us so much already, but I have another question. What do you suggest we do until we hire a criminal lawyer?"

"Lie low. Keep out of the limelight. Don't talk to homicide without representation, and don't speak with reporters-ever. Jed, you carry a lot of clout around here. Call in favors. I'll start working on securing the best criminal attorney in the area the moment you leave. He will instruct you after that."

"What will he advise?" Lila wanted to know.

Cruz picked up the pen again, clicking the top several times. "He'll suggest the two of them go to the detectives with the item and turn the presumed evidence over. What they'll do after that is anyone's guess." He stared at Katie. "The more cooperative you are the easier things will be for you in the long run."

"You mean the DA might offer me a better deal? Fifty years instead of life in prison?"

Neither idea appealed to her. And Cruz and her family weren't really helping. Going to the police may be the right thing, but the right thing sure wasn't the most desirable. Instincts told her, the knife in her possession was in fact the instrument used to kill Hazel and someone was trying to get her to take the fall for the crime. She could stash the damning proof until she discovered who was setting her up since no one else seemed too interested in finding that out. The only risk was the possibility of the law watching her. She must plan her recourses carefully—and quick. Time, or the lack of, would be a major factor.

"Katherine," Lila admonished. "You must keep positive thoughts."

"I am." Katie was usually glad her mother maintained an upbeat attitude. In fact, she loved her for it, but right now, she wished her mom would be more realistic. "I'm positive someone is setting me up to take the fall for Hazel's murder so whoever did kill her can walk free." She flung herself against the chair's back and collapsed. "Face it, mom, I'm now the police's number one suspect. They're not going to look at anyone else."

"That's not your only problem," Cruz warned as he lowered into his chair.

"Cruz is right," Jed agreed. "Someone dangerous has zeroed in on you. I'm guessing if you play complacent, and proceed through the motions, you stand the possibility of going to prison, but this person won't do you any physical harm. If you make waves, they may be desperate enough to go after you."

A shocked gasp escaped from her mother as a hand flew up, her fingers fanned across her chest. "Jed, we need to hire someone to protect Katie."

"Mom, don't over react." Katie focused sharply on Cruz, silently demanding his support. "No one will hurt me."

Jed tapped her on the arm. "Young lady."

Crap. Whenever her father used the term "young lady" Katie was done. The phrase meant he'd made up his mind. The discussion was over, and no use arguing.

"We'll take every precaution to keep you protected. Money is no object here."

"I know, Pops."

As strong as her feelings were for Jack, she wanted to strangle him for notifying her folks. She'd preferred to do this her own way, in her own time.

"Good. You understand once we leave here, you're to go to your condo, pack some essentials, and move back to the ranch until this nightmare is over. And by necessities, I mean only bring what you need. All those damn shoes you love so much stay behind."

Though Katie realized her efforts were futile, she would rather not to live with her parents. "Pops, I don't want to disrupt my life. I've been on my own since high school. I prefer not to—."

"Too late." her dad broke in. "Your life is already disrupted. You're in danger, Katie. Therefore it is necessary to disturb your routine for your safety's sake. No argument."

"Jed makes sense, Katie." Cruz interjected.

Katie stood, her mother followed suit. The women moved away from the men, who'd clustered and become engaged in planning options for her, and probably for the rest of her life.

Lila took Katie's hand and held it between her palms. "We'll have fun. Like when you were a little girl." She beamed. "Christmas is around the corner. I've already started baking. Remember how you loved to help me in the kitchen?"

"I licked spoons and batter from the bowls. And while I still enjoy that, I don't need the added preservatives or extra calories."

Her mother released her and waved. "You and your healthy foods. The best method for eating is from plain home cooking. You grew up that way and turned out fine." She glanced at the men, still in a whispered huddle. "I'll ride with you and help you pack." She leaned in, lowering her voice. "We can sneak some shoes in too. Pops will never know."

"Thanks mom. But I'd rather do this by myself. I have a few things I want to take care of. I'll be a while."

"I don't like the idea of you alone."

"I need these last few minutes. I promise to be careful."

Her family bid Cruz goodbye and walked to the parking lot. Dusk had set in early. The evening was cold but calm. Katie strolled to her jeep assuring her parents she'd be cautious. She guaranteed them she'd call frequently until she arrived at her childhood house.

Neither was happy with her going alone, though they didn't disagree. At least they understood her need for these final moments.

Inside her vehicle, she stuffed a wad of cash her mother slipped her, in case she needed anything, into her purse. Her cell buzzed. She checked the caller ID and punched the on button.

"Katie." Jules voice vibrated from the other end.

"It's me." Katie started her car and turned down her radio.

"Are you still at Cruz's?"

"I'm leaving his office now." She maneuvered her jeep into light traffic. She tapped the gas pedal, passing a dark pickup crawling in the next lane, and pointed the car toward her home. "Apparently the police are aware that I'm in possession of something belonging to Hazel. They are trying to get a search warrant. The news could be better, but it is what it is, so I'm dealing with yet another catastrophe. I'm heading to my place now. I'm going to pack up and move in with my folks."

Jules tone held a trace of laughter. "You knew that was coming."

Katie chuckled wryly. "How has the rest of your day gone?"

"Interesting." She paused. "The meeting Tara told us about was with Vanessa."

"At the restaurant?"

"No. I happened to be in my office and glanced out the window when I spied her getting into Vanessa's car."

"That is interesting. No love lost between those two. I wonder what was so important they needed to meet up on a Sunday."

"Whatever they were discussing included Rhett Oates. He was in the passenger seat."

"Rhett Oates? The owner of Affairs Amore, Hazel's biggest competitor?"

"The same. I thought they might work for him now that Weddings Fantastic's future is possibly up in the air."

"Doubtful. Rhett fired Vanessa from her last job, and I can't see him wanting to hire Tara."

"Didn't Rhett offer you a position not too long ago?"

"Yes he did. The deal was lucrative. I considered taking it. I unsure why, but I got a bad vibe about the whole thing so I turned him down. Besides, I'd set goals for myself. I didn't see the need to change yet. He wasn't happy with me for passing on his offer. I'm thinking my rejecting him wasn't one of my better ideas."

She glanced into her rearview mirror. The pickup she'd passed when she'd left Cruz's office still followed her. It had closed in, and sat on her bumper. Headlights glared into her rear window, blinding her through the mirrors reflection.

Needle pricked across the back of her neck. Was this person tailing her? She deliberately gunned the accelerator. The truck mimicked her movements, staying with her. Not using her signal, she jerked the wheel to the right, making a quick turn, tires squealing as she rounded the curb. The auto did the same, fishtailing as it curved.

"Jules." She hesitated, keeping an eye glued to the image in the mirror. "I think someone is following me."

"Katie, be careful," Jules shrieked. "Stay on the

phone with me. Call nine-one-one."

"I can't do both." She would have laughed, although she failed to find anything about her circumstances humorous. Her foot pounded the floor peddle. She yanked the steering wheel to rapidly changed lanes. Once again, the truck imitated her actions. "I'd rather you remain on the line. I'm coming up to my building."

"You shouldn't go in."

"Then what do I do? Driving around all night is out of the question. I'm pulling inside. If you hear any strangeness from my end or dead air, call the police."

"I need a vehicle description. What kind of car? Do you recognize it?"

"It's a mid-size truck. Later model, either black or dark blue."

"Does anyone you know own something similar?"

"No. And the front license tag is missing, so I can't give you any numbers." She circled into the drive of her parking garage, stopped, and twisted around. The automobile raced past her condo sight, disappearing into the light traffic. She finessed through the garage's gloomy aisles until she found her designated space.

"Katie?" Jules worried voice came from the other end of the phone. "What's happened?"

She put the gear in park and turned off the engine. "I'm home. No one followed me in."

"Thank goodness. I'll stay with until you're inside your place."

"Yes, please." Katie scanned the shadowy area as she exited. She hurried toward the building's entrance, her boots ricocheted against the concrete, emphasizing her isolation.

"I guess you weren't able to see the driver at all?"

She arrived at the entry. "The windows were tinted and it's too dark to see anything clear." She rushed down the hall, key ready to insert into her door. She nearly restrained from breathing until she was inside. "I'm home."

"Is everything okay?"

Katie flipped on the light and skimmed the room. "Nothing's out of place."

"Good. Since you're fine, I have to get back to work. Call me if you need anything."

Katie dialed her parents to let them know she was at her loft, though she omitted her most recent ordeal. Pops would be calling the National Guard to escort her to the ranch. She did her best to shake the incident off, chalking things up as an overactive imagination. Or maybe the police shadowed her.

Except cops would be more discreet.

She climbed the stairs to her bedroom, went straight to her closet for a suitcase. She threw it on the bed to quickly pack her things. After she had everything she needed and a few extras, she dragged her bag downstairs into the living area and loaded her laptop. Her next stop was the kitchen. She crammed some dry goods in two reusable grocery bags, then retrieved a small cooler, opened her refrigerator, and filled the entrails of the ice chest to the brim.

One final task and she was out of here. She snatched a dishtowel off the counter and walked to the coffee table where the knife lay still in its plastic cover.

Time to do a little cleanup.

She didn't understand the basis of DNA or how the process worked except if she'd left anything on the handle then she was sunk. If by chance the piece was clear of her chromosomes, then it would be best they didn't find her fingerprints either. Cover all bases. She stopped and stared at the table. The towel slipped through her fingers and floated to the floor.

The blade was missing.

What the…? She dashed around the room, lifting sofa pillows, cushions, and knick knacks. She fell to her knees to search underneath the furniture. Nothing.

She stood. Hands on hips she glanced about, then she froze. She swallowed back bile as goose bumps crawled over her skin.

What if her intruder returned and removed the evidence—or hid it?

She willed her mind to pull herself together. She rushed into the kitchen and began yanking out drawers, ransacking the cabinet insides. Okay, it didn't make sense for someone to break in and get rid of the knife except if a person was trying to gaslight her or…she couldn't think of any reason a anyone would remove it, unless to hide it to make her appear guiltier.

Her cell buzzed. Her first instinct was to ignore the call, but her mother maybe phoning and she preferred not to set off any alarms. She punched the on button without identifying the caller.

"Katie," said Cruz's deep voice. "I just got word from my friend at the police station. The detectives found a judge to issue a warrant. They'll be at your place to explore, possibly as early as tonight. I can't get a hold of any criminal defense attorneys so they're supposed to notify me when they're on their way. Do not, I repeat, do not let them to do anything until I arrive, understand?"

"Thanks, Cruz," she said in a voice calmer than she felt. "I'm ready."

She slammed a cabinet shut. Time had run out. Since the knife was missing, she should be relieved, but she wasn't. A solid gut punch told her she needed to be more cautious than ever.

Steadily, she picked up her suitcase, food, and laptop case and headed out.

After securing the lock, she left her loft, keeping her pace even as she walked down the hall and into the parking garage, cautiously glancing over her shoulder every few steps. She unlocked the trunk and shoved her belongings into the back, then released the locks with her keypad and got inside.

The passenger side opened.

Katie flinched in the direction and stifled a scream. The police had busted her. A shadowy outlined form dropped into the seat next to her and slammed the door.

"I'd ask where we're going, but I so enjoy surprises."

Chapter 11

A champagne cork popped, followed by the trickle of liquid flowing into glasses. Vanessa's lips curled. She raised her filled flute to ting the crystal against the goblet Rhett Oates held.

Rhett returned her smile as he put the bottle aside, "To the demise of Weddings Fantastic."

"The demise of Weddings Fantastic." Vanessa sipped her drink and skimmed her tongue seductively across her mouth. "Hmmm. Very good. Bubbly." She sat the beaker on a credenza and strolled around the elegant suite until she halted opposite Rhett. "I've accomplished my assignment. Do you have something for me?"

Rhett placed his wineglass on a coaster lying on a table in front of him and slid a palm inside his tailored jacket. He produced a small, but thick, manila envelope and held it out to her. She grabbed at the pack, her fingers snapped together as he snatched it away.

"Your assignment was to bring down Weddings Fantastic. You didn't exactly finish the job."

A flicker of anger flashed over her face. "I was in the process of doing just that before Hazel was killed. I would assume her death is so much better."

Rhett threw back his head and laughed. He brought the packet to her, this time allowing her to remove it from his outstretched hand.

"I'm not complaining she's gone." He indicated at the envelope. "There's more. As soon as this task is complete." He hesitated, displaying an inquisitive look. "You're sure everything is in place?"

Vanessa nodded, opening the packet to remove a stack of hundreds. Her face lit as she fanned the bills out in front of her. Carefully, she restacked the monies, returned the cash to its package, and tucked her payment safety into her handbag placed next to her champagne.

"I spoke to Hazel's daughter. She planned to put Weddings Fantastic up for sale to the highest bidder. I explained I represented you, and you were interested in a private purchase. I also told her you would pay top dollar if she were willing to do a restricted sale. She's all for it. After everything is settled with Hazel's estate, she will meet with her attorney's to draw up the papers." Vanessa smiled. "The company is as good as yours."

Rhett lowered his pudgy body in a nearby Chamois chair and stared out of a high rise window into the night sky. Although the hour was late, and he was at home, he remained dressed in a tailored suit. "Haven't the foggiest how you managed to pull this elaborate scheme off so quickly, though I can't thank you enough for coming to me with such a brilliant idea."

"Just a little ingenuity and imagination."

"You definitely missed your calling, darling. I'm happy you used those special talents for righting evil."

"Thank whoever murdered Hazel."

"My personal opinion but the person who killed the woman deserves multitudes of accolades." He paused, removed a silk handkerchief, and dabbed at his receding forehead. "What's your secret, sweets? What conniving, skillful move did you use to get inside and view Hazel's last will and testament?"

"Can't tell you the resources I use to get into Hazel's private stuff. But I can reveal that I'm privy to the latest news from the police about her death."

"Do share, dear. Explain your abilities to perform such a feat."

"I made friends with the cop from the initial investigation of Hazel's murder."

He chuckled. "How friendly did we have to become to get this inside information?"

Vanessa sighed. "I had to let him put his tongue in my ear. And he got to touch." She made a circle over her breasts.

"Ohhh. So the ladies had a little fun too."

"Not exactly. I swear, if he handles a weapon the way he does boobs, we're in big trouble if this city is ever in a crisis."

"Remember, your sacrifice was for a good cause, and you were able to do what you set out to do. Bury the Nutt. I didn't mean for her to die literally," he shrugged, "but…"

"Her death wasn't a part of the strategy either."

"You sure?"

She laughed and picked up her glass. She wandered to the window and sat in a twin chair across from Rhett.

"To me her dying is like taking the lid off the cookie jar and finding it full," Rhett said. "Instead of us bringing her down, someone did some real dirty work for us."

"Things couldn't have worked out any better."

"I thought putting you on the inside was brilliant,

but I couldn't be more satisfied she's dead." He studied his wine. "I attempted to penetrate Hazel's company and to sway Katherine Drapier over to Affair's Amore a few months back. Bad move. I didn't realize she was such a loyal goody, goody."

Vanessa sighed. "Could've told you."

"You did an amazing job sabotaging her. Without Katherine, the company was doomed, but the downfall would take a while. This way I can buy Weddings Fantastic outright." He smirked. "Granted, Hazel's time as the best party planner was over ages ago, I would've enjoyed assisting her business plummeting into oblivion. I'm almost sorry she didn't live to see it collapse and me snatch it up." He nodded at the envelope's tip, peeking from Vanessa's purse. "Like I said before, there's plenty more. As soon as Weddings Fantastic is mine."

"Plus the job of running Affairs Amore second store."

"Part of our deal." He sighed and relaxed in his seat. "I can't help but wish you hadn't involved Tara."

"Couldn't be avoided." Vanessa raised a shoulder. "I needed someone on the inside to assist me. She's sneakier than she looks."

"She's a liability now."

"She doesn't know that much. Pay her off."

"I've given her a lot of money already. She's hinted she wants more. And for me to employ her."

"Will she fit in this organization? She can file. She's great on computers, but she has absolutely zero creative talent."

"I was thinking of making her your personal assistant."

"What?" Vanessa straightened. "The last thing I need."

"Only be for a short while, doll. She should be watched. We must make sure she remains mostly in the dark. Her closeness will ensure she doesn't learn anything until we can decide what to do with her. But you are correct. She isn't suitable for my establishment on any level." He waved a hand and rolled his eyes. "And her box store attire is ghastly."

Vanessa laughed. "Rhett, you're so bad."

"That's a compliment coming from you."

"I'm not bad."

Rhett raised his brows. "From what I hear, you're pushing for Katherine, an innocent woman, to go to prison for a crime she didn't commit. That is bad."

"We're not sure she wasn't the one who killed Hazel." Vanessa kicked off her stilt-like heals and curled her legs underneath her. "Besides, Katherine's been nothing but a pain in the ass since I entered this business. She needs to go away."

"Such malevolence. I know you prefer not to hear this doll. She's great at what she does."

"So you say." She flicked a lock of hair over her shoulder. "I can't understand why Jack Pharrell is interested in her."

Rhett stopped in mid-drink. "The luscious attorney who's been in the news lately?"

"The same."

"He's got the hots for her? I thought you said he called you to meet for a cocktail."

"Not exactly. He phoned me, but he didn't invite me out. He mentioned he was going to a bar. I happened to show up at the same place."

"Was he glad to see you? Impressed by your boldness or at least flattered from your efforts?"

"Not so much. All we did is drink and he only paid for one of mine. I couldn't get him to move any further."

"Hmm. He must be smitten with someone else if one drink is all your endeavors brought on. Why do you think Katherine is the one he's smitten with?"

"He showed up at her condo this morning, same time I visited. I'm not aware of anything between them, or if Jack even knows he likes her." She shook her head. "A gut feeling. Either way, I hope she's locked up and the key gets lost." Vanessa smiled. "Jackson will recover from his professional faux pas and be a practicing attorney again."

"I assume you'll step in? Put the heavy moves on?"

She lifted her glass. "I'm mapping my strategy as we speak."

****

"Get out," Katie shouted. "I said get out. Leave."

"I heard you." Jack twisted for the seatbelt and glided the strap across his body, fastening the clip. "But as you can see, I'm not going anywhere. Unless you want to physically remove me." He leaned over the console and grinned lazily. "Which could be interesting."

"I don't…" she sputtered and shook her head. "What are you doing here?"

He wiggled further into the seat, making himself comfortable. "You better get a move on. The police will be arriving soon with their warrant. Don't want to them to catch you in the midst of an escape, do we?"

She whirled to him and stared. "How did you—ah.

So much for attorney, client privilege. I'm advising my father to fire Cruz after this is over."

"Don't assume, Katie. I'm not the dumb country boy I once was."

"Right, you're a friggin' expert in human nature."

"Close. Need I remind you the cops are on their way?"

No he didn't. Katie's world was imploding. As if her circumstances couldn't get any worse. Jack, of all people, involved made this current situation more severe. She was always in control. Some accused her of being emotionless when pressure barreled upon her, which was how she succeeded. But she was coming unglued, and if she spent another millisecond with Jack Pharrell who knows what she might say. She glanced at him. Or do.

"Look, I'm going to stay at my parents' house. I'll drop you off at Aaron's and head that way. You can pick up your truck in the morning."

"Liar."

She jerked a glare at him.

"Try again." He folded his arms over his chest, a corner of his mouth lifted. "Study of human nature, remember?"

She hesitated a moment. With exasperation, she turned the ignition and squealed her tires as she propelled out of the parking garage.

"Added attention in this situation isn't necessarily a good thing. Might want to go easy on the getaway."

"Again. Why are you here?"

"Our couple's therapist suggested we take a vacation together."

She released an infuriated growl. "How come you

won't leave me alone?"

"I enjoy your company?"

"Liar," she said through clenched teeth. "Try again."

"That's my story."

"There's no reason for you to be involved in my situation."

He released a huge sigh "Let's say, I'm here because you're a member of a family I care for."

Not the explanation she'd hoped for. "I get it. Pops. He put you up to this."

He didn't answer, giving her confirmation. The idea should make her mad or madder because she was already riled about many other things. Except this new anger had to be put on hold until another time. Still, how did her father convince Jack to pull such an elaborate stunt, and how were they able to figure out her plans. Was she that easy to read?

What's more, why did Jack agree to go along with the idea? She threw a glance in his direction. He was supposed to start work for Aaron in the morning, and she wasn't intending on being anywhere near here by then. She hoped he'd called in.

Jack tilted his head toward the window, seemingly checking the side mirror. "So where are we going?"

"The less you know the better."

"Ahhh. Leaving town in a shroud of mystery. How Sherlock Holmsish. I don't suppose you can reveal as to how long we'll be gone?"

"As long as it takes."

Katie clutched the steering wheel and gunned the accelerator, nearly swerving off the road. The pickup that was following her had parked across the street from her complex.

Jack grabbed the dash. "Easy on the gas, dear."

She checked the rearview mirror relieved to find the truck stayed put.

He peered out the window. "I need to stop by the guesthouse."

"For?"

"Stuff for our trip."

"You made the choice to crash. Not my problem if you didn't prepare. I'm not changing my route for you."

He squirmed farther into the seat. "I can live in stinky clothes if you can."

"Why do you need clothing? Wouldn't a case of beer work better?"

"Splendidly. But we'll have to share your toothbrush." He grinned. "Hate morning breath, don't you?"

She sighed and rolled her eyes. She pointed her vehicle toward her brother's home. Fifteen minutes later, she'd parked in the drive, and killed the motor. "I'll wait for you."

"I don't think so."

"You don't trust me?"

He stretched across the console and snatched her keys from the ignition. "Not for a second."

"Just so you know the lack of faith goes both ways. Thanks for telling on me to my parents. I thought we were past the sixth grade."

"You weren't going to tell them."

"Not everything. From now on stay out of my business."

"Noted. Won't be easy considering the circumstances. Just keep track of my upcoming betrayals for later reference." He opened the jeep's door, stepped out, and peered inside where she remained with her arms folded across her chest. "If I called your folks once, what makes you think I won't do it again?"

She huffed and rammed the door opened with her shoulder.

Jack didn't take long to pack a duffle and within a half an hour they were back on the road. Katie raised her chin and glanced into her rearview mirror. Late Sunday, the streets were dark and empty. A fine mist hovered over the streetlamps giving this journey a perfect setting.

"No one's following us." Jack fished into his pocket and brought out his cell phone.

"I'm aware. Who are you calling?" Her voice screeched, high and shrill. "I swear if you're alerting anyone my whereabouts, I'll haul you out of this vehicle in a split second, and there won't be anything interesting about it."

He held the phone up, and slid off the back, took out the battery. "Needs to be removed."

"Right. We can be traced by the waves pinging towers. Wouldn't turning it off work just as well?"

"Not necessarily. Radio's sendoff signals between the towers within the phone's network, which is a way to track, or they may simply follow via GPS chips. Thought you watched Dateline."

She glimpsed behind the seat. "Mine is my purses side pouch. Would you mind?"

He stuffed his back into his pocket, rotated toward the rear to get her phone. After he punched the key to make the screen disappear, he performed the same feat on her device as he had his own.

"So you believe the police might be tailing you?" he asked as he put away her cell.

Not sure if she trusted him, she debated whether to fill him in on her most recent events. He was her supposed ally, and to some degree, accomplice. Plus, he was all she had.

"Someone followed me earlier. I think. After I left Cruz's office." She went on to tell him about the truck and the knife is missing. "I wondered if my thief broke in and took it back," she suggested after she finished explaining.

"Yeah. Because that's what people who are setting you up, do." He shook his head. "Doesn't make sense. Unless they wanted to ensure you didn't stash it somewhere so the police couldn't find it, which I'm sure you wouldn't," he added with a dash of sarcasm. "Did you look around? Maybe they hid it. Concealed will make you appear a lot guiltier."

"I started to search, but Cruz called and told me to expect the detectives to show up with a warrant. So I high tailed it out of there."

"Good call," he interjected dryly. "Not only are the detectives watching you, a possible killer is on your trail too."

She checked her mirror again. "I think whoever this is wants me to take responsibility, not kill me."

"Leaving town as the police are closing in will only help their cause."

She ignored his observation and drove out away from the city, veering onto the interstate. Eyes bonded to the road, her heart bumped up a beat, her white-knuckled hands gripped tighter to the wheel each time they encountered another vehicle.

They journeyed many miles in silence. The only conversation came when she informed him they were heading into a more remote area and if he needed to use the bathroom, or wanted a snack, they'd have to stop now.

They took a quick break at an isolated convenience store. As a precaution Katie parked far away, in the dark, a long distance from any prying cameras while Jack went inside. Antsy, she waited for him, constantly checking the surroundings. Though it seemed like hours, he returned within minutes, carrying water for her, and a soft drink.

He settled into his seat and popped the lid of his soda can. "Don't suppose I might convince you to do the right thing. The legal thing. Let's turn back Katie. It's not too late."

"I'm a suspect. If the police find a bloody knife in my possession, I'll be arrested. The fact someone is trying to railroad me into a life sentence or worse, doesn't thrill me. I need to get away and think for a while. Figure out who's doing this to me and turn this situation around."

She curved onto an obscure, unlit gravel road and pushed the floor peddle hard enough to show her frustration.

"How do you propose to do that when you have no clue as to whose behind this? Especially out in the middle of nowhere?"

"I have no idea. All I do know is I don't belong in prison, Jack. So if your assignment was to bring me back to be thrown in jail, and then consider your efforts a failure. I'm not returning until I have some answers."

He let out a loud sigh. "I could always call your folks. Tell them where you are."

She slammed her foot onto the brakes. The car swerved left, then right and skidded to a stop halfway into a ditch. She twisted the interior lights to on and stared at him, her eyes, large and moist.

"Give me a chance, Jack. This nightmare has been thrown at me. I haven't had the time to process any of it. Someone is gunning for me. I feel it." To her own ears, her voice sounded shaky. Like she was about to break.

He appeared to consider her request. "I'll give you two days, three tops. Then I'm calling in reinforcements. Neither of our reputations can withstand the implications any longer."

"I don't know if I can figure this out in such a short amount of time."

"I'll help," he stated softly. "But for only three days, Katie."

Chapter 12

The bumpy road swayed the jeep back and forth like a cradle rocking a baby. Katie pushed to keep her mind on the drive, but her thoughts reeled. Jack gave her three days to find out who set her up. She'd argued her point for over an hour to only have him stick to his guns.

They'd been quiet for a while, mainly because she decided to let the subject go until she could come up with a better solution. For the moment, she had just seventy two hours to work with. Three days. Unless she convinced Jack to give her an extension or find an alternate method.

She glanced in his direction. He appeared to be at war with his eyelids. His head rocked with the automobile's shift. Finally, his neck relaxed and his chin dropped to his chest. A low snore whirred from his side of the car. With him fast asleep, she could center on driving, which was where her concentration needed to be. They'd left the smooth blacktop a long time ago, and the rutted narrow stretch commanded her complete focus.

A blanket of clouds covered the moon, altering the night sky into an ashen gloom. The only light were the bright, reedy beams streaking in front of her car reflecting a rise of dust from the road's grit.

She hadn't met another motorist in almost an hour.

They were alone. She eased her clutch on the wheel. For the first time since they left, she felt secure. Despite the perilous roadway, she was safe. How long had she'd sensed such a freeing relief. Two days ago. Her life turned upside down only forty-eight hours before, yet the short span seemed like years.

The soft wheeze beside her triggered a reminder of the man asleep to the right. She stole another peek. Forget about peacefulness. Why he was here? Yeah, her dad probably asked him keep an eye on her. But to enlist him in helping her escape? Pops would insist Jack do everything in his power to prevent her from bolting. So what were his motives? She dared to hope for the best, but only for a second, then she pushed her optimism from her mind. She needed to let the past go.

He was scheduled to start work at her brother's company tomorrow. From what she gathered, he was hurting for cash. Jack wouldn't turn away the opportunity, and she couldn't imagine him standing up Aaron.

She returned her attention to the road. A fine mist had covered the windshield and obstructed her view even more. She turned the handle prompting the wipers to swish in front of her, clearing the condensation from the glass. The vehicle bounced into a pothole as her hand left the steering wheel. Katie gripped tight, holding the jeep steady to keep them on course.

Jack's body jerked with a groan. He shook his head fiercely and then leaned toward dash's digital readout. He turned her and squinted. "Near midnight?"

"We're almost there."

Jack relaxed into his seat, pressed his thumb and forefinger into his eye sockets, and yawned. "Almost where? No reason to keep anything from me now."

Katie didn't respond right away but slowed down. She straightened, lifting her chin for a better view while she carefully maneuvered across another rough patch. "To my grandmother's," she answered after she cleared the rut.

"To grandma's house. As in, over the river and through the woods?"

"Not quite. Though Nana's farmhouse is in a remote area."

He grunted. "Farm? Like with pigs and stuff?"

"No animals." Katie snickered. "Let me clarify. The place used to be a farm. Now it's a house with farming essentials."

"Your grandparents are dead, right?"

"Yes, but we kept the home. The entire family is allowed to use it whenever we want."

"You don't think your parents will figure out where you're hiding?"

"If they assumed I'm," she paused to clear her throat, "on the run, then they'd know which direction I headed. I don't believe they'll let anyone in on my destination."

"They won't need to."

"What do you mean?"

"Property ownership is public record. The detectives will discover your relatives own this place and they'll investigate the area. They'll find you."

Katie considered this. The authorities checking court registers never crossed her mind. "Maybe. The process should take them a while. The homestead deed is in my aunt's name. Plus, we're several counties north. Hopefully that'll buy me enough time."

"It'd better. Use those three days wisely. Get some proof as to who is setting you up. It won't be long before the investigators discover your whereabouts if they're focused on locating you."

"I'm willing to risk it. The house is difficult to find, even using a map, unless you know the location."

Jack turned his head and gazed outside. "Wherever we are, it's dark as hell."

The car dipped then slid as they drove across another obscure pothole. Jack's palms flew to the dash. "Slow down," he said raising his voice. "You're driving too fast."

"We're fine. I've driven this road zillions of times."

The auto leapt from another incline. Jack swore quietly and shifted in his seat. "You're a definite expert in knowing where all the holes are. Have you found them zillions of times?"

"I don't know if you noticed, but this route is nothing but holes," she snapped.

The jeep's bouncing headlamps continued to guide them down the bumpy path. Tires plunged into deep ridges, shaking the vehicle. The engine reared as it fought to climb the uneven terrine's rough hills.

"Damn," Jack shouted, after they'd hit one of the deeper ruts. "This is bad. We ought to turn around and go back before the frame breaks in half."

"Nothing I can't handle."

Neither spoke. Katie kept her eyes glued to the road. Jack seemed to be in a foul mood. If his disposition didn't change soon, and let up about her driving skills, he may be dodging the potholes on foot.

The silence continued. Seconds stretched into

minutes. If quiet could scream it would sound like the nothingness within the contents of her vehicle.

"Jack?" Katie asked her voice barely above a whisper. "How did you know?"

"Know what?"

She slowed the car and looked at him. "What clued you in that I was going to run?"

A corner of his mouth lifted. "First thing I'd do if I were in your situation. Actually, I took off too." He tossed his hair back. "Though my circumstances are different, I also did a disappearing act."

"Right. You chose to return home, instead of staying in Dallas—."

She stopped. In the matter of a few hours, she'd brought the sore subject up three times. She hesitated to voice anything again, especially knowing how uncomfortable the topic was for him.

"You can say it. I screwed up." His hands rested in his lap and fingers interlocked.

"I don't understand why you're still under such scrutiny. Your story is old news now. I mean, if she hadn't made a big deal out of everything this wouldn't even be newsworthy. I'm sure stuff like this happens all the time."

"I can't say too much due to the legalities, but yeah, you're right." He scowled. "The whole thing is about money. For her. The reason this story remains in the local headlines is because she and her new attorney keep it circulating."

"I read the accounts. You don't come off well."

He lifted a shoulder.

"You have a side too, don't you?"

"Everyone does."

"You've been quiet. Why not put your version out so people will know she isn't exactly an innocent?"

"The legal aspects, for one thing," Jack emphasized. "I'd rather my account be revealed in court than in the media, since their tendency is to twist a person's words. Plus a counter attack either makes me seem pathetic or a dick."

"So what exactly happened? I mean if you want to tell me."

Jack released a huge sigh. "You're aware that I worked for one of the biggest law firms in the Dallas area. My specialty was handling faulty claims against insurance companies, or I represent establishments who are being sued after they denied entitlements. Jenna owns an agency that needed my services. To prepare," he stopped to swipe his brow. "She and I met. First in the office...we spent a lot of time together. Things became more informal. We saw each other after hours, for meals, and..." He stopped. "You know the rest."

"You had a personal relationship with her."

"Nice way of saying I slept with her." His lips lifted into a sardonic smile. "Yeah, we were inappropriately involved." He shook his head. "After I lost her case, she turned on me. Accused me of soliciting the affair as a means of payment. She claims I made improper sexual advances and coerced her into bed."

"Sounds awful."

"Especially since the whole thing is a lie. I didn't threaten her, nor did I put on any pressure. Everything between us was consensual. I did the work for a lesser fee because when she came to me, she told me she couldn't afford us at the time. A practice that's not unusual."

Katie leaned around the steering wheel and flipped the defroster switch. "I'm sure this entire episode hurt you."

"Hell yeah, it hurt me. She's suing my firm and me for malpractice and personally for emotional distress." Jack adjusted his vent. "Killed my career."

"What about you, Jack? What about your heart? Did you have feelings for her or was it just—," The word "sex" stuck in her throat. She swallowed to rid her mouth of sudden dryness.

Jack remained silent for a long time. Katie glanced at him. He stared at the wipers brushing across the windshield. The movement appeared to lull him into a trance.

"Jack?"

His jaw tensed. "I don't know how to answer. I told myself this was a casual relationship. No ties, no strings. We're two people who enjoyed each other's company." Jack turned to her. "The outcome has made me cautious. I decided to not get into anymore frivolous entanglements until this is over. Or the whole thing may've killed me on getting involved with anyone ever. I'm playing the wait and see game."

"You're giving her a lot of power."

"Come again?"

"This Jenna woman. You're letting her and the situation control you."

"It kinda does."

"Career wise. You have an attorney and a version of what transpired. I'm betting you have ammunition in your corner to dispute her claim, right?"

"Some evidence has been collected which will

poke holes into her accusations."

"You do stand a chance of returning to your job."

"Possibly. I can also go to work for another firm. Or independently. Either way, my license shouldn't be suspended once this is settled."

"So the employment front is secure. But what about relationships? You're still giving her a huge amount of influence if you stick to your decision against finding someone."

"I've never been great at that sort of thing anyway," he said miserably.

"You can change. She may've hurt you, but everyone's had their heart stepped on at some point. You have to move on."

He went quiet again. "Who stomped on your heart, Katie?"

Katie flinched. Her foot gunned the accelerator. The vehicle slipped.

"Whoa." Her fingers squeezed trying to grip the steering wheel and keep it steady as she pumped the break. "Hold on." The car skidded, and pitched. A scream caught in Katie's throat, fighting to twist in the opposite direction from the slide, but the auto continued to slip, tilting to the side. "I can't stop," she shouted as the jeep veered off the gravel. She clutched onto the helm, her body braced. They briefly became airborne and landed roughly into a trench, where they came to an abrupt halt.

Neither she nor Jack moved.

"Do you always use a ditch as a way to stop?"

Katie unclenched her jaw and exhaled. She released her grasp to put the car in gear and turn the motor off. "Not funny." She ran her perspiring palms across her thighs. "Are you okay?"

"How can I not be with you handling everything with such amazing skill?"

"Not the time, Jack." She shot him what she hoped was an evil glare.

However, the action was probably a waste since they were in near darkness.

He lifted the handle and leaned a shoulder against the panel. The door opened an inch, the edge caught in a clump of mud. A damp flow of air streamed through the crack.

Jack gazed at Katie with a slight grin. "We have a tiny problem." He pushed on the exit again. It didn't move. "Yep, it's stuck. Can you open your side?"

"I think so. The car is leaning more to the right." She boosted the handgrip. The door easily swung opened. She unbuckled her seatbelt, leaned across the console in front of Jack, and undid the glove box to retrieve a small flashlight. She climbed outside. Her feet sank into a puddle of icy slush, seeping over her boots.

A cruel burst of cold air whipped through her. Her shoes heavy, she trudged to the backseat, pulled the handle, and snatched her coat.

Jack undid his belt and threw a long leg over the middle. He maneuvered crossways onto the driver's chair and rolled from the car with a soft groan.

Outside, he extended his torso backward, holding his spine with both hands and lengthened his body. He lifted a foot and examined his mud-covered running shoe.

"My best pair."

"Won't be after tonight."

"Touché."

Katie shined the light at the front of the vehicle. The wheels were wedged into sludge, although the back tires appeared to be okay. "This area must have had a lot of rain recently."

"Really?" Jack snatched the penlight from her and pointed the beam at the jeep.

"Stop being so snippy."

"I'm not being anything, Katie."

"You've been sulking since we left. If I'm such a pain, then you shouldn't have come with me."

"Somebody needs to keep you out of trouble, although my efforts always seemed to bite me in the ass."

Katie crossed her arms in front of her and turned away. "Well, excuse me for trying to save myself."

"I don't to excuse you for anything. We wrecked in the heart of nowhere, at night, and in the rain." He paused and glanced around. "We'll need to use our cells to call for help, though I have no clue if they'll work. I'm pretty sure the towers are limited in these remote parts."

"You're overreacting. The damage doesn't look that bad. Nana kept a tractor in the barn. We can use it to pull the jeep out."

Jack glared at her and shook his head. "Not now. It's too dark. We need to find out how bad we're wrecked."

"We're stuck. Not wrecked."

"You don't know that. We can't go dragging the car through the mud without knowing for sure. We might make matters worse. Besides, Nana's house isn't just around the corner, is it?"

"It's not that far."

"How not that far?"

"About a mile. Maybe two." She took a step. "If we start now, we'll arrive before sun up."

Oversized raindrops dotted their skin as a haunting wail from a lone coyote ricocheted into the disturbing atmosphere.

"You can be there before sunrise. I can't see a thing," he held up the tiny light," even with your powerful flashlight. And I'm not walking in this shit, in the dark, while it's raining with—vampires howling looking for a meal."

"Werewolves howl. Vampires don't have reflections."

"I stand corrected. I'm still not going anywhere."

"Well, what *are* you going to do?"

"I'm staying put. I noticed you packed a pillow and blankets. That'll work for me." He leaned in and popped the back of the jeep, and marched to the rear. He raised the hatch, grabbed several pieces of luggage, and dragged them to the front seat, tossing them inside. "I'm sleeping here. I'll worry about the car and its issue in the morning." Hoisting the remainder of their bags under his arms, he traipsed through the slush, carrying their things to the driver's seat. He shoved them in and slammed the door.

"So you expect me to walk to Nana's by myself?"

He shrugged. "Up to you." He treaded to the backside again and sat on the edge, propping a foot in front of him to untie his shoe laces. He tossed the muddy shoes into the passenger floor board. "There's barely enough room for two." He scooted farther inside as he lowered the hatch. "But I'll share."

Chapter 13

"You'll what?" Katie put her hands on her hips and scowled at the near closed hatch. How dare he offer to share *her* vehicle? Who did this guy think he was?

Jack raised the flap a bit to peer from underneath. "I'm willing to split the backseat with you."

"Excuse me. This is my car, my trip and my—,"

"Not a vacation. You're running away," he interrupted. "To hide."

"Whatever. It's still my escape. You weren't invited." She directed a thumb at her chest. "I'm calling the shots."

He released the handle letting the door elevate. "If you expect me to go to Nana's in the middle of this monsoon, in the dark, then your happy ass is going to have to carry me while holding an umbrella over my head."

She gazed upward, flattening a palm in front of her, allowing the tiny droplets to bounce off her skin. "It's not raining that hard."

"Hard enough."

Katie bit her tongue so not to argue. The drizzle wasn't as fierce as he insinuated, though she had to admit with the strong wind gusts and the holey road, a hike on foot didn't exactly appeal to her either.

Scooting to the rear, Jack leaned between the middle and backseat to release the lever, ramming the second seat down to make more room although he was still too big for the confined area. "Those are my terms. You can't go by 'em, then I'm staying put." He lengthened his body, doing his best to lay straight and undid the top snap of his blue jeans. Zipper parted, he raised his hips to slide them down his legs.

Katie walked to the opening and stared inside with a frown. "What are you doing?"

"I'm taking my pants off." He shoved them over his ankles. "Should be obvious."

"I can see that. The question is why?"

"The bottoms are muddy and wet, which will make sleeping in an already uncomfortable situation worse." He pulled his jeans away from his feet, tossed them over the front passenger seat, and then he leaned forward to grab the hatch. "Nighty Night. Wake me when you get that tractor here." He tilted his body outside and tugged the grip.

A boom cracked from overhead. The sky opened and a downpour gushed. A stitch of panic rose in Katie's chest as large drops pounded the top of her head. "Jack. Wait." She tried to hurry through the slop, grabbing the flap just before it latched.

An ornery grin spread across his face. "Change your mind?"

She shot him an exasperated glare as she climbed inside. She lifted her legs, and rotated on her butt toward the front of the vehicle, then proceeded to take off her muddy boots and socks. After she tossed them to where his lay, she ran her hands down her jeans to wipe away the excess grime.

His gaze glided over her dirty denims. "You're going to leave those nasty clothes on?"

She nodded, struggling with every estrogenic hormone to avert her attention from his bare, muscular legs. "I think it would be more appropriate given the circumstances," she said in a tight, throaty voice. She swallowed and turned away, catching a glimpse of the large bulge situated in the middle his boxers.

Jack stretched across the seat to his duffle, raised the fold, and removed a pair of sweatpants. He slipped them on and then glanced at her. "Better?"

Not really. "Those will keep you warmer."

He returned to his bag and rummaged inside, bringing out several rolled up shirts.

She gestured at the bundle. "What are you doing?"

"I assume because of the rainstorm, you're cancelling your midnight stroll to Nana's." He used the sleeves to bind them together. "You only brought one pillow, and it belongs to you. You'll want to sleep on it. I'll use these to prop my head. But we'll have to share the blanket. It's already cold. The rain will make the night even colder, and I don't have anything to improvise cover." He threw her a warning look as he bent to reclose the backdoor. "You may want to rethink wearing those soaked jeans."

Raindrops had peppered her shirt, but the fabric wasn't so wet. It would dry soon, and was tolerable. Her pants were a different story. Like his, mud had caked around the bottoms and they were soaked through. The moisture traveled to her calves, so high that even her knecs were damp. To sleep waterlogged *and* next to Jack would be a challenge.

She glanced at him, snug in his warm running pants. "I packed several pairs of shorts." She stretched into the front seat, propped a shoulder against the captain chair, and unzipped her suitcase. After a few moments of searching, she found them. She unsnapped her top button of her pants, glancing at Jack. He'd sprawled out, resting on his makeshift pillow, his eyes rested on her wearing a smile.

"Can you turn the other way?"

He grinned widened. "I could."

"You're not going to, are you?"

"Not a lot of ways to move in such a small spot."

No way around it. She'd either have to suffer in her wet clothes or she would have to change in front of him. Though darkness blanketed the vehicle's insides, the penlight lay near Jack's hip—too close to his crotch area for her to risk a grab, and it glowed just enough to give him a clear view of her. If she'd been thinking, she'd have turned the blasted thing off before he reclined. Careful not to look in his direction, she lay on her back, extending her legs and unfastened the second snap of her jeans.

"Hold on." Jack maneuvered his large body to rotate toward the outer window. "I'm not looking. Now you can undress."

Relieved, she attempted to slip her pants over her hips. But the moisture filled denim prevented her from performing any swift movements. She couldn't push them off the way Jack had. Besides even on a normal day, her blue jeans fit snugger than his.

With the hatch closed, lying on her back wasn't working. With some difficulty, she rose to her knees, and twisted her body to force the wet pants over her thighs. The jeep's close-fitting gap didn't give her much wiggle room. She angled to one side and tried to pull a leg out. A foot wound within the soggy fabric.

She swayed and rocked off center. The knee on the floor gave way. She tumbled sideways, and bounced her head off the window when she fell.

Jack whirled around. His expression appeared concerned. "You okay?"

She ignored the sting on her forehead, undid her foot, and pressed into a sitting position. "I'm fine."

A small smile played on his lips, his dark green eyes held a warm gleam. "Pink and stringing. Who'd a thought?"

"My secret is out." She squirmed out of her pants and promptly discarded them, wondering when she'd turned into such a klutz. Jack seemed to bring out her gawkiness. She hurried to put on her shorts, glad to cover up her bright fuchsia stringed panties, which were on display much longer than she'd preferred.

"How come you're so nervous about undressing in front of me?" he asked with a definite sound of laughter in his voice.

"I'm not," she answered indignantly. She yanked the elastic waistband over to her stomach with a snap. "I'm cold." She lay onto the pillow and dragged the blanket he'd already spread up to her shoulders.

"If you say so." He clicked the light switch, dimming the interior. "You do realize I saw less of you now than during your teenage years when you wore those microscopic bathing suits at the ranch pool."

"You noticed me?"

"I was an adolescent boy, and you were a girl in a tiny two piece." He yanked at the cover as he settled, draping an arm over hers. "Enough said."

Katie braced her body. The cramped space didn't give much extent for expansion on either side, and there wasn't any way they could lay without touching. She mentally told herself to relax.

Yeah, relax. Like she would rest tonight. No matter how far he'd tumbled, career wise, or personally, Jack Pharrell was still the hottest man she'd ever met.

Sleep wasn't going to happen.

The warmth of flesh on flesh made her wonder what it'd be like to have all of him across her. Jack's warm skin on hers. She squirmed. Flames ignited in her stomach, the burn plunged, and scorched her between her legs. Nothing concrete pointed in that direction, but they were alone, out in the middle of nowhere. All grown up. Things could happen.

She cerebrally kicked herself. She shouldn't allow her mind to drift like that with him lying next to her. Getting riled up with no satisfaction in sight wouldn't benefit her. From outside, the wind howled, and shook the vehicle. Rain rattled the windows. Except this kind of night whispered cuddling. Or better yet…she inched nearer. Her slight movement stirred him to ease closer into her. He released a heavy gasp. She raised her head—and fell into her pillow. He wasn't breathing hard because of their closeness. He was snoring.

She quietly sighed. They may have united where the backseat and blanket were concerned, but he didn't share her amorous thoughts. She maneuvered onto her side and lifted her head, cautious not to move her arm and break contact. With some difficulty, she folded the pillow and perched at the edge. Her eyes adjusted to the blackness, allowing her to stare at his perfect profile. She ingested a sea of saliva.

He sniffed and pulled the blanket further over his chest. He appeared peaceful. Something he hadn't been since they'd reconnected. Or maybe she only witnessed the darker side of Jackson Pharrell. Almost unthinking, she traced a finger over his stubbled jawline.

"Mmmm," he mumbled. "Feels nice."

She jerked her hand away and leaned closer. His eyes remained shut.

"Don't stop," he murmured in a sleepy voice. "Been a long time since someone's touched me." He shifted nearer and nuzzled her ear.

Her heartbeat raced to Indy car speed. She shivered.

"Cold?" he asked.

"Totally the opposite."

She rolled away, removing her arm from underneath his, afraid to touch him, to be so close. She rested the back of her palm on her forehead. He withdrew his hand from under the cover to reach for her, capturing her fingers, and tugged. She slowly spun onto her side, facing him again.

An arm slid around her waist as he moved closer. Close enough to brush his lips against her neckline, his mouth trailed down an invisible path. She let go a soft moan, gliding her hands over his chest, grasping his shoulders, her fingers digging into his warm covered flesh. His tongue traced over her throat, the scruff of his jawline scratched her skin in the most delicious way.

Katie closed her eyes and arched her back. "Jack."

She inhaled deep, relishing his tangy male scent. She tilted her head and stared into his sleepy, green eyes. The unadorned yearn in his gaze spurred her desires to swell farther. He slid a hand around the nap of her neck, intertwining his fingers in her hair. His cheek stroked hers as his lips feathered over her until his mouth found hers, and firmly closed over her lips. His grip tightened, their bodies merged together.

Kissing Jack. This was something she'd waited forever for, but she wasn't sure if she was dreaming. Her mind whirled as he caressed the inside her mouth with his tongue, taunting, and tasting her with intense discovery. Inner fervor thundered like fiery lava, heating every nerve ending in her body. Sometimes wanting something for such a long time, waiting, then when it finally happened; expectations fell short. But not this. His kisses were beyond fantastic. His mouth, his lips, and his delectable tongue devoured her as he eased onto her.

She needed more. Katie threaded her fingers through his hair. She pulled away to slow the kiss down. Gently she nibbled at his bottom lip, slipping her tongue around his. A faint rumble came from his chest. He intensified the pressure with his mouth. A hand encircled each of her wrists and pinned her to the base where they laid. He lowered further and pressed his hardness between her thighs. Sexual fluxes triggered a surge of sizzling intenseness burning her inside and out. His thick, solid erection thrust against her, his body revealing silently what she'd waited for, for so long.

"Jack."

"Hmm?" he hummed as he nudged away her shirt to kiss her bare shoulder.

"You're holding me down," she panted. "I want to touch you too."

Jack raised his head, his dazzling eyes roved over her. He released her.

Palms placed onto his shoulder blades, she squeezed, savoring the rigidness of his well-formed torso. She continued to explore, finding a way under his shirt, stroking his chest, his hardened muscles as her fingers caressed the soft hair sprinkled across his pecks.

He clasped her hands, bringing them to his lips, lightly kissing each finger.

"My turn," he said in a husky voice. He lifted up the front of her shirt and unclasped her bra without effort. Katie gasped as the coolness swept over her exposed breasts. Jack gazed at her bareness with a smile. "Beautiful."

He stroked the nipple with his fingers, grasping the mound until she quivered. He lowered his head and took her breast into his mouth while his hand inched to the other side. Katie curved her body. Molten heat seared her skin and spiraled between her legs. She bit her tongue so not to scream. He drew her nipple into the tight peak, licking tenderly, before he took the tip, and kissed it with eager greed. Jack urged her shirt higher. His mouth skimmed across her naked chest. His fingers glided over the band of her sleep shorts. He stopped and stiffened above her.

"Shit," Jack hissed. He instantly spun away. "What are we doing?" He yanked his shirt down to cover his abdomen. "This can't happen."

The words tumbling out of his mouth were like massive boulders rolling over her chest. His tone had turned severe. He furthered himself from her, or at least as far as the undersized space allowed.

A knot instantly appeared and squeezed her throat. Her heart almost came to a standstill. "You're right," she lied in a hoarse whisper.

So this *was* too good to be true. She thrust her shirt to cover her nakedness and rearranged her shorts while trying to drive away the humiliation.

"I'm sorry," he said from the darkness. He gulped loudly. "I didn't mean to take advantage of this situation."

A response failed her. She was a willing participant and now he knew. What was she supposed to say? And how would she handle the pain from this horrible rejection. She rotated onto her side, spinning away from him and blinked. *I will not cry, I will not cry.* Weeping wasn't a possibility. She wouldn't allow him to see what his callous behavior had done. She felt like such a fool for putting herself out there. Again.

"Katie? Are you okay?"

She inhaled before she shakily answered him, "I'm fine, Jack. Go to sleep."

He rose onto an elbow and leaned over her. He touched her arm, but her flinch made him yank his hand away. "I don't know what to say. I'm so so sorry."

She revolved onto her back, bravely staring him in the eye. "You don't have to keep apologizing. We both got carried away. It's a good thing you stopped us or we would've made a huge mistake. I actually owe you a world of thanks." She twisted onto her side, no longer able to look at him. Her lids lowered, and squeezed her eyes tight. "Good night, Jack."

Chapter 14

"This house is really old." Jack stopped walking and gazed at the shadowed outline of the two-story structure.

Almost forgetting the strain between them, or that this was the first actual sentence he'd spoken since the previous night's debacle, Katie followed his look and smiled. Even in early morning light the dwelling did appear ageless, although she viewed it more as comfortable. Her family home held countless years of wonderful memories. Recollections of holidays, summers with relatives, many no longer living, became front and center of her thoughts.

"Yes, this house has been standing for a long time. My great-great-grandparents were the original owners, and the estate was passed down through generations." She inhaled deep, filling her lungs with the crisp morning air. "I love the area. I'm crazy about the loft, but if the drive wasn't so far, I would consider making this home."

"Right now, you'd better think of the place as a hideout." He gestured at the sprawling acreage. "How much real estate goes with the property?"

"We once owned several thousand acres though the land has been slowly sold off with only six hundred left. The house is a century and a half years old."

He stared at the home, wearing an expression of

distaste. "Ancient," he said in a dry tone.

Katie assumed he didn't share her passion for family antiquity or her appreciation of the historical buildings situated over the grounds. Though at the moment, she could care less about his tastes.

She led him to an outdated barn and slid the exterior rusted handle. The entry creaked. She leaned in. With all of her strength, she shoved the door open. Jack stepped into the musty scented shed. Katie dusted her hands and followed. Inside the structure displayed an array of cobwebs, tarnished cans, broken barrels, and antique equipment. Each timeworn farm piece appeared to grab Jack's interest. This old stuff, he liked. In the midst of the vintage gear sat a surprisingly newer model tractor.

He strolled to the machine, and slowly paced around it. "This is out of place."

"The land is rented to farmers to produce their crops, but the unused grounds grow over with weeds during the summer." She motioned toward the tractor. "Pops keeps it here for shredding purposes."

A hand traced over the workings. Once he finished his admiration, he hoisted into the seat, his face almost glowing. "Been a few years, but let's see if I remember how to drive one of these babies."

Katie snatched a rope hanging on the wall, and then mounted the tractors step ladder. She climbed until she stood beside Jack, careful not to make any kind of physical contact. He turned the key and the motor cranked. Gears shifted, he backed out of the barn, maneuvered onto the muddy road, and headed toward her stuck vehicle.

Like on their walk earlier, neither spoke. The

awkwardness remained steadfast between them. Katie tried not to think about last night or how the next couple of days would play out. She supposed they'd do like were doing now and pretend nothing happened, although she wasn't sure she was that fine of actress.

The rough terrain had her gripping the stepladder's handle. She kept her gaze away from Jack and focused into the distance. The sun barely tipped the horizon as a frosty haze lifted from a nearby stock pond. The air was cold, but the rain had passed and the strong wind died. A slight breeze remained and wafted the tips of the overgrown brush occupying the unseeded fields.

They found no major damage to the jeep. The effort was minimal to pull it from the mud. Jack helped her return the luggage to the vehicle's rear, hurried to the tractor, and drove away without a word.

She stared at after him as he vanished into the dawn's dazzling glimmer. She wished she didn't have to follow him. Her heart still stung from last night's blow and probably would for the rest of her life. She'd lay awake the entire night, fighting the urges to either burst into tears or smother the man sleeping beside her with her pillow.

Key turned the jeep engine came alive. She gingerly pressed on the gas, taking her time to return. She didn't want to deal with her issues, and she especially preferred not to have anything to do with Jack.

The drive wasn't long. Within minutes, Katie opened her door and stepped out of the vehicle. For a moment, she forgot about Jack and everything else that was wrong in her life. Just the sight of her grandparents' home glinting in the morning sun brought a on a wealth of warmth, despite the biting breeze. Several years had passed since she'd visited, and she'd missed the place. Regardless of her pending troubles, and Jack's presence, she experienced an instant tranquility, more calm than the past few days.

Jack emerged from the barn. "I forgot how hard driving those things are on the body." He placed both hands on his back he stretched, halting in mid-stretch. He stared at a shed next to the main quarters. "Oh, shit. Is that an outhouse?"

Katie glanced in the direction of the broken down outdoor toilet, then turned to Jack. "Wild creatures won't bother you this time of year." She almost grinned. "Too cold." She held in a laugh at his horrified expression. After last night, and this morning's uneasiness, real levity wasn't going to happen. She was tempted to make him use the shattered building. She popped the rear latch and trekked to the back to unload. "Relax. The place contains all the comforts we need. Electricity, indoor plumbing, satellite for television, we even have Internet connections."

Jack leaned in for his bag. "Heat and air?"

Her belongings on the ground and assured Jack had his things, she slammed the door shut with more force than she intended. "Sure. There's a fireplace and you can raise the windows." Handbag in place, she picked up her suitcase, a cooler, and satchel. "How are you a chopping wood?"

He made a noise that sounded like a growl as he hauled his overnight bag over his shoulder. "I suck." He walked to her and took the case and the cooler.

After she locked her car, she prodded into her purse, produced a second set of keys, and fronted the way through the door. They stepped onto a screened porch that stretched the length of the residence, maneuvering past a cistern placed in the center.

She signaled to an opening off the side. "The restroom. Added on long after the house was built."

"No outhouse, but you're nearly going outside to use the bathroom anyway."

"At least you won't encounter anything icky."

"Always see the positive, don't you?"

She switched on the light as they entered a small kitchen. An old time Formica table, surrounded by four, white vinyl chairs dominated the tiny galley. A stove, sink, and refrigerator lined the walls, everything prehistoric. Jack sat the cooler on the diminutive counter and followed her into the living area. A whisper of his warm breath drifted over her neck, making her aware of his closeness.

She hastened her step to create a distance between them, and then whirled around and gestured to a double set of curtain covered glass doors. "That's Nana's old room. I'll sleep in there. The other bedroom across the hall belonged to my aunt. You can take that one." She led him into the hallway, motioned to a sharp angled staircase positioned to one side. "My dad slept upstairs, but the top floor hasn't been aired out in ages. You'll be more comfortable here."

She strolled into the darkened room and flipped on a vintage floor lamp. A dim light flooded the cold area. Faded flowery wallpaper coated the walls. A picture of Jesus on the cross faced an iron bedframe covered in a patchwork quilt sat against the opposite wall. Two windows shielded in worn shades were situated on each side of the bed. Handmade curtains sewn from feed sacks hung over the tops.

"Five star accommodations, huh?"

"Been is worse." Jack sat his bag on the mattress surface, triggering a quiet squeak. He removed his jacket then threw it on top of his duffle. "Much." His nose wrinkled. "What's the smell?"

Her grin extended at the mention of the odd mixture of bleach and ammonia scent. "Mothballs. My grandmother kept them everywhere, and it's been virtually impossible to get rid of the odor. I think she became addicted to the aroma."

He hurried to the window and yanked up the shade, allowing the morning sunlight to filter through. A hand gripped the edge of the sill, his upper arm tensed. Katie squeezed her bottom lip between her teeth and stared. His shirt sleeves tightened around a brawny bicep. Flexing his muscles, he heaved at the ledge before the stubborn glass gave way and lifted.

A blast of cool air smacked her in the face. Katie blinked several times, forcing her gaze from his well-built physique. There wasn't enough ice in Antarctica to take away this guy's hotness, even if she was pissed. How was she going to spend three days, alone with him, knowing what she did?

Jack spun and faced her. "If I must choose between that stink and cold. I choose cold." A charming half-grin prompted a sexy crinkle around his eyes. "No offense to Nana." His smile faded. "Katie, I'm beat and need to sleep, but I think we should talk about what happened last night first."

She held up both hands, palms facing him. "I'm not up for a talk right now, Jack. I want to get some rest too. I'll let you unpack."

Katie rushed to leave. Frigidness might've overpowered his bedroom, but the mention of their shared encounter brought her inner thermometer to sky high then plummet to below zero.

After she'd stashed her belongings, put the groceries away, she went into the bathroom and took a long, hot shower. Since she didn't sleep much the night before, a nap was in the works. She put on an oversized flannel shirt and socks, and climbed into bed. Except rest refused to come. She tried to ignore Jack slept across the hall. With his muscles, and memory of the feel of his lips pressing onto hers, his touch, his hardened body, his dismissal, still fresh.

Her mind churned. How come she couldn't be mad for a while and then let this go? If anyone else had treated her this way, she'd stripped them down and kicked them out into the rain. Why was Jack so different? Why did she allow him and his actions to emotionally beat her down?

Covers thrown back, she rolled to the floor, her stocking feet gliding the length of the worn planks as she snatched her laptop. She stepped softly into the living room, making a stop at a gas fireplace. Flames shot through the metal burners instantly warming her. She curled into an old wooden rocker and opened her computer. With little work from her, the chair swayed back and forth in a hypnotic creak while she forced her mind to absorb the displays on the screen in front of her.

An out of place noise made her glance up.

Jack shadowed form framed the doorway. His bare shoulder braced against the doorjamb, arms folded across his exposed middle, legs crossed, observing her with a serious frown.

She swallowed and choked out, "I thought you were sleeping"

He remained motionless and continued to stare.

"Jack?"

"Thirsty. I need a drink of water." He moved further into the room, bolting toward the kitchen." I don't have to draw it from the well, do I?"

"The faucet works," she mumbled, forcing her attention on her computer. "I've packed some healthy drinks too. You're welcome to one."

"I'll stick with water, thanks." He paused. "Unless you brought beer."

She leaned closer to her laptop screen. "Damn."

He stopped and turned to her with raised brows. "Problem?"

"Internet is iffy. Everything froze. I'm going to lose my shopping cart." She pushed the "enter" button repeatedly. "That's three hours of research, shot to hell."

"Investigating possible suspects?"

"Shoes."

He shook his head. "I thought you planned on discovering who wants to send you to prison."

"On my to do list." Teeth gritted, she rammed the key continuously.

From out of nowhere, rough, warm fingers gripped her wrist. Her entire body stiffened. Slowly, she raised her chin, meeting a green gaze.

Jack let her fist slip from his grasp. "Hitting the button over and over won't unfreeze it."

Katie stared as he backed away.

"Don't buy anything. Save your purchases instead.

Credit and debit cards can be traced," he warned.

"Jack?"

He halted, though his gaze didn't quite mesh with hers. She stared at him, careful to keep her focus on his face. She wouldn't dare allow her eyes to drift onto his naked chest. Her chin dropped "Never mind."

His frowned thoughtfully. "We should talk, Katie."

She shot up a palm and shook her head. "No Jack," she almost shouted.

Thoughts of last night, the humiliation only made her angry. She preferred not to display any heated emotion. He didn't need to know her feelings.

"Yes, Katie." Jack insisted in a quiet voice. His gentle tone took away most of her hostility. "We're here for the next couple of days, and right now everything is awkward as hell. I can't live with this much tension and neither can you. The only way to solve this is to clear the air. Have a heart to heart about what happened."

Katie bit her bottom lip. She couldn't bear to hear why he came to her or worse, the reason he stopped.

"I've already said this, but I'm sorry for my behavior." Hands shoved into his pockets, he sighed and looked away. "I made a mistake. I shouldn't have done anything. It was wrong of me."

Katie clutched the aged wood, her fingers rounded the arms of the chair. "Right. You've made that clear, and I don't need to rehash the episode."

"I want to explain."

"Explain what?" Her voice rose as she edged her butt to the chair's border. Her back straightened. "I understand. I had a crush on you from the moment I met you, a liking that stayed with me until my teenage years. Yes, I behaved badly because of my young age, I didn't know how to act toward someone I was so crazy about. Then I grew up, and you still failed to notice me. I decided to take the initiative. I revealed my feelings the night before you left for college. Instead of letting me down easily, you said…" she blinked back the tears.

Years of pain welled up in her chest. The dam was about to break. She couldn't go further for fear of revealing every spec of agony she'd stored over time. He'd view her as pathetic.

"My response was," Jack continued in a hoarse tone. "To go home, and play with dolls. Learn how to be a girl. And I would never be with someone so annoying."

A tear streaked down her cheek. "You still see me that way. You view me as that bothersome kid with too much testosterone."

He shook his head. "I don't find anything boyish about you, especially after last night. I'm sorry for saying those things to you back then. Very uncalled for, specifically to an impressionable sixteen year old girl. I tried to apologize the other day, but you wouldn't let me." He grinned. "And yeah, you're still a little trying. But it's cute now. Even so, this isn't the right time for me to get involved with anyone. I've already explained that to you."

"There won't ever be the right time for you and me." Her voice cracked. "I'll never be the type of woman you go for."

"Why does this matter so much?"

"Because it does, I mean, doesn't."

"I think so." He took a step closer and bent, making his face level with hers. "What are you saying,

Katie?" Jack eyes narrowed into jade slits. "Or better yet, what are you not saying. Do you still have feelings for me?"

Chapter 15

Katie stared at Jack. "Do I still have feelings for you?" Color crept over her face, though he wasn't sure if it was from anger or he'd hit a nerve. "You actually believe I've been holding on to some teenage dream, especially after the coldhearted way you blew me off? Are you delusional or just that vain?"

He backed away. *Anger, definitely anger.* Dammit, he'd been an attorney for years. He should've used his words better. From her "about to explode" expression, he'd asked the wrong question and turned a tense situation into mountainous. He must perform some damage control before the catastrophe molted into un-repairable devastation.

After last night, he was unsure they hadn't already reached desolation. He'd constantly scolded himself over his behavior. He allowed his personal needs to overtake his common sense and he'd taken advantage of her old feelings. His current yearnings were nothing more than the lack of being close to a woman for months.

"I'm sorry, Katie. I shouldn't have asked you—," he rushed, ramming his hands into his pockets. A corner of his mouth lifted. "I seem to be apologizing a lot lately."

"Maybe you should do a blanket one. Cover everything from past indiscretions to your present behavior. And for any stupidity that may occur in between."

Sarcasm. His attempt at charm didn't work. He needed to do something else or she might pick him up and toss him out on his ass, locking the doors behind her.

Outer limits country wasn't his thing.

"I should," he agreed. "I do. I don't know what made me ask that. Forgive me. Last night." He swallowed and hurried on before she could stop him. "Due to my circumstances, I prefer not to drag you into my mess, particularly when you have other—things—to deal with. You understand, right?"

"Sure. I see." Her gaze dropped. She stared vacantly at the floor.

"Do you?" His gut told him she wasn't being straight about her feelings, but because she seemed determined to make him believe otherwise, he wouldn't pursue the subject.

"Your involvement with me could create a messier problem for you too."

He sighed forcefully as he studied her closer. Up until now, he'd worked hard to avoid even a meager glance at her but the draw was too strong. He could feel his lips pressed on hers. The taste of her sweet, intoxicating tang lingered.

The shades were drawn, keeping the room dark with a trancelike mistiness. Flames danced from the fireplace and cast a soft, enchanted glow around her, haloing her mussed tresses.

She'd relaxed in an old-fashioned rocker, dressed in an oversized flannel shirt, laptop opened, resting on the arm. The scene created an enticing setting. The alluring vision along with the knowledge of how her body felt had him all but sprinting to her.

Jack gave his follicles an extra tug as he sifted his fingers through his hair. "I have serious trust issues. My problem, I know, still it'd be a huge disaster to get romantically involved."

She lifted her eyes and gazed straight at him. "So why did you? How come you kissed me if you're in such a bad place?"

He shook his head.

"You've been adamant about not getting close to a woman, yet you did it anyway."

He pursed his lips and blew out a stream of air. How would he answer her without making things worse? The truth wouldn't work, but it's all he had. Yeah, he'd be a jerk, but at least he was an honest one. Hands withdrawn from his pockets, he lifted his shoulders and held his arms out to his sides. "No clue."

"You don't know?"

He dropped his hands and stared. For a moment, he forgot they were on the verge of a major blow up, or at least she was. Her taut, slender body reminded him of a graceful cat. Bare legs—lengthy, well-formed, toned legs he shouldn't look at, but couldn't help staring— were tucked underneath her. His gut heaved a massive, alarming jolt.

He gulped. The little room overheated. Women didn't make him nervous, and he'd never been at a loss for something to say, but the sight of her and, those shapely limbs blacked out any concept of common sense. The tiny section in his mind where he stored bad ideas and even worse choices prodded him unmercifully.

Get the girl out of your head. Not the time or place. Ever.

"I was with you because I got caught up in the moment."

Her brows rose.

"Rotten excuse. I'm a man and you're a woman. You looked beautiful, all messy, and sexy. You smelled like rain, and you were touching me. I lost it." Images saturated his thoughts. He shook his head to get rid of the memories. "I screwed up, and now we're dealing with the fallout of my mistake. Can't I just say I'm sorry and move on? Must this be so fucking complicated?"

"The situation became complicated the second you pushed me away."

He held up his forefinger. "You can't tell me you've never lost control in the heat of the moment, and then realized the behavior unwise. You even indicated you were glad I stopped us. This situation is a perfect example."

"It is," she agreed in a small voice.

"Why take things so personal. It's not about you. My circumstances have left a huge hole in the pit of my stomach and while I hope to recover," he lifted and released both shoulders, "I haven't."

She straightened and dropped a foot to the floor and pushed the rocker with her toes.

"So are we okay? Am I forgiven?"

She stopped rocking, biting her bottom lip as if to consider his request. "We'll put the incident behind us. Chalk it up to bad decisions on both our parts."

"Thank you." Relief swept throughout him. He may make through the next couple of days after all.

"Except..." Katie leaned against the chairs side, arms crossed over her chest. "You're letting a single incident mar your judgment. Not every woman is so cruel."

She couldn't just let things go. He eyed her outstretched limb, his gaze glided downward to her purple socked foot. The insides of his mouth dried, like the Sahara. He wanted to be done talking about—anything. "This wasn't the first time I've been let down. Jenna was the last of many. I can start at the beginning, to my mother and her lack of maternal instincts."

"She was that bad? Jenna?"

Jack cleared his throat and spoke in a jaded tone. "She made sure every local media outlet aware we had an intimate relationship while she was a client. She claimed I seduced her, and insinuated the correlation jeopardized my ability to represent her in a competent manner." He re-jammed his hands into his pockets and swore softly. He hated discussing the subject, but if he must to ease her irritation, he would. "Bad enough she declared I used sex as additional payment, then to insinuate I didn't act professional, or in her best interest was a knee to the groin accusation. What occurred between us was consensual, and I made no demands, implications, or promises. And she's ruined me."

"You're saying it's okay?" She shifted in her chair and frowned. "For an attorney to sleep with their client?"

Not the first time someone asked him this question, but explaining to her was more difficult. He heaved a long, raspy breath. "Lawyers are one of the few professions where intimacy with cliental isn't taboo-or illegal. Though sexual involvement is discouraged in most practices and the ethics of doing so is debatable."

Toes bent, she pushed the rocker back and forth, an ancient squeak the only sound between them for several seconds. "What you're saying is this behavior isn't unusual in your line of work?"

"I can't speak for others." His voice rang hoarse in his ears. "This was a first for me. I'd never gotten involved with a client before."

She stopped rocking and looked him up and down.

His eyes narrowed. "You don't believe me, do you?"

Katie smiled as she closed her laptop and sat the pc onto the floor next to her. "Of course I do." Her mouth opened, like she was going to add something, but changed her mind.

"Go ahead."

Her gaze connected with his. "Didn't you stop to wonder if being with this woman was a bad idea? That perhaps you shouldn't."

"Hell yeah." He fidgeted. "No question. I knew this could all blow up and bite me in the ass." Easing backward to the couch, Jack lowered onto the cushion. "And yes, I thought of walking away more than once."

"So why didn't you? I mean, you're not some hormonal teenager. As an attorney, self-control should be a natural part of your persona."

"Should have, but did not happen. I get to be a double dumbass on this one, hence my reasoning for not getting involved with anyone at the moment."

"Was there a lesson buried in the experience?"

"Ancient saying, we never really grow up, we only learn how to act in public therefore, I guess I learned that I'm not too old to do something stupid." He snuffed a laugh. "I found out I still don't always think with my brain, although I'm making a conscious effort to do so now. She apparently wasn't using her mind either. Her focus seemed to be on my bank account, which she assumed was a lot bigger than it actually was, and stiffing my company." Then he shook his head and mumbled, "I can't believe she took everything this far."

"Women are emotional creatures, Jack. Hell hath no fury as they say. Perhaps she developed actual feelings for you, and she became ticked off over your lack of commitment. Maybe she thought the relationship was more than sex."

"Doubtful."

Katie stared at him sharply. Her look of reproach grabbed him and squeezed his gut. The woman lived in a romance novel where she believed in fairies and Santa. A pleasant, peachy perspective.

He studied her face glowing in the blaze. "Believe what you want. She was no innocent. Cruz discovered that my company isn't the first law firm she's sued. She's done this before."

Katie took a moment before she spoke. "So she's about the money."

"The almighty dollar. Believe it or not, Katie, some individuals revel in green."

"You're getting let down again," She warned deliberately. "By hanging out with Vanessa. You're bound to be burned another time."

He'd wondered how long it would take for her to bring that up. "No worries. Nothing happened with Vanessa, nor will it. I only called her after several beers, I might add. We had, maybe a fifteen minute conversation."

"She insinuated you went out. Like on a date."

"I'm aware. But that's not true. I happen to mention the bar I planned on going to later in the evening while on the phone. She showed up. I bought her one drink. We spent a couple of hours together, had a few laughs, and I left. Alone." Tired of these discussions and even more frustrated at his physical response to her, Jack rose to his feet not quite meeting her gaze. "Can we please let this go?"

"You're the one who brought up the subject."

"I'm getting water now."

He stomped toward the kitchen. Inside, he snapped the light switch to on. Rummaging through the cupboards, he searched for a glass or a cup but the majority of them were empty. All he wanted was a drink of fricken' water. He slammed a cabinet door and opened another.

How dare she look so enticing? She seemed oblivious to the fact he found her attractive, and to make matters worse, she appeared dismayed over his recklessness. He was a guy, for Christ's sake. He did guy things. Another cabinet bare. He banged the door harder. Even a place this outdated ought to have some sort of glassware.

"Why are you beating up my grandmother's house?"

He jerked and twisted around. Katie stood in the threshold of the tiny room. Their eyes met, but his gaze dropped and lingered to where the top two buttons of her sleep shirt was left undone. The gap formed a perfect V and revealed her smooth skin over the apexes of her pert breasts.

She closed the space between them, giving him a better view. The vision blended with her fresh scent, and zinged him directly into his exploding hormones, which spewed to the point of rivaling a teenager's.

"Jack?"

He forced his eyes upward and gazed at her face where she returned his stare with an impatient glare.

"What's with all the noise?"

He swung away from her and groused, "Can't find a glass."

"No need to tear the place down." She swept past him, opened the far cabinet, removed a jar, and handed it to him.

He took the flask and inched away. "What is this?"

"A canning jar. Nana used them for drinking glasses. She didn't waste money on anything extravagant."

"Glasses are extravagant?"

She angled her head and smiled. "Nana thought so."

Jack held the container under the faucet and flipped the handle, filling it with water and muttered, "Might as well be camped out in a damn cave."

"Why are you in such a foul mood?"

He whipped around. "Because I want to…" His gaze drifted to her mouth. Her tongue nervously ran over her full lips, moistening them.

Kiss you.

Heat flared inside his belly, scorching his insides like a firestorm boiling through his body. He wanted more than just a kiss. A hell of a lot more. He shook his head and blinked, then downed the lukewarm water in one swallow. Damn this woman with her sexy legs and exquisite cleavage. The idea of a cold night in an isolated farmhouse, snuggled against her, or better yet inside her, in front of the fire had a definite appeal, no matter how ill-advised. He'd had enough of behaving rashly. Still, his libido would soon overrule his brain if he didn't get away from her. "Because you want to?" Index fingers pointed, she circled her hands in a wheeling motion as if to prompt him to complete the thought.

"Nothing."

She sighed loud and spun toward the doorway.

"What happened with your fiancé?" he blurted.

Katie turned and stared at him. "We…," she fumbled and folded her arms across her stomach, almost defiantly. "What?"

He cleared his throat, not understanding where the sudden question about her love life came from, but since he brought the subject up, "I've confessed my humiliating transgressions. Your turn to answer some questions. You were engaged and you're not anymore. How come?"

She ducked her head and mumbled, "We weren't meant to be."

"Don't buy it."

"Buy whatever, that's the reason." She raised her chin and laughed resentfully. "We wanted different things. I had personal goals and was driven to achieve them and he, he wasn't."

"Meaning?"

"Meaning." She tightened her arms around her waist, clutching her biceps. "Too often men find my family's money more enticing than me. Usually I can tell the difference, but this guy…" She gazed at him.

Her eyes held a trace of sadness. "I do understand about those who revel in the green."

"I'm sorry, Katie. I didn't realize."

"I don't want your pity, Jack."

"I'm not giving you any pity—"

"Yes you are," she interrupted, her voice raised to a harsh pitch. "You've always misjudged me. I have feelings, Jack." She spun toward the living area. "I'm exhausted, and I'm going to bed."

Without a glimpse in his direction, she brushed past him, hurried into the next room, and disappeared. The click of her bedroom door closing echoed through the silent house.

Jack crossed into the main area to douse the gas flames, then stood with his hands on his hips and glowered into the darkness. *That went well.* He should be happy he'd pissed her off and made her go away. Instead her ire left him unsettled.

Inside his room, he dug into his bag and extracted his favorite sweats. Pretending to sleep in that cramped space last night, so close to Katie, had drained him. He needed to rest. Changed and in bed, he lay on a too thin mattress, which resembled a torture device. The springs whined at his every movement. Hands linked behind his head, covered to his neck, he stared at the ceiling as his mind drifted.

What was he doing here? He should be at his new job, which Jed assured him he'd square with Aaron if he'd keep an eye on Katie and bring her home. A feat wouldn't be easy or as quick as he first believed. Anything to take care of the princess.

So here he was. Looking after the Drapier's little darling.

Someone he used to couldn't stand.

Used to.

He threw the covers off and rose from the too soft pillows that's comfortable days were long past. When did he start liking her? True, he discovered on the day they'd reconnected that he wanted her physically, except this was more than about sex.

Jack liked Katie. Unreal. He found her smart, entertaining, funny. Cruz was right. She'd blossomed into a damn good-looking woman. He walked to his doorway and stood in the threshold, staring across the hall where she slept.

He owed Jed and Lila, no doubt. But the price he would have to pay in return may've risen too high.

Chapter 16

"Ugh!" Vanessa slammed the door followed by the click of her high heels against the travertine tiles. The tick faded as she trekked onto the carpet. Tara trialed close behind, her feet hurried in double time to keep up.

Rhett raised his chin from his electronic tablet. "Darling, this is my home. I had the door shipped from East Asia. Hand carved. The beveled glass inside is etched to perfection and most expensive. Please be careful."

Vanessa flung her body onto a settee and dropped her bag onto the floor, not caring about the damage she might've done to Rhett's stupid entryway. The man was loaded. He could afford to replace whatever she ruined.

Rhett returned to his tablet. "What is the current catastrophe are we dealing with?"

"If I'm forced to go out on one more date with this dull, bore of a cop, I'm going to throw up my entire insides."

Rhett slid his pad onto the glassed coffee table, and leaped from his chair. "Not on the Berber." Hands held up on either side of his head, he wiggled his fingers. "Should I get you a pan?"

Tara, who'd walked to the far end of the room and parked on a fainting chair, eyed Rhett with a smirk. "Just an expression. She's not really going to barf."

"Barf," he repeated. He flashed an irritated glance

at her, and then planted his fists to his hips. "Such a poetical term for the word vomit."

Vanessa lounged on her back, clutching her forehead. "My head is pounding."

Rhett looked away, still annoyed, but Tara's concerned gaze remained on her. "Is there anything we can do?"

Vanessa dropped an arm over her eyes and groaned louder. "Yes. Leave me alone."

"Perhaps you should go to your own home, if solitude is what you crave," Rhett suggested. "I'd also appreciate you remove those impalers disguised as shoes from my sofa. The fabric is a rare silk. Costs me a fortune."

"I have aspirin," Tara expressed in a hopeful tone.

Vanessa peeked from underneath her forearm. "Aspirin won't work." Though disagreeable, she consented to Rhett's request and shifted her feet from the couch's pillow. "Run to the drugstore downstairs and get me something stronger. There's bound to be some over the counter meds for migraines."

"It's awfully late. I doubt they're open."

Vanessa wrestled to her elbows, her eyes flickered instant anger. "Then go to another pharmacy. I need medication before my brain explodes."

She slumped to the sofa's cushion. Rhett paid a pretty penny to live in this piece of luxury. He could phone the concierge, and the staff would deliver anything a tenant or guest desired. Except she was ready to get rid of Tara. The girl may be competent in many areas, but she got on Vanessa's nerves.

Tara huffed as she rose. She stomped to where Vanessa had dumped her pocketbook and bent to snatch something from the inside. "I'll be damned if I buy you anything with my money when you act like a bitch." She twisted a plastic square between her fingers. "I'm using your credit card."

Vanessa sat up and shouted, "You are my subordinate." She flopped back onto the couch. "I wish you'd remember that sometimes."

Clumping to the exit, Tara banged the door.

Rhett flinched as he watched her leave. He turned to Vanessa with a frown. "I not sure how much longer I can stand that appalling woman."

"You're the one who insisted I keep her."

He lowered to his chair. "Doesn't explain why you brought her here."

"She's my assistant. As much I detest the idea, she goes where I go."

He raised his brows. "She accompanied you on your date?"

Vanessa pushed her body up to sit, planting her feet onto the floor. "I wish."

"Bad?"

"Horrible. He took me to a snack shop for dinner. At the mall." Vanessa squealed, still unable to comprehend this dude who thought she'd be willing to spend her evening in a shopping center's delicatessen. "Can you believe he's trying to impress me, to get me into bed, and he buys me a sandwich?" She made a motion over her tailored, designer dress." Do I look like a submarine, hoagie kind of women?"

"Cops salary. Or lack of. Doubtless all he could afford."

"He might as well apply for welfare if that's the best he can do."

"You may be giving off the impression you're a cheap date."

She glared at him, but her venomous scowl didn't seem to bother him.

"This is your vendetta, sweet cheeks. You must endure the man's parsimony to achieve your goal."

"I'm done enduring anything after tonight. His usefulness is long over." She leaned forward, picked up her purse, and removed her cell phone. "I'm ditching this guy."

"By text?" Rhett looked incredulous as he watched her punch the letters on the miniature keyboard. "How cold? Especially since he did, however unwitting, give you information about Hazel's case. You ought to at least call to give him the bad news. In person would be better."

Vanessa ignored his suggestion and continued to move her thumbs swiftly over her screen. She could care less about how she unloaded the dupe. Past tired of his tedious cop stories, and his constant telling her he found his work so rewarding that it made her want to gag. Hazel's murder was the most exciting investigation he'd been involved in since he'd joined the force. Fortunately for her, he couldn't wait to spill details. Now she didn't need the silly cop. She'd always been able to cajole her way through any situation and come out on top with little or no help. His involvement just made things go quicker.

"Done." Vanessa replaced her phone.

"You're sure this decision is a wise one? You may need to extract more data, and you've cut off your information line."

"Everything is in place. I don't require anything

else from him." She raised her chin, and smiled. "I can re-erect the relationship if I need him."

"You're certainly confident."

"Never been a guy I couldn't get. More than once, if necessary."

Rhett cleared his throat. "How goes the romance with the handsome, but tarnished attorney?"

Her smile faltered. "Still in progress."

He smirked knowingly. "Hasn't fallen for you yet?"

"Things with Jack aren't going as swift as I anticipated which is okay. He must get his act together and be a practicing attorney again before I'm willing to make my move. I refuse to take on his problems."

"Publically, of course. Don't tell me you wouldn't be opposed to secretly dabbling in his briefs."

She laughed. "That's a possibility. He has such potential for the future once his little storm blows over. I'd rather wait."

"I'm confused with your fascination concerning this man. Granted, his pictures show he's attractive enough, yet his employment status is on hold, and his reputation is shot. What's the appeal? "

"The guy oozes charisma. He's associated with the right people who may not support him publically, but my sources say they back him privately. He'll be forgiven and eventually successful again. His contacts will be useful for my career at Weddings Fantastic. Once he's cleaned up, he'll be delicious arm candy."

She didn't understand her interest for Jackson Pharrell either. All Vanessa knew was she wanted him. Maybe because she'd gotten a whiff Katherine Drapier had the hots for him, and her inability to get him.

Vanessa loved the idea of attaining something that women couldn't.

Rhett shook his head. "I still don't see how an association with him will benefit you. Even if he overcomes these allegations, he will be tainted for a long time."

"We'll make a marvelous couple."

"What about Katherine? You're sure she's on her way out of the picture?"

"She will be soon. I feel it. We're not too far from putting Katherine away forever."

"You're not too far from putting Katherine away forever." Rhett corrected, a flicker of misgiving sparked in his eyes. "I possess no ill will against the girl, other than she turned down my job offer. Such a shame." A hand flittered in the air. "We would've made an awesome team. Maybe once I acquire Weddings Fantastic, I can lure her back, if she doesn't go to jail."

"Rhett."

"Oh she's pricy, but the girl's talent is unmatchable, and people wrangle to use her to do their affairs."

"Rhett." Vanessa jumped off the sofa and stomped a foot. She glowered at him, fingers extended across her hips.

He pulled his bottom lip to appear chastened. "Sorry, dear. At one point, I didn't care who took the blame for Hazel's demise, but I've reconsidered. You're insisting on pinning a murder on this poor woman is a damn disgrace. She exhibits such a gift." He raised his eyes and sharply looked at her. "I know I've asked you before, but what is your problem with Katherine, anyway? She must have done something dreadful to make you so intent to ruin her life."

"I want to manage Weddings Fantastic, and she's in my way." Vanessa clamped her mouth shut and returned to her seat.

"Hard to believe that's your only hindrance against the girl. I sense other objectives." He held up a hand and turned away. "No. Changed my mind. I don't want to know. All I care about is I acquire Weddings Fantastic." He paused. "Word from my attorney the private sale is going smoothly. I've signed the contracts and issued a check, I'm waiting on the Nutt side to complete their end."

"Can't wait till all of this is over." She lips turned up slyly. "I'll have everything I want."

Rhett shook his head with a tsk.

"Excuse me," Vanessa fumed. "You're the one who wants to buy Weddings Fantastic, remember. You were okay with going with the slow method, and run Hazel's business into the ground so you could buy her out. I developed this plan on spec. I came up with this idea quickly after I'd discovered her untimely demise."

Rhett picked up his electronic pad, and bent to study the screen, releasing a soft hum. "Yes. I'm aware. For years, I wanted Hazel Nutt out of my hair, and I thought acquiring her business as an extension of Affairs Amore would be a sound investment. I bet she'd be doing backflips in her grave if she realized I'm planning purchase her precious company."

"Be careful. She may come back and haunt you."

He lifted his chin and gazed at Vanessa. "Don't speak of such things."

She chuckled. "Surely you don't believe in ghosts."

"I do imagine some spirits roam because they

cannot rest for whatever reason. Hazel Nutt was a horrible human being, and did many bad things to a lot of people. I wonder if her soul will ever be at peace in the hereafter."

"If you insist in accepting such foolishness, then—"

"It is not foolishness," Rhett interrupted.

"Okay, well look at it this way. Her wandering specter might be upset you've purchased her firm, but she loved me. She'll be thrill I'm running it."

"Yes, unless she discovers you were in cahoots with me. Then she'll haunt us both." He glanced up from his pad. "Which reminds me. We don't want to make anyone suspicious when this transaction transpires. It might take a while before we announce you as the company manager. I may be forced to continue to employ you undercover for a bit longer."

"Rhett, you promised. I put myself out there. I could end up in jail with Katherine if anyone discovers my part in you getting this business."

"All your choices."

She glared at him, her back erect as she straightened. "You agreed to make me manager of Weddings Fantastic as soon as the purchase went through." Vanessa steamed. She needed Rhett's financial backing to continue with her strategy. If he bailed, all of her hard work, and her future would be lost. She wanted to head this company, and Rhett was her ticket to getting there.

He raised a shoulder. "This arrangement isn't in writing."

"A verbal agreement is binding."

"Again, no proof." He sighed and picked up his

tablet. "I'm not totally opposed to you running the business, but there is the matter of you taking kickbacks from venders. I have to consider your reputation. Explain to customers and associates why I'm rehiring you after I terminated you for such deception, and now allowing you to lead my second organization. This matter will take time and finesse."

She relaxed, slacking into her seat, silently simmering. She had no intention on waiting for her rightful place at Weddings Fantastic. She'd sacrificed too much.

"Nevertheless, the argument is moot since the purchase has yet to be complete." Rhett studied his device. "So did our little sandwich shop cop reveal to you anything about Hazel's murder case?" He gazed up and lowered his voice. "I won't ask what you revealed to him."

She kicked off her heals and curled her legs under her. "Apparently someone called in a tip. Katherine is possession of something that may link her to the murder."

Rhett's eyes widened. "Interesting. Did he give you any hint as to what the item might be?"

She shook her head.

"Who called the tip in?"

"Anonymous."

"Sounds promising"

"It would be," Tara let the door shut with a soft click. "A judge issued a warrant to search her home, but another judge annulled it. No investigation."

"You're kidding," Vanessa nearly shouted. Then she spoke calmer, "Probably a friend of Katherine's rich daddy. I'm sure he keeps the idiot in his back pocket."

"Jed Drapier is a straight up guy." Tara walked further inside, and laid a paper bag next to Vanessa, and then returned to the far side of the room. "Well respected throughout the community."

"So the warrant was repealed." Rhett glanced from one woman to the other. "Did they give a reason?"

"The tipoff is from an unidentified source. It equals to not sufficient enough evidence for any investigation," Tara explained.

"If she has something to do with Hazel's murder then it shouldn't matter who told the police. They ought to be digging." Vanessa wrinkled her nose and sniffed. "I bet if the detectives looked into her past, they'd find Katherine not to be as perfect as she likes everyone to believe."

Tara made an odd sound then spoke in a near whisper, "she's not."

Vanessa frowned. "What are you saying over there?"

"I heard other things too."

They both stared at Tara and when she didn't elaborate, Rhett prompted, "Don't keep secrets, girl. Spill."

"Katherine's disappeared."

Rhett gazed at Vanessa. "Maybe your assumption is correct. She is Hazel's killer." He chuckled. "Which upped her another notch on my ladder."

"Where is she," Vanessa demanded.

Tara shrugged. "No one's talking, but the police find the move very curious, and want to speak to her again."

"Too bad you broke up with your cop boyfriend,"

Rhett smirked. "I bet he's in the know."

Vanessa reached for her cell phone.

"There's more," Tara announced. Vanessa froze. Tara grinned triumphantly. "Jack's with her."

Silence draped the room for a full minute.

Vanessa's eyes narrowed. "How do you know?"

Tara's smile widened. "He's missing too. My classmates stay connected through social networking. Several saw Katie and Jack together the other night. Someone even said they were seen kissing outside the Broadway Bistro."

"Ooohhh, this is delicious." Rhett clapped his hands. He lowered his voice. "The plot thickens."

"I bet her wealthy daddy encouraged him to go with her." Vanessa rose from the sofa and plodded to Tara, placed her fists on her hips and glared. "Do these contacts of yours have any idea where they are? As much as this town enjoys gossip, surely somebody knows."

"People are guessing." Tara paused. "I doubt if anyone would tell, though." She blinked innocently from behind her thick lenses. "Everyone likes them. No one will rat them out."

Vanessa slapped her arms against her side and paced. Those two need to be found immediately. Apprehended. Katherine belonged in jail and Jack…she didn't know what to do about him. At some point they'd be having a serious heart to heart where his loyalties lie. Granted, he wasn't aware of his allegiances yet, so she'd give him a pass for now.

"We must find out her hideout, and alert the authorities."

Tara's voice grew softer again. "I may know."

Vanessa stopped moving and stared at her assistant.

She pushed her glasses up her nose and cleared her throat. "I'm sure I know where Katie is hiding." The corners of Tara lips lifted higher. "It'll cost you."

"Cost us?" Vanessa shouted.

"Not me," Rhett stated firmly. "I don't give a shiny rat's booty where Katherine and her defiled attorney are shacking up." Rhett studied his nails. "And I've paid you enough. In addition to your salary as Vanessa's assistant. You will not receive another penny from me."

"You're lucky we're including you at all," Vanessa said.

"But you did include me." Tara's tone sounded smug. "Rhett paid Vanessa to sabotage Weddings Fantastic and Hazel. The police might find this information very interesting, seeing Hazel is dead."

"You have proof to use against us, don't you," Rhett stated, dully.

"Of course I kept records of everything. That's my job. As things are, it may be in your best interest to keep the authorities focus on Katie in this murder investigation. Among other things, my info could generate some bad publicity for Affairs Amore."

Vanessa looked anxiously at Rhett, who sighed. "So what do you want?"

Chapter 17

Jack threw the quilt back and spun out of bed moments before the sun peered through the window. "Shit its cold," he whispered, chafing his bare arms. An icy draft screamed underneath the glass's slim cavity, prompting shudders to shroud his body. He hurried to the crack and gulped a mouthful of clean air. At first the chilliness was uncomfortable, but the crisp morning gust morphed into a pleasant change. For years, he'd lived immersed in city smog and grimy haze. He'd forgotten how a rural breeze relaxed him. He remained by the gap for several minutes, relishing in the freshness before he pressed the edge and shut the pane. While he found the fragrance enjoyable, the frosty stream of air quickly negated the brisk tang.

Already in his sweats, he stumbled to his bag, dug out a shirt, and heaved it over his head. He snatched his toothbrush and quietly maneuvered through the corridor, past the staircase, and onto the porch bathroom.

It didn't take long to satisfy his needs, especially since the lavatory was more bone chilling than outside. After he'd finished, he noiselessly returned to his room. At the entrance, he stopped. His gaze lingered at the closed, dingy painted door across the hallway. Not a sound came from within. Katie must still be asleep. Of course, she was. Unless she'd tossed and turned, and now she lay awake staring at the ceiling. The way he had most of the night.

He shook his head to return to the present. He'd never get his concentration back on track if he didn't stop thinking about her. He needed to move past Jenna, her betrayal, and learn to trust again. He refused to have two emotional fuckups in a row.

Stepping into his room, he rifled through his duffle to retrieve his spare running shoes and socks, and slipped them over his feet. Ready for his morning jog, Jack rose from the bedside, returned to the window and viewed outside. He had no idea where he was, he just knew Katie drove him to the boonies.

He searched for a place to run. Dilapidated farm buildings were set off from the house. A winding, dirt road snaked away from the home and disappeared into a thatch of dense, dry grass. His tractor drive had already made him aware that the path was full of potholes. Dangerous for runners.

He continued to study the property. A pond sat nearby. Sunlight glinted off the water as the morning's draught thrust miniature rollers over the surface. A small weedy trail ran around the fishpond might work. Ready to get started, he left the bedroom and walked into the living area.

He stopped short and stared, powerless to tear his look away.

Katie lay stretched out on the sofa, a throw covered her legs. Still dressed in her too large flannel, the top of her smooth breasts peeked from the exposed gap.

His gaze stopped at the delightful aperture for several seconds before he took in the rest of her.

Her propped knees supported her laptop. A frown

sat firmly in place across her brow, giving the appearance she was in deep concentration. A sudden swelling materialized, and wedged in the middle of his throat. His palms moistened. A warm tingle pricked over his body, shooting through his inner sensors into an unknown cosmos.

He inhaled again and combed his fingers through his hair as he strolled to where she lay. Jack bent over her computer, and glanced at the spreadsheet displayed over the screen. "Whatcha doing?"

Her head snapped in his direction. "I didn't hear you come in."

Her voice held a major coolness, a degree lower than the freezing wind outside. Still annoyed from the night before.

"I was trying not to disturb you, though I suppose I messed up." He lowered to perch on the side of the cushion next to her, leaning in, grazing her shoulder with his. Careful, he kept his eyes focused onto the computer screen and disregard her shirt's revealing gap.

"What is all of this?"

Shifting away from him, she returned to her work and hummed softly. "Research. I'm trying to discover whose set me up."

He took in a lungful of air, catching a whiff of her clean, feminine scent, halting in mid-breath. This needed to stop because he was losing this fight. He couldn't quit thinking about her. No matter what he'd told her, his frame of mind regarding his former nemesis was too big to fight. Bottom line. He had it bad.

Even though she appeared to be pissed at him, he'd gotten the sense her feelings for him were still strong.

Unfortunately, they couldn't happen, and it would be in both their interest to part ways sooner than later.

"So exactly how are you conducting your exploration? I understand the bunch of names and their association to Hazel." He pointed to the monitor and waved a finger in front of several rows. "What do these columns mean?"

"You are correct." She indicated toward the first row, and explained, "This list is former clients, consultants, and venders who've had unhappy or dissatisfied dealings."

He studied the extended roll. "All of those people are pissed at her?" He chuckled humorlessly. "Surprised it took so long for someone to knock her off."

"These are the only names I'm aware of."

"You didn't answer my question. What's this other stuff?"

"This column specifies what she did to them in various degrees. They're customers she overcharged, insulted, and employees she fired without cause, or venders she cheated. The next row is the element of anger or frustration they expressed from their business transactions with Weddings Fantastic. This last line is threats made against her." She glanced at him. "Any one of them could've murdered her."

He continued to examine the display. "I see you included the venders we encountered the other night."

"I have my doubts about them, but it makes sense to consider everyone."

"It more than makes sense." He motioned at her lists. "They definitely didn't sound like they would miss her."

"Hazel was known for thriftiness. She'd pick apart a bill so not to pay her venders in full, regardless of the contracts. Most stayed ticked off at her, but their choices in the field are limited so they had to deal with her."

"Not so much. Either they work for her or they don't. Simple."

"Not so simple. I can't prove it, but I'm pretty sure Hazel kept a file of dirt on everyone she did business with."

"A file of dirt?"

"You know. Something in their history they preferred to not let the entire world know about."

"Ruthless woman. How is it no one ever sued her if she operated so crooked?"

Katie wiggled to sit straighter. "Oh, customers did file lawsuits. Hazel had a slick attorney who got her out most of the legal situations or she'd pay them off."

"Paid who off?"

"Not venders, of course, but clients who threatened to go to the media."

Jack laughed caustically. "I'm surprised she was able to keep her dishonesty under wraps and her company afloat."

"I don't know how she stayed in business, either. I think her secret is she hired competent people."

"And fire them?"

Katie sighed and nodded. "She was known for creating reasons to get rid of employees."

"No one safe?"

She made a face. "Only Tara."

Jack brows rose. "Didn't expect that."

"Don't mistake her frumpiness for stupidity. Tara

was on, twenty-four seven. Her capabilities went beyond the actual consultants. She's quick at solving problem, and she maintains excellent records. She was good at finding and keeping secrets, which was invaluable to Hazel." Katie gazed at Jack. "I'm sure Tara's loyalty is geared toward her own motives, but for she was a great asset to Hazel."

"Who'd a thought?"

"I know, right?" Katie returned to her work, relaxing against the sofa's arm. "What are your views on my system?"

He lifted a shoulder. "I mean, yeah you made a list of possible suspects, but an inventory of names isn't going to help you much."

"I've only just begun."

"What's your next step? You need concrete evidence to take to the authorities. Proof. I mean, stabbing is personal. Someone was very angry at her." Jack gestured at her presentation. "You have to go from this list to something more tangible?"

"I know," she replied in a frustrated tone. "This is just a starting point."

"Maybe we can brainstorm later and possibly think of something."

He continued to stare at the screen as he deliberated, doubting any brainstorming would be forthcoming. After he returned, he'd need to deal with what he considered the tough part of his morning. He dreaded what was to come, but he and Katie had to have a serious discussion.

"Do you want breakfast? I packed food."

The idea of a meal sounded appealing. He hadn't eaten since they left, and his last feast was his usual weekend cuisine of pastries and beer. He was hungry. "I could go for something after I get back."

"I'd made oatmeal. I brought blueberries and flaxseed, which works better for you?"

"Uh, neither." He almost gagged. "I'd rather eat mud as opposed to oatmeal."

Katie returned to her computer work. "Plenty outside."

"I suppose I need to drive to the nearest town and buy some groceries."

"The closest place is an hour away and there's no fast food. Just one general store and the supply is limited. They only sell seasonal stuff."

A sixty minute trip didn't appeal, but for a marginal spread, Jack may consider doing that. "Coffee? Surely you brought caffeine."

"Too many unhealthy side effects, and it's addicting."

"You don't you drink coffee?"

"Rarely."

"How do you wake up? How do you move?"

She dipped her head toward a half full plastic bottle sitting by Jack's feet. "My pick-me-ups. You're welcome to try one."

He bent and lifted the bottle. Pealing back the foil lid, he sniffed, and jerked away, giving an exaggerated heave. "You drink this?"

"Every morning. The benefits are amazing."

"Like it makes you want to puke from the smell alone? What's in it?"

"Alkahine, rice protein, organic hemp, spirulina, raw cocoa powder, udo oil, maca powder, and glycobalance and some blue green algae."

"Rice protein, raw cocoa, and puke colored algae?" He made a face. "So I what you're telling me is there's nothing eatable in the shitload of previsions you brought?"

She continued to study her laptop. "You can't be choosey, Jack. You came uninvited. Next time you crash a getaway, you need to be more prepared."

"You got me there. And to think, I just restocked on beer and toaster pastries."

She lifted her head and wrinkled her nose. "For breakfast?"

"The stomach wants what the stomach wants, Katie."

"My aunt may keep some instant crystals in the pantry," she murmured, returning to her work. "You're welcome to check."

"Mmmm, instant."

"You're awfully grouchy."

"I'm grouchy because I haven't had any caffeine."

"See. You're addicted. You ought to think about kicking the habit and switch to something better for you. Your intestines will thank you."

He rose from the sofa to check. "My insides are cement coated." He would've preferred to have coffee after his run, but he wasn't ready to leave her. "Are there actual cups or do I have to use Nana's jelly jars?"

"Mugs are on a shelf above the sink."

Back in the kitchen Jack filled a cup, and placed it into a prehistoric microwave, and punched in the time. He searched the cloth bags hoping to find something decent to eat. He found a ton of healthy—he hesitated to call what she ate actual food. The bottom of one bag, he unearthed a box of salt-free crackers and organic peanut butter. Thinking this might be eatable, he prepared several while he waited for his water to heat. After the bell dinged, he opened the door and retrieved the steaming mug, adding a generous spoonful of crystals, and stirred slowly. He carried his coffee and a filled napkin back to the living room and walked to the rocker.

He cleared his throat and placed his drink onto a small, rickety table next to the chair and unfolded the paper towel in his lap. "Katie. We need to talk."

Her chin lifted, blinked confused, and put her laptop aside. "Sounds serious."

"We should go home." He studied the spread on his cracker. "Today."

"Today?" she repeated, her voice rising. She grabbed the blanket and yanked it chest level, like a shield.

"Yes. It's the right thing to do."

"You mean y*our* right thing to do."

"Exactly. Fight this through proper channels."

"I am fighting." Her lips went white from anger. "You said you'd give me three days. We've been here for a few hours. I've barely made any progress. I need to find out who is doing this to me."

"A list isn't progress, Katie. Other than shoe purchases, what else are you going to do?"

She shot him a death glare and huffed. "I don't know, because I haven't had time to figure anything out."

"You don't have a plan."

"I'm developing one."

"By making a list? You're not even sure of all her unhappy clients."

"I'm going to…" she released a long sigh. Her anger altered into exasperation. "I have to figure this out. I can't go to jail, Jack. I didn't do this and don't belong in prison. Besides, I look terrible in orange stripes."

"That's what you're worried about?"

"I'm bothered by a lot of things. You're the one who said to be careful where the authorities are concerned. They're under pressure to make an arrest and they'll fit me into the evidence they have."

A tide of guilt ran through him. His warning was true, though now he wished he'd used different terminology in his caution and not sounded so dramatic.

"You're right," she continued. "What I'm doing is detrimental to my cause. I think I need to focus my energy in one direction."

"Which direction might that be?"

"Vanessa is behind this setting me up. Except I have no inkling how to prove it."

Jack shook his head. "Vanessa may be crafty. I don't think she's devious enough to disengage cameras, break into your condo unnoticed, and drop off a murder weapon. At least not by herself."

"Are you really that blind?" She dropped her feet to the floor and fell into the back of the couch. "I'm sure she did plant the knife, and she initiated the police investigation against me."

"Let's look at this, objectively. Say you're right, and she's trying to send you to prison for the rest of your life."

"She is."

"What does she gain?"

"She gets me out of the party planning business."

"Those are some extreme actions for someone who just wants to get you out of a profession. From your account, her reputation is tarnished from the kickbacks and other deceptions with her former employer."

"Yes, but her ability to be so deceitful ought to give you a clue how damaged her character is and what she's capable of."

"Okay, I concede, she's a rotten human being. I don't doubt she sees you as an enemy and competition in the industry. But one person, meaning you, isn't going to prevent her from being prosperous if she's talented. Are you the only roadblock to her success? Is she that good? Are you the only one in her way of becoming a wedding coordinator superstar?"

Katie lifted a shoulder. "She's okay. There are plenty of others whose talent equaled hers, some are better. I still think she's doing everything she can to get the police to look at me."

"You're probably right. Remember, she's only manipulating what the cops will find out anyway."

Katie's shoulders sank, her expression appeared dejected. Jack resisted the impulse to go to her, to comfort her. His growing need for her was becoming more difficult to resist. Celibacy was killing him. Just this last thirty minutes with her, even with her angry at him, made him want to rush over to the sofa a rip that shirt off her.

And though he told her it was the right thing to do, which he believed, his reasons to leave also selfish. Which brought him to his decision. If they didn't get out of here soon, he'd give in to his urges, and he feared he'd fall for her more than he already had.

"Maybe," she conceded. "She's working awfully

hard to make sure they discover things about me, and I bet she's blowing innocent occurrences out of proportion. Now, there she has a talent."

Jack met her gaze. "If that's true, have you considered she's trying to avert her attention away from herself?"

Katie frowned. "You mean, like she killed Hazel?"

"I don't know if I'd go that far."

"Or she's somehow involved in the death," Katie suggested. "It'd make a lot more sense than her going to such extremes to get me out of the party planning business. If she was successful, then in a roundabout way, she'd be killing two proverbial birds. Hazel and me."

Chapter 18

"What is Vanessa's motive?" Jack drained his coffee cup and set it aside, then wadded up the napkin that held his crackers and crushed the paper towel between his palm and fingers. "Her intention was to get you fired, and she accomplished that, so what's the point of her killing Hazel too?"

"I don't have all the answers," Katie argued. "My instincts tell me she's involved."

"Vanessa is a lot of things, many not good, but I'm sure she's not a murderer. I doubt she's done anything but alert the authorities of your termination."

Katie sucked in a gasp. She'd grown weary of Jack protecting that woman. Every time she hit the mythical ball in Vanessa's direction, he fielded it for her.

"How come you always defend her?"

"I don't." He aimed an index finger at her. "This is your problem. You can't get past this obsession concerning the woman. She's a troublemaker. Period. But she's smart. She won't go beyond certain boundaries and allow herself to submerge into too much hot water. That would defeat her purpose, and definitely spoil her fun."

"Fun?" Katie paused at this. "She's the one who pointed the police my way. You're saying this is her idea of a good time?"

"Again," he crossed his arms over his chest, "they

would've come to you on their own because of your dismissal. She may have sped up the process, but that's all she achieved. And yes, I think she gets perverse enjoyment out of your getting sacked and causing you the added trouble."

"She's more warped than I ever could've imagined." Katie shook her head. "She's given the detectives twisted information, I'm sure. If they find the knife, along with her feeding them, I'm sunk."

"That's why we should return. So you can search, and see if the knife is still at your place, and fight this unknown person."

"I already know who that is. Vanessa. What I don't know, is how to prove it."

Jack blew a puff of air to show resistance. "All she's done is state her opinion to the police. They work off facts. She has no verification, nothing concrete against you, not one piece of evidence to support her claim."

She glared at him. "What is it with you and her? I'm beginning to believe your little get together at the bar was more than a chance meeting."

"I told you what happened."

"Are you sure you remember? You've been hitting the booze hard lately. You may've done things in your beer induced haze you don't recall."

"To-fucking-uché." Jack scatted to the edge of the rocker, and shot to his feet. Hands on hips, his nostrils flared. He glowered at her, his voice low and controlled. "I suggest we end this conversation before I say something I'll regret later." He walked to the doorway, stopped, and turned to her. "I'm going for my run. We'll leave when I get back, you need to be packed."

"Jack."

"Not open for discussion, Katie." He stomped to through the kitchen, and onto the porch, letting the doors slam behind him.

"Whatever you say, Jack." She leaned down and snapped her computer lid shut. "Might as well get started." Rolling off the sofa, she scooped up her laptop, and walked to the bedroom.

As instructed, she retrieved her suitcase she'd left opened on the floor next to the bed and placed the luggage on top of the mattress. Because they'd barely arrived, most of her things remained packed so it didn't take her long to throw her belongings inside. After she changed into clothes, she hurried to the bathroom to brush her teeth and put on a little makeup. Then she rushed back to her room to repack her toiletries, loaded her computer, and hauled everything to the kitchen.

The clock above the stove told her Jack left fifteen minutes ago. She assumed he'd run for about twenty more, therefore, her timeframe was fleeting.

The refrigerator open, she carefully placed her cold items inside the cooler she'd sat by the appliance after she unloaded last night. Once filled, she crammed the eco bags with food, but set aside the peanut butter and crackers.

She carried her possessions outside and to her jeep. After her things were stored, she walked to the driver's side, and unlocked the car door. She stared off into the desolate fields wishing she'd paid attention to which way Jack went for his run.

She gazed at the house. His phone. Did he take it with him? Probably not. What would be the point, if he'd removed the battery? She preferred he not have immediate contact to the outside. She returned inside, and down the hall, trying to remember if the sweatpants he wore had pockets and was there any sign he was carrying anything in them.

She skidded to a halt at the entrance of his room. Clothes were scattered across the floor. The covers on the unmade bed, twisted, and hung from to one side, like he'd experienced a restless night. The small dresser was clear of any of his personal effects. In other words, no cell phone. Disappointed, Katie turned to leave, but stopped at the exit.

A muddy pair of jeans was in a heap in the far corner. He'd worn those pants the night before, and he'd carried the cell inside the pocket. Maybe he hadn't bothered to remove it. She dashed to where the jeans lay and bent to pick them up. She froze. A shadow passed in front of the window.

Jack had returned. He'd be inside within seconds. The boom of the screened door ricocheted and bounced against the jam. Katie dropped the pants. He'd probably come straight down the hall, instead of the alternate way, through the living room. She couldn't escape without him catching her.

She searched the tiny space for a place to hide. The closet. His entire wardrobe seemed strewn everywhere. Evidently he wasn't using it. She sprinted to the small enclave, twisted the knob, and yanked. The door didn't budge. She tugged again, but nothing happened, probably due to the house settling, many times over the years.

The light tap of footsteps echoed up the hallway grew closer. She dove to the floor and rolled under the bed, the same moment Jack entered. Katie lay on her stomach, and gazed past the bedframe's iron bar, not moving a centimeter. He stood directly in front of her. He toed off his sneakers, and peeled away his socks, then bowed to rummage through his duffle. If he rotated an inch, he'd discover her. Fortunately, he appeared focused on the contents inside his bag. He seized a pair of clean blue jeans and a toothbrush, straightened, and moved away. He shuffled around, his bare feet scuffing against the worn floors.

Katie remained immobile except to turn her head and follow the lower halve of his legs activities. Noises on wood indicated he placed some items onto the dresser, and then he exited.

Katie stayed put until a rush of water whistled throughout the home, squealing from the old pipes. Jack was in the shower. She scrambled from underneath the bed springs, jumped to her feet, and tiptoed through the hallway and outside to her car.

A faint twinge of guilt twisted inside for what she was about to do. But this was a sooner rather than later circumstance. She was already developing an escape plan, needing more than three days to complete her private investigation and now Jack shortened the time to zero.

She patted her jacket for keys. Nothing. She slapped her jean pockets. Empty. She glanced at the house and gasped. They must have slipped out—in Jack's room.

Inside, relieved the water still flowed she dashed back to his bedroom. She fell to her knees and peeked below the bed. A small heap rested in the middle of the underside. She stretched beneath the mattress to snatch the wayward set and glided out, hopping onto the balls of her feet, as she slipped the keychain into her coat pocket. She hastened toward the door, sliding to a stop just beyond her flight. Her pulse leaped. His cell and battery lay on the dresser.

Backtracking, she grabbed the phone and shoved the device into her other pocket and hurried out of there. She sped down the hall and onto the porch.

Palming the screen, she gave it a hard push. One foot outside, she was ready to flee, but an odd quiet stilled her. The water was no longer running.

Jack walked out of the bathroom, followed by a thin, stream of fog. A two-day scruff covered his jawline, his hair slicked back, as beads of liquid trickled down his damp skin. Bare-chested, wearing only a pair of faded jeans, his nipples tightened from the frosty breeze blustering amidst the opened enclosure. Her head almost spun from the luscious view. She forced herself to calm down. This wasn't the time to lose control.

His jaw hardened at the sight of her. "Are you packed?"

Katie nodded.

"Good. I'm going to finish dressing, and get my stuff. Then we'll go."

"Jack." She realized what she was about to do would put an end to any hope of a relationship—well that was pretty much a bust anyway. But the smidgen of friendship left between them was soon gone too. She hoped she might ease her upcoming betrayal.

"No arguing, Katie. We're doing the right thing."

She flashed a nervous smile in his direction. "I wanted to apologize. For my comments about your drinking. I was out of line. It's none of my business, and I based my assessment on a single encounter."

Jack looked uncomfortable. Seconds ticked before he spoke again. "Actually, I thought over what you said while out running." He inhaled and exhaled loudly. "You're right. I've been hiding in a beer bottle. I need to get a grip and cut back my intake. The escape is becoming more than a habit. I owe you a world of thanks, so thank you for having the courage to bring the subject to my attention."

She shrugged. "Least I can do since you've helped me."

"Yeah, well, I know it looks like I'm trying to railroad you into the police custody."

"You kind of are."

"Katie, if they are looking at you closely, your disappearance will only broaden their suspensions. You must go back and face this. Running away isn't going to help, even if you discover who's behind this."

"You're right, Jack." She sighed and then smiled. "I needed some time to calm down, and think too. Put everything in perspective."

"Good." He gave an affirmative nod. "Let me get my things, and we'll be on our way." Jack stepped into the bathroom, gathered his dirties, and walked inside without speaking again.

"I'll wait for you here."

Katie paused, not making a move until she was sure he was at the back of the house. It'd take a full ten minutes for him to dress and stuff his scattered belongings into his duffle.

She calmly strolled outdoors, and onto her loaded jeep. She slid in, resisting the urge to tremble as she inserted the key. Twisting the ignition, the vehicle came to life. She pushed the shift into reverse and turned to check behind her. All clear. Facing forward, she rested a foot on the gas. A motion inside her peripheral made her freeze.

She stomped on the break and returned the gear to park. The driver's side door flew open. Katie didn't need a glance to know what happened. Steadily, she cut the engine and emerged from the car. Jack closed in on her, pinning her against the jeep, his hands on the roof, arms confining on either side of her shoulders. Angered heat radiated from his near naked body.

"This disappearing act is getting old, Katie."

"Do you have a GPS planted on me?"

His face turned a bright crimson. "Why do you always make things so damn hard?"

"I'm making things hard? Your skin doesn't need to be saved, so it's easy for you to say, let's go back and face this."

"Wrong. I might be in trouble for being with you or knowing your whereabouts without contacting the police." He stepped closer, jammed a hand into her coat pocket, and retrieved his cell phone, holding it up. "You planned to leave me high and dry."

"I'll do what it takes NOT to go to prison."

****

Jack sighed. He wasn't going to get through to her. His efforts to stronghold her were futile. A fact he should've realized. He ought to have suspected something was up when she agreed to leave so easily. She'd fought him on just about everything with the exception of their stolen moments in the back of the jeep the other night. There she was as agreeable as hell.

But he didn't need to focus on that.

Frustrated, mad, and cold, he shoved his phone into his pants pocket and stomped away. He stopped and spun around, arms held out to his sides. "Okay, Katie. You win. What's the plan?" His hands dropped. "I want to help" A cloud of misgiving wavered in her eyes. "I'm serious this time. No tricks or anything."

"How can I trust you?"

"The same way I trust you."

"You don't."

A side of his lip curved. "There's your answer."

"We're at a stalemate." She pushed away from the jeep, leaving the driver's door gaped. "You're free to leave, Jack. I can do this on my own."

Jack pursed his lips so not to smile. "Don't doubt it for a second. But I think I'll hang out. I want to see how this ends. What's your strategy?"

"I need some. Maybe you can assist me, and by assist, I mean us not going to the police until we have something to take to them."

"Understood. First thing we should do is look somewhere besides Vanessa." He held up a palm as she opened her mouth to protest. "I'm all for considering your idea, but after we explore other options. Let's take your things inside and go through the list of possible suspects, and study each person in detail, one by one. Aaron's company has given me access to conduct background checks. Some pretty deep ones. I'll log into the account and we can build from that and see what we come up with."

"Oh Jack." She rushed to him and threw her arms around his shoulders, embracing him before she realized her actions. Soft, warm palms skimmed across his chest as she backed away. Hands covered her mouth. She stared with a horrified expression. "I'm so sorry, I didn't mean…"

He nodded and swallowed. "Heat of the moment." He walked to the rear of the jeep trying to shake the brief encounter, and failing miserably. "Raise the lift and I'll unload your stuff. Then we'll get started on our investigation."

Katie stretched inside for her keys and pressed on the pad to unlatch the lock. Jack lifted the hatch and leaned inward to retrieve her bags. A dull gleam, embedded next to the wheel-well caught his attention.

"What the hell?" He crawled inside to get a closer look. He tugged to peel the carpet away, and jerked backward, landing on his butt. He stared at his discovery, holding in a monstrous gag.

"Is something wrong?" Katie appeared behind him, with a worried expression. He glanced at her before he returned to his find. "Jack? What is it?"

He motioned for her to come closer. Carefully, he separated the outer layer from the interior. "This," he showed her.

Katie leaned further in. Her eyes grew bigger than the moon. The missing knife. "How did that—" She gasped. Her hands flew to her cheeks.

"Look at the amount of blood caked on the blade. I'm more sure this was the murder weapon. The question is; how did it get inside your car?"

Chapter 19

"I can't believe this," Katie mumbled, though she wasn't sure she was coherent. She handed Jack a towel and garbage bag, and climbed into the jeep after she'd fetched the provisions from inside. "How did that get in here?" she asked for the hundredth time.

"No clue." Jack shook into a shirt she'd brought him. He covered the knife with the cloth, and cautiously placed the blade into the plastic sack, careful to keep his fingers away from anything incriminating. "Do you have a spare key to your jeep?"

"At the loft."

"You sure?" He glanced at her. "Someone's been going in and out at will. Could've taken it."

She touched her forehead, swiping a windblown lock of hair from her eyes. "You're certain that's what was used to kill Hazel?"

He threw a glance in her direction. "Unless you make a habit of hiding plasma coated knifes in your car."

"I do carry spares for wedding cakes. You'd be surprised how many couples forget to buy one."

"Oh, I don't think I would be that shocked." A worried frown spread across Jack's face. "You don't look so good."

"Something a girl never tires of hearing, especially after the implication of her being a murderer just increased times a million."

"I mean your skin is pale. Like you're going to pass out."

"I was about to tell you the same thing," Katie gazed back at him. "You're a little pasty, too."

He hesitated, as if debating whether to speak again. "Blood and I don't get along."

"You and what?"

"The sight of blood makes me nauseous. Sometimes just the memory can turn my stomach inside out." As if on cue, he paled, slapped a palm over his mouth to cover a gag reflex.

Katie fought back a gurgle of laughter. Even with the severity of the situation, she delighted in Jack's humanness.

"Go ahead. Laugh." He wiped a trickle of sweat from his brow before he continued to bind the plastic around towel multiple times. "You want to."

"No, I don't," she denied, but couldn't stop her smile from broadening.

"This is how I'm convinced you're not a murderer. You're a terrible liar."

She laughed out loud. "To see you, a big, strapping guy brought down by a spec of dried blood is funny."

"Happy to make your day." He laid the covered weapon on the floorboard and brushed his hands.

Katie got control of her outburst and gave him a sad smile. "A flash of humor makes everything better. For a second, anyway." She continued to gaze at Jack. "It's like they're watching me, anticipating my next move."

"Didn't you say someone followed you earlier?"

She nodded and drew her jacket closer, not so

much from the cold, but because from the unknown exposure.

"You're a pretty easy read these days. Anyone who is acquainted with you well enough, and understands how you work can track you with no trouble. Remember, I figured you were going to bolt." He snapped a glare at her, as his mouth straightened. "Twice."

"Sorry." she said in a small voice.

He refocused his attention recovering the mat. "That knife is thick. I don't see how we missed it. We practically slept right on top of the damn thing."

"That edge is sharp. We're lucky neither of us were cut, the way we…" Katie stopped, not sure how to go on or if she should. She stared at Jack. Her current problems faded away at the mention of the other night. Memories from their closeness revved Katie's pulse into overdrive.

The corners of his mouth lifted as he gazed back at her. "I doubt either of us would have noticed if we'd been fatally stabbed."

Neither tore their eyes away. The air turned thick. Reflections of those moments brought on a slew of sensations that crashed into the pit of Katie's stomach. Excitement swirled throughout her body from the mere thought of Jack's lips on hers. He discharged a noisy, unsteady breath. His expression revealed, those fiery seconds were on his mind, too.

A burst of frosty wind reeled through the opened jeep, cooling them instantly. A quiet rumble crackled from above. They glanced outside, surveying the sky. Black clouds shadowed a strong draft. Rainclouds revolved overhead and draped the atmosphere.

"Weather doesn't look good," Jack murmured huskily as he observed the gloomy vapors circling lower. "Why don't you go inside before the storm hits?"

"What are you going to do?"

Only in a t-shirt and hair still damp, he scrubbed his palms over his bare arms. "Freeze my ass off while I do a thorough search. Make sure there are no more little surprises stowed away in here."

"You'd think we've found everything."

"The way things are going, I wouldn't be shocked if a copy of Hazel's will turns up—with you inheriting all she owns. That would for sure seal the deal in making you the prime suspect."

"Do you want me to help?" She was climbing out of the vehicle as she posed the question. She needed to get away. This new evidence and his cynical suggestion didn't alarm her as much as the two of them in such an enclosed space with fresh of memories floating around. "You may discover something else bloody and faint."

"I'm fine."

She pointed to one of the old barns and raised her voice above the roaring gusts. "I'll wait in here, close by. Call me if you find anything else."

Katie unlatched the bolt and shoved the wooden door ajar, using a larger rock to hold it open. The musty, scent of hay tickled her nostrils the minute she entered. She walked to the far end, finding a broken bale and sat down to contemplate. She should be deliberating the weapon, and the insinuations connected because the killer most likely put it there. Her thoughts remained on Jack instead, and how she ought to check her feelings, for good. He'd made his intensions clear.

217

Even if he wavered a bit, she was sure he'd stick to his convictions in the end.

****

Jack watched Katie tread to the barn until she disappeared inside. This was crazy. He was here to help her. Bring her home, back to her family, and face the predicament ahead of her. Yet all he could think about getting her naked and follow his primal instincts. These reactions could stem from the unfinished encounter from the other night, and his need to complete their backseat tryst overpowered his common sense.

Or perhaps he'd just lost his mind. He preferred to believe his enamored disposition was due to his long stretch between carnal encounters, but that was no longer the case. He was beginning to feel something for Katie Drapier. Something indescribable. Confusing.

What bothered him more was his awareness of her sentiments for him. She may deny, but they experienced the same emotions and those feelings were growing stronger. If they stayed together much longer, who knew what would happen. Jack sighed and glanced in the barn's direction. He knew.

Time to divert. Get her home, and then get her out of his life before he made a colossal, irreversible mistake.

He lifted his chin and stared out the car window. Lightning flashed, followed by piercing booms overhead. The storm was moving in quick. He should hurry.

Complete his search. Proceed to his next task.

****

Inside the barn, Katie removed her jacket. She lay back, pulling an old blanket over her legs, and enjoyed the course, flexible straw beneath her. For a brief instant, she allowed her problems and the man of her dreams to drift from her mind, and just appreciate the simplicity of how the hay felt underneath her.

Streaks of lightning flickered outside. Thunder rumbled. The shed dimmed, as the sky opened. Fat raindrops pounded the tin roof. A harsh wind shrieked through the cracks of warped boards. The door creaked, escaping her makeshift doorjamb, and banged against the building. Katie pushed to a sitting position, ready to dash into the rushing rain to readjust.

Jack hurried though the opening. His clothes, soaked from the downpour, and had glued to his body. All wet again. Amazingly sexy. He caught the door, and closed it behind him.

"Please tell me you didn't find anything else." Her gaze didn't waver as he approached.

He lowered onto the hay next to her. Icy beads spewed as he shook the moisture from his hair. "Car's clean."

"What's our next move? Go inside and do research?" A blast from overhead vibrated throughout the barn. "After the storm passes?"

Jack paused. He bit his bottom lip as if he were deliberating. "We need to leave. Go home."

Katie groaned a huge sigh. "I thought we'd settled this whole thing earlier? I am not going anywhere until I have solid proof to turn in to the police showing I'm not Hazel's killer."

Jack pressed a thumb and forefinger into his closed eye sockets before he looked up "I don't know how to put this, so I'm just going to say it. My reason for wanting to go has nothing to do with Hazel's murder."

Katie had a retort ready, but before her mouth opened he turned to her. "I need to get away from you."

His words struck her as if he'd pommelled her stomach with his fist. "You're driving me crazy. If I stay around you much longer, I'm going to do things I shouldn't. Like finish what we started the other night." He sifted a hand through his wet hair again and rotated away. "I could care less about the killer right now. And that's wrong. What's even worse is, all I want to do is rip your clothes off and," he stopped and turned back to her, pinning her with a spellbinding gaze. "You know what comes next."

Tiny quivers summer-salted inside her chest. He wanted her. Except he wasn't saying he liked her. Instincts told her he did, but she'd been wrong before.

She refused to be anyone's fool again. Especially Jack's. On the other hand, she sensed her imminent arrest was on the horizon, and the police might show up at any time. Perhaps she shouldn't worry about his reasons and live for the moment.

"So why don't you?" she asked in a soft voice, holding her arms out to her sides. "Rip away."

He shook his head vigorously. "Katie, I can't. We can't."

She moved closer and traced a finger over his dampened arm, spreading the drops across his skin. "Why not, Jack? I'm willing and your vow is stupid. We both want this."

"I have no clue if I can fill your emotional needs afterward. I'm already fucked up. I won't take advantage of your situation."

"I'm aware, Jack. You need to also understand at this point that doesn't matter." Katie smiled slightly.

"True, your life is a mess, but so is mine. I might go to prison. This may be my last chance, to," she leaned nearer so her lips hovered below his, "you know." She bravely brushed her mouth against his.

He didn't blink. The instant fire in his eyes answered any reservations she may've had from her actions. He wrapped his arms around her and said hoarsely, "I would hate to be the one to squash your final opportunity to," he smiled. "You know."

Katie raised her chin, opening her mouth slightly. Jack pressed his lips into hers, savoring her wordless offer. A velvety moan escaped as her arms automatically glided across his shoulders. Mouths open, the kiss sizzled. Ravenous tongues interlaced, setting her insides on fire triggering her entire body to shout. Gently, he steered her into the hay's softness, keeping the bond between their warming bodies joined. He lowered his weight on top of her.

He abruptly interrupted their kiss. "You're sure about this?" he asked in a rough whisper.

She pressed her fingers deep into his shoulder-blades and dragged him to her. He found her lips again, pushing his body into hers. Her hands slipped round his biceps, flowing over his chest, loving the feel of him beneath her palms. He groaned, shoving his hips against her, thrusting a rock-hard erection into the softness between her thighs. She opened and raised her legs, attaching around his and squeezed. Another thick growl vibrated from his throat.

Slightly rising, he urged her shirt over her head. The bra quickly followed. The cool air tensed her nipples. Or maybe Jack's hungry look was the culprit of her tightness. A hand slid across her bare skin. He stroked one breast then moved to the other, his mouth closed hungrily over her nipple. His tongue drew over the tip. She arched her back, squirming in delight with each caress. Heat amplified, spiraling and throbbed in the middle of her legs. A primitive moan ripped through her. His touch, even his kisses wasn't enough. She wanted more. She needed more.

As if reading her thoughts, his fingertips skimmed over her, stopping at her waist to unsnap her jeans. He rolled away and quickly removed her pants and panties at the same time. Longing filled his gaze as he took her in. Normally, she would have experienced shyness from the look, but the only thing on her mind now was to get him naked too. She raised high enough to tug at the hem of his shirt.

He elevated his arms, allowing her to pull the wet garment over his head. The corners of his mouth turned up into a naughty grin as he lay down, giving her access to the top button of his pants. Katie didn't think twice. Within seconds his jeans and underwear were tossed somewhere into the unknown.

She gazed at his nakedness as a smile crawled across her lips. She'd been waiting for this for years. She should be nervous, but she wasn't. With a hand, he took her wrist and steered her lie back. Fingers traced over her skin, finding their way to the middle of her thighs. She was moist and warm. Ready.

He kissed her gently as he stroked her, driving her to the threshold of recklessness, her interiors overflowing with demand. She reached for his penis. Rock-solid, it flinched at her touch. He moaned, forgetting the foreplay and lowered his body onto hers, easily gliding into her.

Their hips automatically moved in a slow rhythm. Katie gasped as he edged deeper inside. He clasped her mouth with his. She hugged him tighter as he rode her faster, harder, prompting her consciousness to waft. They swayed together back and forth, the movements, strong and smooth.

Sizzling sensations pulsed as she neared the point of ecstasy. Explosions burst. Her fingers dug into his skin. Her mind vacated as her body detonated, bracing into rigidness before she released a soft, but clear moan.

Jack beamed, brushing his lips over hers, pushing into her again. She flexed her inner muscles around him. He groaned. His strokes were slight at first, but within instants, escalated into heated friction. After only seconds, Katie's body locked, clutching him to her. She muffled a shriek into his shoulder. Jack shuddered, and then toppled onto her.

Neither moved. Jack finally raised and smiled. "That was—wow."

"Yeah," she sighed.

"You're okay?"

"Better than." she yawned sleepily.

Jack spun off her, snatching the blanket wadded at her ankles, covering them both. "I think we'll consider that our practice run for your last time." He leaned over and kissed her temple, and grinned.

She raised her brows and smiled back at him. "Oh?"

"Yeah, we may have several more tries at this before we get to the finale."

Chapter 20

"Wake up."

Jack sighed with a smile, his eyes shut. "Gimme minute, babe," he mumbled.

The woman exhibited pure stamina. She'd worn him out. In a good way. He nestled into the hay, pulling the covers to his neck, not quite ready to answer her bid. Between rests, they had sex the entire afternoon and well on into the evening. Yet he couldn't get enough of her. He definitely made up for the last four months. He'd hope to continue his catch up mode throughout the night, and for once, he didn't think she'd argue with him.

He rolled in her direction, prepared to let her have her way with him yet again. "Mmmm, okay. Now I'm ready."

"Yeah, you are." A beefy hand gripped his arm and jerked him to his butt. "Time to get up, lover boy."

Jack's eyelids flew opened. A light shined into his face, blinding him. The person holding the beam, pushed hard into his shoulder. "What the fuck?" He squinted putting a hand in front of him, while trying to wiggle free of the uncomfortable grasp. "Who the hell are you?"

Silhouettes of two large men stood on either side of him. A glimmer sparked from one's chests. Uniformed men. Shit. They'd been found. He hoped Katie stayed calm and didn't do anything stupid, like put up a fight. So far she'd remained silent.

"You Jackson Pharrell?"

"Yeah," he answered, in his best tough guy voice. "You've neglected to mention your name."

"Byron Klix. Deputy Byron Klix." Klix released his shoulder and stepped back. "We're here to take you home."

Jack smiled and gestured at his lack of clothing. "I'm not dressed for travel."

"Not my problem, stud. You're wanted for questioning in Hazel Nutt's murder."

"I'm the one who found her body, and I've already told the police everything I know."

"We're aware."

"So why do they need to speak with me again?"

"You're with Katherine Drapier, right?" The deputy holding the light moved the cylinder closer to Jack's face, causing him to blink repeatedly.

Katie. Jack's lips dropped into a frown. She'd fallen asleep in his arms. Naked. The normal Katie would be screaming, fighting for cover with these two goons being this up close and personal. She was awfully damn quiet. Too quiet.

"Where's your girlfriend, Romeo?"

Jack glanced to Katie's side. His throat tightened. An upsurge of rage filled his chest. She'd done it again.

"Good question."

"You're hiding her," the second cop accused. "Tell us where she is or you'll be in a lot more trouble than you already are."

So close. He thought he may have a shot of getting his life on track and return to Dallas, and live the way he used to. He squinted at the dent she left in the hay. He'd been screwed again. By another woman. One of these days he'd smarten up.

He shook his head. "Guess she took off. Don't ask me where, cause I have no clue."

"I bet you don't."

Jack shrugged. "You can search me."

A shit-eating grin spread across Byron's face. He nudged the other guy. "I don't think he knows, Pete."

Pete chuckled. "You mean to tell me, she flew the coop and left you?" He gestured at Jack's nakedness.

"Either that, or I'm doing some very strange stuff by myself."

"Seen weirder," Pete the deputy commented. "Hope you had a good time."

Jack didn't respond. Fantastic and beyond is what he had. Unfortunately the ending was the all too common crash and burn.

Byron threw his half dried pants into his lap. "Get dressed," he told him. "We've got a long trip ahead, and though I'm tempted to take you in like that, I'm prone to believe you've been punished enough."

****

Seated in the back of a cop's four-wheeled drive, Jack stared out the window with a deep frown. Where'd Katie go? He assumed she'd remained on the property since her vehicle hadn't moved. Though he'd overheard a conversation between his new friends, a search warrant, along with the tow truck had been called. A forensics team would be leading the pack, and they'd find the evidence against her soon. Yeah, he was wading knee-deep in shit, but his situation didn't compare to Katie's plight.

He leaned into the seat as they maneuvered the muddy drive. Why did he even care? She'd used him, leaving him to deal with the consequences. Just like Jenna. Except, what happened between them didn't possess similarities to Jenna.

This seemed…real. But that's crazy, because here he was, being hauled away in a county car while she hid somewhere on the premises, probably watching him leave. Maybe even doing that cute thing with her mouth, when she wanted to smile, but tried not to.

Stop thinking about the good stuff.

Several automobiles passed them on the dirt road of the Drapier property traveling in the opposite direction, heading for the house. Jack swiveled his head as they went by. Unmarked cars.

"What's going on?" he asked, casually. "Looks like a swat team swooping in."

"Yeah, we reported your girlfriend missing while you changed. Ask if we should do a search, seeing as her cars still parked, figured she's hanging around somewhere. Sheriff said authorities from your hometown are on the way, and for us not to do anything. Since this is a high profile case in your region, it'd look better if they found her."

"Surprised they didn't have one of you stay behind. You know the area."

A sheriff's department car turned the corner as they entered the main road. "Sheriff is handling this one himself," said Byron sarcastically.

Jack nodded. "Likes the glory, huh."

"Apparently wants his fifteen minutes." Byron sighed. "Only reason we showed is because we happened to be in the neighborhood when the call came in."

Jack frowned. "Any idea who turned us in?"

The deputy shook his head. "Think someone you know guessed your whereabouts. We were supposed to watch the place until the big guns arrived. Only by chance we found you asleep and," he chuckled, "bare assed."

"Never going to live that down."

"You'll be the top story at Peeper's Bar for a while."

Pete twisted to give Jack a onceover. "You seem like a smart guy. Young, successful. I bet you got the ladies coming after you from every direction. How'd you get taken in by this one?"

"I consider myself intelligent. Except with woman," Jack shook his head with a cynical laugh. "I'm dumber than most."

"Don't feel bad," Byron said. "All of us have been tempted by a primo piece of ass."

Jack bit his tongue. Though not in his best interest to alienate these guys, he wanted to tell them Katie wasn't a hot lay. She was a special lady. Although she'd screwed him, in many ways, he didn't think of her as a causal sex partner, which frightened him more than made him furious over his current position. He stared out the window as they pulled onto the main highway.

He needed to keep his head on straight and concentrate on his future instead of worrying about her. She had her family, and their bank account. She'd probably come out of this with nothing more than a tap on the wrist. He, on the other hand had no one. The Drapier's might help, seeing his state was because of their daughter. But he didn't have their name behind him to get him completely out of this sticky situation. He was on his own.

****

Katie peered outside the window as the vehicle drove away with Jack in the backseat. She bet he was livid, believing she deserted him, letting him take the blame.

Nothing could be further from the truth. She intended to return to the barn.

Like why wouldn't she, after they'd spent a glorious afternoon in each other's arms. She wanted more of him, and got the impression he felt the same.

She'd dressed, and gone inside, needing to use the bathroom, leaving him to rest before the next round. That's when she heard the car drive up. Alarmed, she'd peeked outside into the darkness. The SUV left their headlights on, and the occupants carried a flashlight. Both gave her enough light to see they from the sheriff's department, which meant one of two things. Someone reported some strange activity at Nana's and they were here to investigate, or they'd come for her. The latter seemed the most probable.

She'd continued to observe through the glass, thankful she didn't flip the switch, leaving the room dark. The men milled around the property, neither inspecting any buildings. She thought they may be off the hook. It appeared by chance one shined his beam inside the barn.

He'd motioned to his partner. They disappeared. Not long after they escorted Jack outside, wearing his wet clothes. One brought him into the house and vanished toward the back. The other guy stood at the

SUV, holding a mike to his mouth. Jack reappeared, redressed, with a jacket. He and the cop trudged past the rooms, and outdoors where they put him into the car, thankfully, not handcuffed. Then they drove away.

Surprised the deputies didn't search anymore, she slipped out of the bathroom, and onto the porch. Her first instinct was to run to her jeep and escape. But what about Jack? She couldn't leave him in the counties hands. Yet, if she made an appearance they'd arrest her. Those guys weren't here to discuss the weather.

Headlight flashes flickered from the drive. Several cars approached. She backed against the far wall, sneaked toward the front door, and she crept inside. Hurried, she flew up the flight of stairs, into her dad's old room and sprinted to a filmy coated floor to ceiling window that faced the outer property.

Uniformed officers emerged from their vehicles. Her life had turned to shit and it was about to hit the proverbial fan in the matter of seconds. If they had a warrant, which she assumed they did, they'd come in to investigate, and they would find her.

Her grandmother's closet. The entire floor lifted and provided a tunnel as a getaway. She and Aaron used to play inside. An escape hatch built by her ancestors, supposedly to flee from any enemy attacks during some war. It may still be usable. If the passageway remained clear, she could disappear. All she had to do was get there before they came in. She rushed to the stairwell opening and stopped.

This wasn't about her anymore. Jack was in trouble because of her. The right thing would be to call her parents, and tell them to contact Cruz, and then give up to the authorities. She retrieved her phone from her pocket, engaged the battery, and pushed the on button. The display lit up. Knock's came from the front of the home.

"Katherine," someone called. "Sheriff's department. We know you're here, so open up."

Barely breathing, Katie strained to hear. Faint voices drifted through the wind, but she couldn't catch a word. After a long pause, they banged again. She didn't move. Another stretch of nothingness followed. She'd left the screen unlocked, and door unlatched. They simply opened up and walked in. Footsteps resonated below. No time to make any calls, but she needed a lawyer to meet her at the police station. She scrolled to Jules number and typed a message:

Help! About to be arrested.

She pressed the send button and prayed Jules wasn't too busy to check and read her texts.

Sounds came from the foot of the stairs. "Katherine?" A light shimmered up the stairway. She took a deep breath, put the phone back into her pocket, and stepped into the doorway.

"Yes?"

"Hands up where I can see them." Katie gulped. The officer had a gun pointed right at her chest. "Slowly, come down."

The rest of the events were nothing short of bizarre. Holding her hands high in the air, she descended, stepping carefully. Her heart thumped at top speed, as she made her way down, cautious not to perform any action perceived as threatening and provoke the person aiming the firearm to shoot.

Once she reached the bottom, the officer lowered the pistol. Relief swept through her. Her reprieve was fleeting. Immediately, another deputy grabbed her arm and jerked around.

"Place your hands flat against the wall and spread your legs wide apart."

Katie followed their instructions without comment. They patted her down, removing her phone from her pocket. Breath held she kept her entire body motionless as a stranger's fingers gripped into her skin. The person touching her stepped away.

Slightly violated, Katie released a loud sigh, and blinked hard. Tears brimmed, though she was uncertain if she needed to cry from fear, release, or something else. Either way, she preferred not to show infirmity in front of what looked like an entire army of law enforcement.

An officer yanked her arms behind her back. Solid steel gripped her wrists, trailed by a decisive click that rendered her defenseless. "Katherine Elizabeth Drapier. You're under arrest in the murder of Hazel Nutt," the deputy told her and continued by reading her rights. "Do you understand?"

After she affirmed she understood, and she would speak to an attorney, she was roughly guided through the house and outside to a waiting car. She bit her lip, as she passed a group going through her jeep. The officer guiding her, shoved her into the backseat of a sheriff's department vehicle, and left her alone to stare a mesh partition.

So this is what it felt like to be a criminal. She'd only thought losing her job, being a possible murder suspect and, going into hiding because of it was humiliating. This experience sank below demeaning, and the worst was still ahead. She hoped Jules received her texts and able to get her some help.

Two officers got into the car, both sat up front. Within seconds they'd left the property and the mayhem behind. Other than speak on the radio, no one said a word. She couldn't think about her situation, if she did, she'd burst into tears.

Her focus remained on Jack. Why did they take him? Other than coming with her, he had nothing to do with Hazel's death. Maybe they questioned him and released him. She had to know.

"Where is Jack? Jackson Pharrell. He was with me."

Neither answered her.

"Come on, innocent until proven guilty, remember?"

"Oh, we have proof against you, lady."

The other officer laughed. "Don't think daddy's friends in high places or his millions are going to get you out of this one, sweet cheeks."

"I'm not discussing anything until I speak with an attorney."

"Then be quiet."

"You can at least tell me about Jack. What happened to him?"

"Any plans you made with your man are going to have to be put on hold for a while." She chuckled. "I mean forever. Your shady lawyer boyfriend is considered as a co-conspirator in Hazel Nutt's murder. He's going to rot in jail. Just like you."

Chapter 21

Katie needed to sleep. The drive was long, tedious, and impossible to rest in the backseat, especially with her hands restrained behind her. The officers transporting her could care less about her wellbeing, which added to the unpleasantness. Once they arrived at the police station, her capturers almost drug her from the car, and brusquely escorted her through a backdoor, void of any onlookers or reporters hanging around the entrance. A new group of law enforcers took over the moment she entered the building. While her scenario didn't get more enjoyable, this unit appeared professional, unlike the "tough bunch" that brought her in.

"Ms. Drapier," said the formable looking detective who'd met them. "Take the handcuffs off," he instructed. The cop whipped her around a little harder than necessary. "Easy," the investigator charged. "We don't do that kind of stuff in this office."

The deputy looked peeved but complied. Within moments he'd removed the bonds. She rubbed her chafed wrists, wondering if asking for something to sooth the irritation would be worth the effort. The new detective introduced himself, though she forgot his name the second the introduction was over. He guided her into a less crowded section of the station, and relieved her of all personal items, followed by a request that she sign for them. Next, he directed her through the photographed and fingerprinting process. Then he sat her in an empty office and explained she'd been officially booked. After the formalities were completed, he went to the other side of the desk to sit.

"Any questions?"

"What's going to happen now?" she asked timidly.

"You've requested a lawyer, and from my understanding, he is on the way. Once you confer with your attorney, we'll interrogate you. Then you go to a jail cell. The prosecutor's office will decide if we've built a strong enough case against you, and what charges to file. Several things can occur after. You could be arraigned which, means you'll go before a judge and plead guilty or not."

"I'm not."

The detective eyed her. "The prosecutor might take the facts before a grand jury, and let them determine if enough information has been gathered for a trial. Or he may conclude he doesn't the evidence isn't sufficient to hold you at this time, and release you, with the option of arresting you again if more proof comes to light." He hesitated. "Anything else?"

"What about bail?"

"Usually set at the arraignment, which will occur anywhere between forty eight to seventy two hours." He cleared his throat. "If a judge sets a bond."

"So until then—I'm going to jail now?"

"Yes."

"Are my parents here?"

"I understand they are in the waiting area."

"Can they visit me?"

He shook his head. "Not at this time."

"I need to know what happened to Jack."

"Who?"

"Jackson Pharrell. He was with me, and taken away before I was, um, captured. Is he here?"

"Can't discuss him."

She swallowed the argument that'd lodged in her throat. She needed to know what happened to him, but she was in no position to help herself, much less give Jack assistance.

"The cell has a bed, right?"

"Yes ma 'me," he answered almost gently. "Would you like coffee or a cold drink?"

She shook her head. "A bathroom?"

He rose from behind the desk and called a female officer, who took her to the ladies room. She stood watch, after instructing Katie not shut the stall door.

The lack of privacy only extended her disgrace, but she figured for now she'd better get over it. This may be how she lived for a while.

The detective was waiting outside the restroom. "Your attorney is here."

He led her to a small, white room. No windows and one door. A plain table sat in the middle with two straight back chairs on either side was the only furniture. She didn't sit. Instead she paced the floor, despite her tiredness, wishing this whole nightmare was finished. After was seemed like day and a half, Cruz walked inside with a partner.

She rushed to Cruz, happy to see a familiar face. "Thank you. Thank you so much for coming."

He took her hands and led her to the table. "You look drained. Here, sit down." He soothingly pushed her into the chair. "This is Martin Lolle. He's a criminal attorney and he'll be representing you. Your dad had him flown in from Houston. He's the best defense lawyer in the state. Do what he says."

"Mr. Lolle," she acknowledged.

He was a short, diminutive man, with a slight receding hairline. Large, thick glasses covered his middle aged face. His expression reminded Katie of a dog who wouldn't release a bone no matter what. She wasn't certain if she got positive or negative vibes from him. One thing for sure, she didn't want him as an enemy.

"Ms. Drapier," he said in calm, but firm tone as he laid a briefcase on the table. He opened the lid and brought out a thick folder, which he placed in front of him. "We don't have a lot of time. Let me explain what is about to happen." He didn't wait for a reply. "You'll be questioned by the police. You will not answer their inquiries. Repeat. Do NOT say a word. I'll do the talking." He stared straight at her. "Do you understand?"

She bit her lip and nodded.

"This should go quick. Once they're finished, they'll place you in a holding cell until the DA makes a decision. If an arraignment is required, bail will be set or denied. We'll pull a few strings. Our choice judge is affable."

"By affable, he means your dad and his honor are acquainted," Cruz put in.

"Even then, he may still set a high bond or deny, because you did flee. We're hoping he'll consider your overall record, ignore your recent transgression, and be lenient." The door opened and two detectives entered. Martin's gaze pierced into her. "Are you ready? Do exactly as I've instructed you. Got it?"

The integration went as Katie's attorney described. Hands clutched in her lap, her bottom lip tucked between her teeth, she did her best to remain motionless while they peppered her with inquires. Everything happened fast, and though she didn't speak, the procedure was the most unnerving she'd been through thus far.

The detectives stood to leave.

"Another moment?" Martin asked, indicating toward Katie.

They nodded as they exited the room.

"You did very well, although your facial expression altered a smidge when they probed about you being near the Nutt home on the night of the murder." He glanced at Cruz. "I'm sure they caught that."

"They already know the answer."

Before she could reply, Martin leaned across the table putting his face close to hers. His bottle cap glasses magnified his eyeballs. His irises looked as if they swam in a fishbowl.

"Careful what you say inside," he whispered. "Don't trust anyone or give out any information."

"In other words, don't make friends," Cruz advised.

"Whatever you do, keep your mouth closed."

"Can I see my parents?"

"Not tonight, I'm afraid." Martin gathered his paperwork and stuffed the mass into his briefcase as he stood. Cruz followed suit, and quietly called for the guard.

Katie rose from her chair too, her knees wobbled

from fright at the sight of the huge man who'd entered to take her to her new lodgings. "What happened to Jack, Cruz? Where is he?"

"Up to his eyeballs in stupidity."

The guard replaced the dreaded medal cuffs around her wrists, and then she was steered out of the room before she could ask anything else.

"Hang in there, Katie," Cruz called as the man led her away.

Thankfully, they didn't make her change into prison garb, and they locked her in a secluded area, alone. Maybe her father's influence was the reason they sectored her, no matter, she was happy for the solitude. She lay on a puny mattress, so tired she fell asleep within seconds.

"Wakey, wakey, jailbird."

Katie blinked repetitively and slowly sat, trying to distinguish her whereabouts. She shook her head and glanced around, taking in the dingy, cemented dungeon. Right. She was in jail.

"You okay?"

She gazed across the small area. Jules leaned against the bars, peering inside.

Slowly, Katie rolled off the bed, her body screeched from lying on the pad seemingly made of granite.

Jules nodded at the stained, steel toilet braced to the wall. "They've provided you with some lovely accommodations."

"County spares no expense." She walked to where Jules stood, and hugged her though the rods. "How did you manage a visit? Without a guard to watch over us."

"You want my secret to getting a free pass?" She

smiled. "You're aware how the system works. You know someone who knows someone and all kinds of doors open."

"And you're acquainted with?"

"Chuck at the front desk. One of my best customers."

"Ah, yes, Officer Chuck. Hasn't he tried to date you for like, years?"

"We're doing dinner and a play Saturday night. So not my type." Jules gripped the iron bars with both hands and pretended to bang her head them. "The things I must do for my friends."

"You've gone over and beyond this time."

"I had to make sure you were okay. I'm not allowed to stay long." She flashed a smile and spoke through clenched teeth. "Can't get my new boyfriend in trouble."

"How are my parents? Are they here?"

"Yes, and understandably upset. But they're doing everything to get you out of this jam."

"And Jack?"

Jules laughed sarcastically as she crossed her arms across her chest. "He and his two arresting officers are tighter than cemented bricks. He waltzed out the door right after I arrived. The three of them were having the best time. On their way to breakfast, I believe."

"My deputies were total assholes. They must be overcompensating for their tiny badges. They said Jack is considered an accessory in Hazel's murder."

Jules flipped her palm. "He's not anything. You're worried over nothing."

"It's not nothing. He's here because of me."

"No he's not. Chuck said they found specks of

blood belonging to someone other than Hazel. Jack's a possible match, although DNA tests won't be back for weeks. He claims he cut himself in a fall. They apparently believed him because they released him."

Relief swept over her. "Oh thank goodness."

"Priorities, Katie. I mean you do realize you're the one in jail, right?" Jules reminded. "At least for the next seventy-two hours."

Katie glanced around. "Small space, no windows, no color, decorations are a disgusting toilet and a dirty cot?" She nodded. "Oh yeah, I'm mindful of my predicament."

"Then stop dwelling on Jack. He didn't seem too upset over your circumstances."

"Do you think he's aware that I've been arrested?"

"The whole town is, so I'm sure he knows."

Katie grasped the iron shafts, leaning her forehead against them for support.

"What Katie?" Her expression turned grim. "Something happened between you and Jack while you were out in the middle of nowhere?"

"Don't want to talk about it," she mumbled, as she released the bars and hurried to lie down onto her saggy bed, feeling she may be sick. He hated her. He'd gotten the wrong idea, and now they were done forever.

"It's worse than I thought." Jules appeared dismayed. "Okay, calm down."

"I'm calm. I just need," she stopped. "I don't know what I need." She sat up and stared at Jules. "Yes I do. You must do a favor for me."

"Dating Chuck isn't enough?"

"I realize I'm asking a lot, but this is huge."

Jules sighed. "Tell me."

"Find Jack. He's furious with me, because he thinks I snuck away, leaving him to get in trouble." She rose from the bed and rushed to Jules, shaking her head. "I didn't. I went inside to go to the bathroom before the deputies arrived. I even gave myself up when the second set of authorities showed up. I could've escaped through an old war tunnel located in my grandmother's closet. They would've never found me. Jules go find him and tell him," she pleaded. "I need for him to understand."

Jules nodded. "I will." She embraced Katie through the bars. "I hope it'll give you the results you're expecting."

Jules left, but Katie felt little relief. She lay on the cot. Her only interaction was with a guard who brought her lunch, which consisted of a green begonia sandwich, a bag of chips and a bottle of juice.

She bypassed the sandwich, tried a chip, and found the entire sack to be stale. The only thing remotely palatable was the drink, and after checking the ingredients she discovered what she'd already assumed. Full of sugar and preservatives.

Starvation may not be a bad way to go if her situations didn't improve soon.

Another guard walked inside the chamber, pressing a knob that automatically opened the door to her cell. "You're free. Charges are dropped. You can leave."

Uncertainty rose in her chest. "I'm what?"

"Don't pay me to asked questions." He grinned. "I just do what I'm told."

She jumped off the bed and nearly skipped through the steel bars. Freedom. No more musty air, thin mattresses, and she could go to the bathroom without an audience.

"Down the hall, second door to the left. People are waiting for you."

She hurried to follow his instructions.

"Want your lunch?"

"No thanks," she hollered as she ran. She found her parents, and bounced into their arms, hugging them both, her eyes full of tears.

Her attorney, Martin was with them. "DA has decided the evidcncc isn't strong enough to take before a grand jury."

Her brows shot up. "I had the knife."

"Not a secret, Katie," Jed reminded her.

"The DA seems to think the set up against you is too perfect. Staged." Her mother hugged her again. "But the most compelling, is they've pinpointed the time of death when you were at the ranch."

"Mr. Lolle is well worth the money, but you're not off the hook, young lady. They can review and arrest you again if they find more evidence," her father warned. "Why didn't you tell us that you drove past Hazel's the night of the killing?"

"I should've. I was so scared of what the implication might mean. I went by going from your house to Jules's place. I thought about stopping, decided it wouldn't do any good to talk to her. She'd made her decision." Her shoulders slumped. "I suppose my cell pinged the tower and gave me away."

"Yep. Which could've sent you to prison for a long time. Still could," Jed cautioned.

Her eyes watered. "I'm not able to deal with this right now, can we please leave?"

"Your jeep's impounded, so you'll have to hitch a

ride with us," Lila told her.

"Why?"

"The murder weapon was hidden inside. They are checking for prints." Jed gave Lila a frustrated look. "Except those Barney Fife's probably destroyed any real evidence. You'll have to use one of the work trucks."

"What happened to Jack?" Katie asked after she collected her belongings.

"He's already gone home," her dad said, opening the door leading to the parking lot.

"You sent him with me to bring me back, didn't you, Pops?"

"I did. Paid him well to do it."

Katie stopped walking. "You gave him money? To be with me?"

"You're a stubborn women, Katie." Jed laughed. "No one would take on that job for free."

Her heartbeat came to a near halt. She didn't have any illusions that Pops had convinced him to come with her, but to pay him. Her elatedness from freedom dissolved into disappointment. Slowly she climbed into her parent vehicle, her legs felt almost too heavy to lift. She lay in the backseat, feigning exhaustion, but truthfully she didn't want to talk to anyone.

But she needed to speak with someone. Jules. She had to stop her before she delivered Katie's message. As soon as she left her parents, she punched in her friend's number.

"Katie," Jules answered excitedly. "I heard. I'm so happy for you."

"I know, right?" She cradled the phone between her neck and ear as she wheeled her way out of the long graveled road. "I'm excited but I can't think about that right now. Listen. Don't bother about giving Jack that message. I'm not too late, am I?"

"Ah yeah, Jack. No, I haven't spoken to him, yet." Her voice had an odd pitch.

"Good," Katie said relieved. She was unsure what her next step would be. This was something she'd have to think over carefully.

"Katie?" Jules almost squeaked from the other end of the line. "He's here. Jack is here. At the restaurant. And he's not alone."

Chapter 22

Katie stormed into Jules restaurant. Never had she gone from elatedness to fear to anger in such a short amount of time. She marched to where Jules stood. Her friend wore a stern scowl, arms folded tight across her middle. She guarded the entrance of the dining area like a vulture keeping watch over deceased prey.

"They're still here?"

Jules nodded toward the corner. "Look for yourself."

Katie stopped at the entryway and steadied for what she was about to view. The noon crowd packed the place. She searched the room until she spied them. In an intimate booth, near the rear. Jack and Vanessa appeared to be enjoying a private meal along with a very friendly conversation. Vanessa had apparently said something that made Jack tilt his head and laugh. An unfamiliar sensation crawled inside Katie.

Katie didn't hesitate to mull over her next move. "Stand back," she growled.

She stomped through the throngs of tables full of patrons, her focus centered on the couple. Jack faced the front of the restaurant. He leaned in across the table, his attention fixated on Vanessa. A faint smile touched his mouth. His gaze wavered. He straightened, his unreadable stare aimed on an approaching Katie. She paused at the table's edge and glared at him.

"Well, well whatd'yaknow." He folded his arms over his chest and relaxed his frame. A cynical smile played at his lips. "Houdini reappears."

"Katherine. You're out of jail." Vanessa's surprised expression told Katie she was shocked by her sudden arrival, though she quickly regained her smugness. "I'd have thought the police would be fitting you with a shiny, new set of ankle bracelets."

Katie ignored Vanessa and continued to glower at Jack. Hands rested on her hips, brows raised, she nodded in Vanessa's direction. "You want to explain?"

"Not really," Jack replied nonchalantly.

"Your father must have paid a pretty penny to free you," Vanessa put in with a chuckle.

"Oh he paid all right." Katie's voice was dangerously low as her narrow-eyed glare bonded on Jack.

Jack looked uncomfortable, but only for a millisecond. His demeanor swiftly reverted to unmoving. "I needed cash. What can I say?"

"You could say a lot of things," Katie choked back her disbelief. His disposition had turned so…cold. She was such a fool. "You neglected to disclose that little detail."

"You also forgot to include a minute factor," Jack countered. "Like you went past Hazel's house the night of the murder?"

"Yes, I did drive by Hazel's home. But my whereabouts during the actual crime cleared me of any wrongdoing, which I already knew. I didn't see the need to bring up the point. You, on the other hand..."

"Add it to the list, Katie. I have bills to pay. I won't apologize for doing what I had to do."

Vanessa's eyes brightened. A palm covered her mouth to conceal a shrewd grin. "Am I to understand Katherine's father rewarded you to go on her little escape adventure," she laughed. Her hand dropped, making her smile evident. "I'd hoped you had better sense than to run off with a presumed murderer. I'm glad I was right."

"Vanessa, this doesn't concern you," Katie snapped.

"No Katherine," Vanessa countered in a snide tone. "Jack and I are enjoying a lovely lunch. You're the one who barged in uninvited. The person this doesn't concern is *you*."

About to retort, Katie froze. Her adversary's words hit her square in the gut. Vanessa was correct. Jack's date with Vanessa wasn't any of her business. Katie and Jack lived for the moment, and now their time was over. Obviously, he'd finished with her and had moved on to someone else. Her stomach whirled, her head spun. She feared she'd pass out if she stayed another here second. Without a word, she took a step backwards then she turned and rushed to the outer vestibule toward the exit.

"Katie" Jules shouted. "Wait."

Katie halted and rotated to face her friend. "I can't," she blinked hard, holding in her rage. "I need to get out of here." With both arms braced, she shoved the heavy doors, making her way outside into the cool, autumn afternoon.

****

Jack wasn't hungry when he'd arranged this lunch date. His appetite diminished even more after the encounter with Katie. Although angry, it took every effort to not chase her down and... He didn't know how he'd be able to maintain his sanity, but somehow he must.

Careful to keep his face neutral, he gazed at Vanessa. "Sorry about the disturbance."

"I'm not." Vanessa smiled, running her fingers over a hand he'd laid on the table. "What do you say we take this some place more private? That way we won't by interrupted by such undesirables."

The corners of Jack's mouth lifted as he did his best to put Katie and her fury on the backburner. "Sounds like a plan. Unfortunately, I've scheduled an appointment with my attorney." He paused to glance at his watch. "As a matter of fact, I'm due to meet him in about ten minutes. I'm going to have to end this." His lips elevated higher. "For now."

"I like that. Why don't you call me after you're finished with your meeting? We can continue this at my place."

Jack scooted out of the booth and stood. He threw some bills onto the table and nodded. He left Vanessa sipping her wine, hurrying to get out of there. He'd almost reached the door when Jules stepped in front of him. Jack abruptly stopped.

Fists on his hips, he rolled his eyes. "Don't have time for this."

Nor did he want to hear what she had to say. He was already aware what an asshole he was, but he had his reasons. Reasons he wouldn't be disclosing to Katie's friend.

Jules jabbed a finger into his chest. "You can make time, you son of a bitch. Katie has never done anything but like you, and you always treated her as if she doesn't matter. Well, let me tell you, she does count," her voice elevated to shrill as she pushed her finger further into him, "she's out of your league."

"No argument there," he agreed wearily. "Now, can I please leave?"

"You just don't care, do you?"

"I don't? She's the one who disappeared while the deputies hauled me off. I'm surprised she's still not in hiding."

"She's not because she gave herself up. For you. She knew of a place to go where they wouldn't find her but her worry over you, however undeserved, made her turn herself in."

Jack inhaled, unable to exhale. Words failed him. Powerless to speak, he moved around Jules and rushed outside, needing fresh air. Katie went to jail for him. Needless to say, no one had ever done anything like this. If he didn't already feel he was a cad, he certainly believed himself one now.

Cruz waited by Jack's truck. He chuckled as Jack approached. "What happened in there?" He sidestepped Jack to gaze at the eatery's open door where Jules remained. "Katie just high tailed it out of here, and Jules is staring you down like she wants you dead."

"I'm aware. Not sure how I'm still breathing." Jack unlocked his vehicle for them to get inside, in a hurry to vacate the location. He needed to think. The sooner he got away from here the better. "I must have killed a sacred cow in another life, and now I'm being punished for my evil deeds in this one."

Cruz shot him an inquisitive look from the passenger side. "Why in the world would you agree to meet Katie's worst enemy in her best friend's restaurant. I mean, dude, what were you thinking."

"Evidently I wasn't." He switched the ignition, and stomped on the gas, dashing away from the disturbing incident. "I didn't realize the place belonged to Jules, nor was I aware Katie had been released from jail." He threw a glance at Cruz. "What's the story there?"

"Yeah, I was in the middle of texting you when the war of your female admirers broke out. She's in the clear. For now."

Jack's surprised expression turned to relief. "Even with the cell records of her being in the vicinity of the murder and the found evidence? I'd think the prosecutor would be drooling with all the proof."

"Phone also proves time of death and her whereabouts don't add up. Believe it or not, we elected a decent DA. He spoke with Martin. They feel everything seemed a little too neat. Katie's not a stupid person. First, why keep the knife? Second, her family owns a huge ranch on the outskirts of town. Easy to get rid of any evidence and it'd never be discovered."

"I'm glad he's seeing the big picture."

"It doesn't hurt Katie is a Drapier."

"All the more reason to find the real killer or this will hang over her head for the rest of her life."

"Why are you so hell bent on helping her?" Cruz asked. "I don't recall you being a big fan when we were kids. I'd be mad as a hornet she let those cops take you away while she hid."

Jack remained silent for several seconds as Cruz's question hung in the air. He needed to process all he'd learned from Jules and deal with his conflicting feelings but he didn't have it in him right now. "No clue."

"I think you're into Aaron's baby sister."

251

Jack's mouth straightened. He liked her a lot, so much he was almost willing to forget the pact he made with himself. Except he couldn't. He wouldn't. "Jules is right. Katie's out of my league. My goal is to find Hazel's real killer, and then I'm going to leave her alone."

"Probably a wise move."

Neither spoke for some time. Jack steered the truck in the direction of Cruz's office. They were supposed to meet about the upcoming conference with Jenna's attorney's, but in light of recent events, he no longer cared what happened with Jenna or her lawsuit.

"Was the crazy worth it?"

Jack slowly nodded. "I think so."

"What'd you find out?"

"Vanessa benefits from Ms. Nutt's demise. Rhett Oats just purchased Weddings Fantastic from Hazel's daughter in a private sale. Name ring a bell?"

"Yeah, but I don't know from where."

"He owns the other big wedding planner agency in town."

Cruz snapped his fingers. "Right. Daphne and I talked to him about doing our ceremony. She liked him okay, but to me he resided on the left side of slime."

"Vanessa is going to work for him."

Cruz made a face. "Again?"

Jack frowned, not understanding the implication.

"He's the guy who fired her for taking the kickbacks."

"That makes this all the more curious. According to Vanessa, she's set to be Weddings Fantastic's new manager."

"Strange."

"Oh, it gets stranger, my friend." Jack paused. "Hazel's will states, the company was to be left to her daughter, and then be sold to the highest bidder. Vanessa revealed to me that she discovered this tidbit by accident, and the one who put Rhett in touch with the daughter for the private sale."

"Interesting," Cruz mused. "And timely."

"Isn't it? Rhett Oats snatched up the business in a clandestine deal before Hazel's body turns to soot."

"Sounds too—convenient. Haven't heard any mumbles about the will from the detectives or the DA so it must not be an issue. But then again, I'm not privy to all of their information. Did Vanessa reveal how she came to find out the contents of Hazel's will?"

"She did not. When I inquired on her methods of obtaining the knowledge, she became vague other than to say it was a coincidence." Jack's voice turned shaky. "Katie insisted all along Vanessa had something to do with Hazel's murder, and I didn't listen." He hesitated. "Now I'm unsure."

"Do you believe Rhett's involved too?"

Jack lifted a shoulder. "No clue. He and Hazel were business rivals. Might be worth looking into."

Cruz looked at Jack. "Sure sounds fishy."

"Don't it? Let's add another wrinkle. Vanessa also informed me we would be neighbors soon."

"How's that?"

"Supposedly, Hazel left her the house on Mulberry."

"That is—weird." Cruz stared out the window. "How long has she worked for Weddings Fantastic?"

"About six months." Jack bit at his bottom lip.

Neither spoke for a while. Jack contemplated his

later date with Vanessa and wondered how he was going to get out of it. She would not be pleased when he cancelled. He only agreed to go to play along because he didn't want to alert her of the real reason he arranged the lunch. No need for this to go any further.

He pulled into Cruz's office parking lot and put his truck in park, but left the engine run. Instead, he let it idle as he stared out the windshield, his mind turned.

"Something about that will bothering you?" he finally asked Cruz.

"I'm getting a bad vibe about the whole thing. Besides, the strangeness over the sale, why would the women leave her home to someone she's only known for a few months." Cruz threw Jack a side glance. "I'm wondering if we should maybe go see..."

Jack jerked the gear in reverse and backed out of the lot. "Way ahead of you."

Chapter 23

The men made the thirty minute drive uptown into a newer section of the city. They parked at the curb in front of a contemporary brownstone and emerged from the truck.

Jack gazed upward, toward the large second story window, admiring the oversized red bricked building. "Fake document making must pay well," he commented dryly.

"Rumors say he does a lot of work for illegals. He gets about three thousand a pop."

Jack shook his head. "Certainly doing better than me."

Cruz chuckled. "Me too. Four years of college and three at law school and I can't afford a place like this. Did he even finish high school?"

They strolled through a wrought iron gate, continuing up the sidewalk, the lawn and flowerbed immaculately manicured despite the time of year. Cruz pushed the bell located next to a beveled glassed door. A high pitched yip came from inside.

Anticipation welled into Jack's chest. Their former teammate may provide the missing link to Hazel's death. He wanted to make sure Katie wouldn't be a suspect again or have anyone believe she got away with murder because of her families association. "Think he's here?"

"It's the middle of the day and he works from home. Where else would he be?"

The dog continued to yap, but no one answered. Cruz punched the buzzer again. The pup barked wildly.

"Hang on, I'm coming," came a voice from inside. "Come here Remy." Everything went quiet. The door opened. "Cruz?"

"Hey, Winnie. How you doing?"

"Can't complain, but I do." Winnie filled the entrance and then some, gently cradled a teacup size puppy in one large hand. He pulled the door wider and peeked around Cruz and smiled. "I'll be damned. Jack Pharrell." He shifted the dog to the other side as he walked out onto the stoop with an outstretched hand. "Been a long time. How the hell are you?"

"Great, Winnie." Jack accepted the offered palm. The man hadn't changed since high school, sans the beard and multitude of tattoos. "Good to see you too."

Winnie indicated toward the inside. "Come in." They followed him through a grand entryway and into a hall. "What brings you guys to my neck of the woods?"

"You call this woods?" Jack laughed, while taking in the spiral staircase, elaborates light fixtures, and modern art positioned on the walls. "This place is outstanding."

"Thanks. The wife picked it out."

"The wife?" Jack whispered to Cruz, who nodded.

"We need to talk to you for a few minutes," Cruz said. "Is now okay?"

"Now's as good as any." Winnie led them through the modern decorated hallway. "We'll go to my special room. More privacy." He fronted them into a space that rivaled a sports bar. Still holding the dog, he spread out his free arm. "My official man cave." He chuckled but appeared proud. "What'll y'all think?"

"Impressive," Jack commented.

"The wife allows me my sanctuary. The rest of this place belongs to her." Winnie switched the now docile pup back to the other hand. "Well, I do have my home office upstairs." He paused. "Let me put Remy in his kennel."

"Does Remy belong to the wife?" Jack asked.

"Nope." He scrubbed the dog's head and gazed at the pup lovingly. "This little fellow is mine. I'll be back in a few and then we'll talk. Make yourselves at home."

Neither man sat, but explored with a hint of envy. Cruz released a soft whistle. "This is some spread," he said admiring a sixty inch TV mounted on the wall, with two smaller ones positioned on either side.

"You're not kidden'." Jack ran a palm over an extended bar, coming to a halt beside a pool table situated in front of a stained glass window. Though he was never into material stuff, he had to admit Winnie's private area impressed him.

"Ya want a beverage?" Winnie asked as he reentered. He moved behind the bar. "I got a little bit of everything."

About to ask for a beer, Jack hesitated. "A Coke, if you have one."

Cruz shot Jack an odd look. "The same."

Winnie pulled the handle of a small refrigerator, brought out three soda cans, and handed them to the men. "Too early for anything stronger." He motioned at a pair of leather sofas.

"I didn't think it was ever too early for you," Cruz said to Jack.

Jack popped the Coke tab and took a lingering sip. "Cutting back."

Winnie put his can aside. "So what do you guys need from me?"

Jack cleared his throat and clutched his drink in between his hands. "We're here about a document."

"A document?"

"A possible illegal one."

Winnie looked uncertain and pulled at his chin. "Ah hah."

Jack studied his old friend. A slight trace of fear ran through him. Everyone, including the authorities was aware of Winnie's dealings though he didn't admit to anything.

"Winnie, we don't want to get you in any trouble," Cruz clarified.

"Good. Hate to think my former football teammates would turn on me." He squirmed in his seat. "So what kind of document are you guys investigating?" A gleam in his old friend's eye told Jack he already understood.

"Hazel Nutt's last will and testament," Cruz explained.

"Hmm. Heard about her untimely demise. Couldn't happen to a nicer person."

Jack's brows rose. "You're familiar with Hazel?"

"Yeah. She refused to do our wedding." He scoffed. "Didn't want to work with my kind, whatever that means. Katie Drapier agreed to help us on the side. Did us a real good job. Had the ceremony at the Hyatt. Held the reception in the ballroom. Pretty place."

"You got married at the Hyatt?" Jack queried amused.

"Wore a tux at my bride's insistence."

"Specially made in denim," Cruz interjected.

"Katie is a special lady. Nice. Doesn't act like she comes from money." Winnie smiled. "Hate for her to get railroaded into anything."

"You were aware she was being set up?" Cruz asked.

"Bank my life on it."

"Any idea of who was behind it?"

Winnie rose from his seat and strolled over behind the bar. He bent down, leaving the peak of his large back exposed. Seconds later he stood, placing a stack of papers in the middle of the counter and patted them. "I'm making homemade tortellini for supper. The wife's favorite. I need to do a quick check. Back in a minute." He grinned and nodded toward the mound before he left the room.

Cautiously, Jack and Cruz rose to their feet, and crept to the pile. They peered over the forms.

"Is this…?" Jack studied the top line. *Last Will and Testament of Hazel Nutt.*

"Hazel Nutt's original will."

Huddled together, the men skimmed the document. They looked at each other and back at the paperwork.

"So Hazel's final wishes were for the company to go to her daughter and have Katie run Weddings Fantastic. If the descendant no longer wished to own the business, it was to be offered to Katie at a cheaper price," Cruz summarized.

"Evidently she didn't make any changes before she died. This puts a whole new spin on things." A wave of agitation skated through Jack.

"It certainly does," Cruz agreed. "Here's a copy of

the forged will and signed receipt of the purchase."

Jack peered at the signature. "Vanessa," he said unsurprised.

"Makes her look guilty as hell."

"Probably should speak with Rhett Oaks too. Find out if he's involved."

Winnie returned. "Got to the stove just in time. Pasta had floated to the top and needed to be removed from the hot water." His look bounced from Jack to Cruz. "You guys discover anything useful?"

Cruz gave Jack a quick glance before he returned to Winnie. "Can we borrow this?" he pointed to the will.

"Keep 'em." Winnie waved at the papers. "That's the original. I save copies in case I need a little insurance. Kept that one down here instead of my office, cuz I figured someone might come asking. Do with it what you want. None my beeswax as long as you don't bring me any shit."

"We can avoid shit, since your name doesn't appear anywhere on here." Cruz picked up the will and folded the paper into a three sectioned crease. "We owe you one, Winnie."

The two men headed out of the man room and toward the exit. Winnie followed them.

"Keep Katie out of trouble."

"That's what we're trying to do." Jack grasped the doorknob, and gave it a gentle twist. "We'll find a way to get these into the right hands."

"Good deal." Winnie chuckled. "I'm glad somebody caught my addition."

They both stopped and eyed him.

"Caught what, Winnie?"

"Vanessa getting the house was my idea. She never questioned it, though I figured someone would."

"Didn't fit," Cruz said. "Hazel barely knew her."

"Have an expert check the signatures. They might be a tad off." He grinned.

"Glad you stopped by. Come again and we can catch up. Gotta go now, make my meatballs, and sauce before the wife gets home."

They walked outside. Relief zipped through Jack. Katie would be in the clear. He turned to his old friend. "By the way, Winnie, who did you end up marrying? Anyone we're acquainted with?"

"Marcie Patterson," Cruz said out of the side of his mouth.

Jack's expression displayed surprise. "The prom queen?"

"You weren't the only football hero she dated, Jack." Winnie laughed. "I was luckier than you though. She married me."

****

Jack and Cruz entered the plush offices of Affairs Amore. A receptionist with a trendy haircut wearing a chic ensemble glanced up from her computer as soon as they walked through the door. "May I help you?"

"We'd like to speak with Rhett Oaks." Cruz told her. "Is he here?"

"Do you have an appointment?" she skimmed an opened scheduling book spread across her desk.

"No," Jack said. "We're not—."

"You're a first," she interrupted excitedly. "We've never done a ceremony for a gay and interracial couple."

Jack raised his brows. "What?"

"Everyone says Rhett is the best." Cruz nudged him.

"He's got about ten minutes to spare right now." She rose from her chair, eagerly. "I'll tell him you're here."

"We're a couple?" Jack hissed after she disappeared.

"Chill. We're whatever it takes to get us through the door."

The room wasn't decorated as Jack imagined a wedding planner's agency to be. He expected a lavish extravaganza full of frills and lace. Instead this resembled his law offices.

The woman returned moments later, her face beaming like she'd just discovered fudge. "Mr. Oats will meet with you in the conference room. Follow me."

Cruz grinned at Jack. "Follow her, sweetie."

"Shut up," he muttered.

Rhett waited for them inside a neutrally decorated board room. Brochures and photographs were displayed over a long table. His welcoming smile faltered the moment his guests crossed the threshold.

"Kinsley," Rhett admonished the young assistant. "You've made a terrible faux pas. These gentlemen are not a couple."

Jack smiled. "But we are interracial." His expression turned stern. "Sit down, Rhett. We're here to have a discussion."

A clearly nervous Rhett slowly lowered to his seat. Jack sat on one side while Cruz took a chair on the other.

"What's the story on you buying Weddings

Fantastic?"

Hands clutched in front of him, Rhett shook his head. "No story." His tone even. "A rumor circulated that the company was to be placed on the market. I inquired about a private sale and made an offer. A good one, mind you. Hazel Nutt's daughter accepted my bid. Papers have been drawn up and signed. All nice and legal."

"Not so," Cruz informed him. "Hazel's will was forged. The business wasn't supposed to be for sale. I don't know what you paid, but you might be out some cash, and in possibly some legal trouble, to boot."

Rhett shot up from his chair. Hands on his hips he shouted, "That little bitch. I knew I shouldn't trust her."

"Vanessa King?" Jack asked.

"Of course, Vanessa King." A pale Rhett walked over to a credenza and opened the cabinet. He brought out a decanter filled with an amber liquid. He poured a generous portion into a small glass, gulping most of it in one swallow before he refilled. As almost an afterthought, he spun to his guests. "Sherry?"

Both men shook their heads. "I'm guessing you were unaware Vanessa had a duplicate, phony will made?"

Rhett brought his refilled glass to the table and returned to his seat. "Vanessa came to me the day after Hazel was killed. She said she had an inside track on the Weddings Fantastic fate. Hazel's daughter wanted to sell the company as soon as possible. Vanessa was aware I'd been looking to expand from when she worked for me. She offered to put me in touch with the offspring and act as a go between if I were willing to pay her a fee and make her Weddings Fantastic manager after the sale was complete. I was interested in acquiring the business for several reasons, so I agreed to her terms."

"That's it," Jack said doubtfully.

Rhett nervously adjusted his tie. "I may have paid Vanessa to get hired by Hazel and to destroy her establishment from the inside so that I could buy Hazel out."

Cruz's brows dropped. "You fired Vanessa for taking kickbacks, correct?"

"I did. She begged me for a second chance. My goal was to run Hazel out of business for some time. For Vanessa's redemption, I suggested she convince Hazel to employ her at Weddings Fantastic and utilize the same tactics. Common knowledge Hazel loved to pinch pennies and would love the corrupt concept. She'd even find a way to justify it."

"So you paid her to institute a bribe policy," Jack said grimly, thinking now it was clear why Katie lost her position.

"No, I compensated her to bring Hazel and Weddings Fantastic to a point where she needed to sell and I could purchase. She was doing a fantastic job, I might add."

"I suppose Hazel's death fit right into your plans," Jack commented.

Rhett nearly smiled. "It certainly didn't hurt."

"How come you didn't contact Hazel's daughter yourself?" Cruz wanted to know.

Rhett sighed. "Although Hazel and her offspring were at odds, her girl still held some kind of perverse loyalty to her mother. Since I'm Hazel's bitter enemy, her daughter considers me a foe also. She would never speak directly to me without a go between." He shrugged. "It's how things are." Rhett hesitated. "So now what?"

Jack eyed Cruz across the table, getting that Cruz was feeling the same as him. Vanessa had duped Rhett. "It'll be for the courts to decide."

Cruz rose from his seat as Jack got to his feet. They headed toward the door, but Jack stopped and turned to face a paled Rhett Oaks. Jack put a finger to his lips. "On the QT. If Vanessa finds out we're onto her, we'll know where it came from."

"I'd piss on a hotwire before I lift a pinky to help that woman."

Chapter 24

Jack entered the guesthouse from what seemed like forever. He wrestled out of his jacket, and tossed it at a nearby peg, missing the hook by a mile. Leaving the coat rest in a heap on the floor, he dodged sawhorses, and paint cans to get into the kitchen.

He wished it felt good to be home, except the mess the laborers left prevented any elation. He hoped they'd complete the work before his return. Aaron assured him they scheduled only minor renovations, but this job had grown into a full blown makeover.

Even with the chaos, this night would be his first in total solitude in a while. He looked forward to privacy and contemplation, especially since he'd completed his obligations.

He and Cruz took Hazel's authentic and phony wills to the authorities as soon as they'd left Rhett's. The rest laid in homicides hands. He received word the detectives picked up Vanessa for questioning, and they hoped for a confession by the end of the evening. After he dropped Cruz off, he'd gone to Jed and discussed the payment over his trip with Katie. Once they finalized their transaction, he headed home.

He walked to the freezer, took out a frozen pizza, and shoved the pie into the microwave, then opened the refrigerator for a beer. His mouth watered as he twisted the cap. The first he'd had in days. Drink to his lips, he stopped, and sat the beverage on the counter. He'd made a number of recent changes, no sense in backtracking. Keep moving ahead. He retrieved a water bottle and looked around the room. Next change. Find a different place. Stop freeloading. Start living his life again. Or maybe living for the first time.

Katie. He could no longer ignore his emotions. For a guy who kept relationships at bay, he was in an unusual spot. He didn't normally think beyond phase one, because there wasn't a phase two. Even with Jenna, who he thought he might have feelings, were not close to what he'd experienced with Katie. With her, he wanted to push his trust issues aside and discover the next chapter and beyond.

Except she was out of his league. He hadn't needed Jules's recap, although now he couldn't forget. If they could overlook their differences, he'd messed up beyond repair. Katie would never forgive him. With Vanessa on the verge of an arrest, she was in the clear. She didn't need him anymore. Time to fast forward.

The microwave dinged, but his hunger had disappeared. Restless, he needed to get away from the restoration clutter and the confusion inside his head. Outside, he got his duffle from his truck, and returned to dig out his favorite running shoes.

Into the evening, Jack did his best to unwind, eager to run, although the sun had set. He focused on exhaling each time his right foot slapped the walkway. His head cleared, all problems faded as his pace strengthened. Sweat poured from his skin. He pushed himself to go faster.

Hugging the corner, he entered Hazel's neighborhood. A first since he'd discovered her dead.

He soared around the block, trying to keep his mind free of the bloodied memories. The recollections became too strong. He slowed as he approached her house, stopping when he reached the front. Hundred year old oak limbs clicked above him, propelled by the cool breeze. Streetlamps lit the sidewalk, lights beamed from the surrounding homes, but this one sat dark. Other than a piece of crime tape blowing in the wind, Jack would have thought the owners were out for the evening.

A furry, flash of gray darted in front of him. Jack caught himself before he tumbled to the cement. He laughed. His feline friend was up to its old tricks. The kitten batted an object, tingling over the concrete. A glimmer from the kitty toy grabbed Jack's attention. He scowled. The cat whacked the play thing in his direction, hitting the toe of his shoe. It came to a stop in front of him. The feline scampered away, ducking underneath a hedge.

Jack bent to pick up the sparkly object and turned it over several times.

Something familiar…a memory from the murder scene flickered though his mind.

Especially in such a brutal fashion. How would…? He pocketed the item took off for the run of his life.

****

Katie carried her belongings through the parking garage, glad to be home. Her mother insisted on taking her to dinner, since her father had some business to attend. They'd had a nice, long visit. Now with a full belly, she wanted to take a hot bath, and sleep for a week. Then she'd move on to plan B. Although, she didn't want to consider the future, since she wasn't sure about the present. The police may arrest and charge her again for Hazel's murder, but Martin assured her the possibility had lessened and most likely wouldn't occur.

Then there was Jack. She still couldn't fathom his coldness at the restaurant, or he'd taken money from her father to go on the run with her. Or worse, he dined with her arch enemy at her best friend's place. She should be relieved after everything, but all she could feel was sadness. And used.

She tugged her things down the hallway, parking her luggage by the entrance while she searched her bag for keys.

"Katie?"

She swung around. "Tara?"

Tara pushed her glasses up her nose and smiled. "I've come at a bad time."

"No, you're fine," Katie lied. The last thing she wanted was company, especially someone from Weddings Fantastic, but since Tara was here, she didn't have much choice. "Just let me unlock and get my stuff inside."

Tara picked up a couple of Katie's bags and helped her haul them in after Katie pushed the door open.

"Set everything to the side," she instructed Tara. "I'll put them away later." She led Tara to the living area and motioned for her to sit. "I'm happy to visit." she paused. "But it is late and it's been a long day."

"I understand you're exhausted after your ordeal, therefore I won't take up much time." Tara removed her coat and undid her scarf before she took a seat. "I'm not sure if you're aware—Rhett Oats has purchased Weddings Fantastic."

Katie blinked in surprise. "No, I hadn't heard.

Certainly a quick turnaround."

"Yes. Some ongoing legal issues are being debated about the sale, although Rhett assures me he'll prevail."

"Legal matters?"

Tara waved her hand. "Nothing you should be concerned about." She crossed her leg and tugged at her skirt. "The reason I'm here is because Rhett wants to offer you a position—as manager of Weddings Fantastic."

Speechless, Katie's brows shot up. Manage her former company. Would going back to work for them nullify her old contract? Did she want to return?

"This is a lucrative post, and you'd maintain full control of the office," Tara continued.

Katie put a hand across her chest. "I'm so surprised."

Tara rose. "Take some time to think it over." She placed a card on the coffee table. "You can call Rhett at your convenience and discuss the particulars."

Katie stood too. "You're working for Rhett, I assume?"

Tara nodded as she picked up her coat. "Yes, I'm his personal assistant. The same job I did for Hazel, only making a lot more money."

Katie took a moment to process this information. She remembered the meeting Jules mentioned not so long ago. Another thought hit her. "What about Vanessa? Is she working for Rhett too?"

Tara's smile widened. "You've been out of the loop." She walked around the table coming to a halt next to Katie.

"I don't understand."

"Vanessa is at the police station speaking with

detectives. They believe her to be the murderer."

Katie's pulse zoomed. She stared at Tara, overwhelmed by this second piece of staggering information in the matter of seconds. "Homicide thinks Vanessa killed Hazel?"

Tara advanced toward the door. "She tampered with Hazel's last will and testament. Actually, she had a new one made where she would benefit. Pretty ingenious. You must admit she worked hard to point you out as the killer."

"I thought she had it in for me all along. But to alter an official document. Not too bright on her part."

"No. The will is Rhett's problem, although he's confident he'll resolve the difficulty."

"How'd they discover Vanessa's meddling?"

"Funny. Your -,"Tara stopped to clear her throat, "friend Jack and Cruz Zapata found the evidence. Took it to the cops and the rest as they say, is history."

Jack. He'd helped her. The huge catch in her chest released a smidgen. More questions mounted, but she'd save them for later. Katie grinned. "You've given me the best news, Tara. Thank you so much."

"You deserved some goodness for a change."

"This is so wonderful. I always figured Vanessa was a troublemaker. Did you know she broke in here and planted some incriminating evidence in my sofa for the police to find?"

"Not surprised." Tara turned to the door and touched the knob. "The woman has no conscience. I'm glad everything worked out."

Katie chuckled. "You and me, both."

Tara laughed too. "I bet you panicked when you discovered that chef's knife."

"Yes, I about…"Katie froze. "Wait. How did you know it was a chef's knife? Few people were privy to the information. The report was never made public."

Tara dropped her hand and circled to face Katie. "I guessed." She shrugged. "I mean she was stabbed. Makes sense, right?"

Katie stared at her former coworker. Anxiety gripped her chest. She wanted to believe Tara, that she'd put two and two together, but her instincts gave her a solid shove.

"Oh, Katie." Tara slowly walked toward her. "I wish you weren't so smart."

"You." Katie backed away. "You murdered Hazel. Why?"

"Do you have to ask?" Tara stopped. Arms out to her side, she lifted a shoulder. "I mean, isn't it enough that some people just need to be killed?"

"That's your reason?"

She drew a loud breath. "I drove Hazel home the day she fired you. As usual, I asked her if I should prepare dinner. She said she wasn't hungry, but wanted me to make a tuna salad sandwich for later. She also requested her customary vodka tonic. On her third drink, she started rambling about company problems, how clients kept choosing Rhett over her. Nothing uncommon. She always did this after a downing few. She was despondent your termination, and had second thoughts. Then she switched gears. She'd discovered earlier her computer had been hacked, and she'd decided someone was working for Rhett from the inside, which was how he gotten to so many of her potential customers. All of a sudden, she accused me. She claimed I had the technological knowhow to perform the treason." Tara's eyes went misty.

"You do," Katie said quietly.

"How could she believe I'd do such a thing? The woman had no concept of devotion."

"Did you sell her information to Rhett?"

"Of course not." Her voice vibrated. "I retained access to her info. That was my job. I never did anything other than what was expected of me. Which I told her, concluding with her precious Vanessa was the one doing the dirty deed. I even had proof. And you know what she did? She went off on me, wanting me to explain my motives for not coming to her with the details before."

"Why didn't you?"

Tara smiled. "Because Vanessa paid me via Rhett not to."

"Let me see if I understand. Vanessa worked for Rhett to—I presume to ruin Hazel and you knew. Rhett rewarded you financially to keep quiet, yet you still consider yourself loyal?"

"That was Hazel's response."

"What was your answer?"

"She paid me squat and I needed the money." Her grin faltered. Beads of perspiration formed across her brow. "Then she fired me. Right in the middle of making her tuna salad sandwich." Her expression turned sheepish. "I might've lost it a little after that."

"A little?"

"I suppose I need to watch my temper when I have a knife in my hand."

"And you've been trying to frame me for killing her all along."

"Nothing personal, Katie. You were the logical

choice." She picked up a large decorative pot.

Katie forced herself to sound calm. "I suppose I was." She backed away. "I won't tell, Tara. She let me go, too. I'm not sweating her death, especially with Vanessa taking the fall."

Her eyes narrowed. "I wish I could believe you." She bolted toward Katie with a lunge and swung the urn.

Katie ducked her head, and sidestepped Tara. The vase hit the wall and smashed into tiny pieces. Katie backed around the sofa, her eyes never leaving Tara. Tara bolted toward her again. She jumped aside, and bumped into the coffee table. Her body tipped sideways. Tara used her instability to her advantage, rammed into Katie, and knocked her to the floor, falling on top of her. The much heavier woman pinned her to the ground. Tara pressed her legs into hers. Katie's arms flailed. Her only defense was to slap. Tara slightly raised and balled a fist, punching Katie in the face. Blood splattered from somewhere, pain reverberated throughout her, stunning her.

Katie couldn't move. Tara grinned as she straddled Katie, removing her scarf from her shoulders, and wound it around discombobulated Katie's neck. She yanked, squeezing Katie's throat.

Katie's hands flew to the wool material, fingers grasping at the roughened threads. Tara pulled tighter. She strained to reach Tara's hands, but she held the ends too far away. She tried to roll, grappling for air. Her legs escaped Tara's hold as she kicked wildly. She fought to breathe until her passages clogged. Oxygen ceased to flow. Her arms fell to her sides, limp. Life slowly dissipated from her body. A hazy image of

Jack's face appeared before dismal blackness overcame her.

****

Jack ran to Katie's loft, knuckles ready to pound the door down. He stopped to listen. Strange sounds came from inside. This was all wrong. Forgoing a knock, he pushed at the door. Unlocked. He barreled in, hesitating at the sight.

Tara was bent over Katie with a muffler coiled about her neck, twisted tight. Katie's head flopped from side to side. Her skin white, her eyes budged from their sockets.

Without thinking, he launched into the air, reaching Tara with one jump. He snatched her hair and jerked her backwards. She screamed, stilling for a moment, and then tugged the wrap more snugly. Jack released her, grabbing her hands, trying to loosen her grip from the material.

"Let me go, you son of a bitch."

Jack didn't bother to reply. Her clutch was firm, and he couldn't mover her intertwined fingers from the yarn. Swiftly, he raised his forearm and slammed it into her, bumping her away from Katie and slackening her hold.

Katie's lifeless body collapsed to the ground. Her breathing appeared to have stopped. He stooped to find her pulse.

Tara smiled. "Too late, hero. Your girlfriend's gone."

Anger shrouded him blind. He whirled around and punched her in the stomach. She heaved as she bowed, clutching her abdomen. He dislodged her fingers, grabbed her shoulder, and flung her diagonally across the floor with added force. Momentum smashed her into a wall and toppled her to the tiles in a fleshy heap. She didn't move. Jack assumed he'd knocked her out, but at this point he could care less if he'd killed the bitch. He'd happily serve his time.

He knelt over Katie, placing his fingers on her wrist. Relief swept over him. Her heartbeat was weak, but she was alive. He unwound the scarf and held her close, silently vowing to never let her go.

****

The tightness in her throat eased. Air spread throughout her lungs. Was this death? She inhaled, deep, enjoying the fresh flow of oxygen. How could she be dead if she was able to breathe?

"Katie," came a smooth, male voice. "Everything's okay. Open your eyes."

She gradually raised her lids. She blinked, clutching her neck. She gazed up at Jack, who cradled her in his arms. "What are you doing here?" she asked in a hoarse voice.

He grinned, and held up the scarf. "Saving your ass, as usual."

Her eyes widened at the sight. She struggled to sit. Jack braced an arm against her back. "Easy. You need to stay put."

She ignored his warning and continued to rise. "Where's Tara?"

Jack bobbed his head toward the far end of the room.

Katie spun around. Her would be killer lay sprawled across the floor. She appeared to be asleep, but Katie knew better. She returned to Jack. "Is she dead?"

"I wanted to kill her." Jack glanced to where an unconscious Tara lay. "When I found her strangling you."

"How did you figure things out?"

"Hunch." He dipped a hand into his pocket, producing a shiny hair clip. One like Tara wore. "This was at Hazel's house. A cat passed it along."

"Furrsy? A big, gray boy?"

"You've met, um, Furrsy?"

"He belonged to Hazel."

"He saved your life. This," he held up the barrette, "and a comment Tara made at the murder scene."

"Why didn't you say something before?"

"With everything going on, I guess it slipped past me. The hair thing triggered the memory. I'll explain more after you're checked out."

Panic rushed through her. She turned frightened eyes to Jack and clutched his upper arm. "She tried to kill me."

"You're safe now." He wrapped his arms around her and kissed her forehead. "The police are on their way and so is an ambulance."

"Pops offer you more money to watch over me again?"

He pushed her away. "You're really going there?" He grinned. "He didn't pay me a penny. I turned the payment down."

She stared at him. "You needed the cash. Why would you do that?"

His arms tightened as bent and brushed his lips against hers. "Think about it."

Chapter 25

Katie stood at the opened barn door observing the afternoon sky. Rainclouds had moved in and threatened to steal the last morsel of daylight. A large, gray cat circled her ankles before it bounced atop a shaky, old stand and nudged her arm. She complied with the cat's request, absently scratching the feline behind the ears. The animal tilted his head back with a soft purr until the noise of fresh raindrops vaulting off the tin roof triggered the tom to leap from his perch and disappear behind a mound of haystacks.

"Only a shower, Furrsy," Katie told the feline with a grin.

A distant sound of an engine combating the muddy roads pulled her attention away from the cat. She gazed through the expected drizzle and waited for the truck's headlights to come into view. After several minutes, Jack's ancient pickup appeared, maneuvering in front of Nana's house before coming to a stop. He threw opened a door and darted into the rain.

Twitches hurdled inside her stomach. He'd given her shivers since she was a little girl. She'd never get over this man. Her insides had been in a tizzy since he'd phoned her earlier, a call she'd missed. He left a message, saying he and Cruz were about to meet with Jenna's lawyers, and he anticipated the outcome to be positive. He also stated they needed to talk and preferred to do that in private. Would she meet him at her grandmother's house?

She hoped for the best, though tried to keep her head, and expected the worst. If this was the anticlimax for them, she prayed he would let her down nicer this time. Then she'd deal with his final rejection and move forward. He jogged through the rain, triggering Katie to release a resigned sigh.

He caught sight of her as he approached and grinned. "See you got my message." He seized her arm to guide her back inside, brushing the dampness from his neatly trimmed hair with his other hand. "Damn, I'm tired of rain."

"At least it's not snow."

"There you go with your annoying optimism again." Furrsy darted from his hiding spot and ran to Jack, rubbing his ankles. "Hey ol' buddy." He bent to pick up the cat, and scratched its head.

She eyed him. "So are you going to tell me how everything went?"

He sat the feline down and grabbed her hand, directing her toward the busted bale of hay and sat, half dragging her with him. Memories of their last time here brought a heated tinge to her skin. She ducked, hoping he wouldn't notice her embarrassment. A finger slid underneath her chin, guiding her back to study the fading marks on her neck. "These look better."

"Yeah, but my eyes are black from where she punched me. Broken nose."

He looked closer. "You can hardly see them."

"The wonders of makeup." She paused. "Are you going to tell me?"

He grinned. "Tell you what?"

"I'm guessing by the twinkle in your eye, your license is no longer suspended, and you're free to practice law again?"

"Better." He loosened his tie. "Jenna dropped the lawsuits against me and my firm."

"That's wonderful, Jack." He'd waited so long for this moment. Katie was thrilled for him, although she realized the forthcoming implications. "Did she have a choice?"

"She could've continued, but if she chose to go that route, we would've brought out she's done this to three other lawyers and their companies, which is all we've discovered so far. I'm sure if we dug deeper, we'd find more."

Katie fiddled with the bottom button at the edge of her coat. "I suppose your company is ecstatic over the outcome too."

"More than ecstatic, if that's possible. They're making sure the news is spreading over the Dallas area."

"Wonderful. Not only are you exonerated, you'll come through this with your reputation in tact also."

"For the most part."

"I assume you can return to work whenever you're ready?"

"My office is waiting for me."

"Too bad you rented your house or you could move into your home. How much is left on the lease?"

"Six months, and month five is almost up."

"Seems like everything has fallen into place for you, Jack."

"For you too."

Katie sighed.

He leaned in to examine her again. "You aren't having second thoughts about letting Rhett keep Weddings Fantastic or turning down his offer to manage, are you?"

She shook her head. "After what he pulled, he doesn't deserve it, but I'm letting him keep it. My goal is to start my own company, and that's what I intend to do. As long as he released me from the five year wait, I'm happy. He even agreed to give me recommendations. If someone is needed his services on a day he's booked, he'll suggest my company as an alternative, which is huge for just starting out."

"Awfully nice of him," Jack commented wryly. "I'm still not convinced he wasn't aware of Vanessa's dirty dealings to get his hands on Weddings Fantastic."

"Me either. Since she had no proof, she's left holding the proverbial bag. I thought she'd be smarter."

"Greed does funny things to people. Her court date is set, by the way."

"Do you think she'll go to jail?"

Jack shrugged. "Depends how much she can schmooze a judge."

"Would I be considered too evil if I hoped for a female judge?"

He laughed. "After what she tried to do to you, I don't think the too evil exists." He paused. "You're upset about the whole Tara thing, aren't you?"

"How could I not be," Katie conceded. "After all, her downfall started at my condo. I'm glad she signed a full confession explaining how she killed Hazel, and her attempts to make me look guilty before she…I thought the police took away anything a person may use to take their own life."

"Sometimes things get missed. And I don't believe they deemed her suicidal. Ironic she hung herself with the same scarf she tried to kill you with." He slipped his arm around her shoulders and pulled her closer to him. "It was her decision, Katie."

Katie inhaled and nodded. "I'm aware. I've known her since grade school, Jack. I hardly called her a friend, especially after she tried to set me up, but the thought of her killing herself disturbs me."

"We should talk about happier things."

She turned to him with raised brows. The last week had been a whirlwind. Homicide investigations, Jack's hearing, and Katie involvement in sorting out the issues of Hazel's wills. They hadn't seen one another since the police and ambulances surrounded Katie's loft the night Tara tried to kill her, much less spoken of their stolen moments here in the barn. Even with the turmoil, she couldn't fall asleep without a ton of questions rolling through her head concerning Jack.

Jack cleared his throat and shifted, removing his arm from her shoulders. "I understand you're not comfortable discussing," he stopped, "certain things, but we should talk about us, Katie. Like what happened in this barn." He grinned. "Before they hauled me off, almost commando to the police station." His expression turned serious. "I prefer us not to have any unresolved issues between us so we can move forward."

Katie braced herself. Fear of his next words overwhelmed, but she had to hear, to know, so to take the next step in her life. "Okay, Jack," she said in a voice scarcely above a whisper. "I like you a lot. I have liked you since I was a little girl. Heck, I might be in love with you." She turned to look him square in the eye." How's that for not discussing certain things?"

Jack held her gaze for several seconds. He spun away to stare in front of him as if taking in her words. "Jules said you were too good for me." A pause followed. "I tend to agree."

Katie's heart stopped. Surly after everything they'd been through, he wasn't going to end this with the clichéd, "it's not you, it's me," line. "My family didn't raise me to believe anyone was better than anybody else. You know them well enough to get that."

He slightly nodded.

"Then stop trying to use that as a defense. A person can't help how they feel, Jack. If your feelings aren't the same, that's fine. Just man up and tell me."

"I don't," he said sharply. Katie bit her bottom lip to hold in a slew of emotions rising in her chest. "There is no "might" for me," he continued. "I am in love with you." She released a breath and stared at him unsure if she heard him right. "But I can't give you the life you're accustomed to right now. Most of my money went into this lawsuit. It'll be a while before I recoup. I'm working in a small firm, so I won't be making a lot just yet."

She frowned. "I thought you worked for one of the largest firms in Dallas?"

"Nope. You're not the only one who made some changes professionally. I resigned, and I am joining Cruz. He needs a partner, and I'm his man."

"Which means you're staying here, and in love with me."

"Bout sums everything up. How do you want to proceed?"

"I want to proceed with you."

He smiled. "Can you learn to live on what we make? And cut back on your shoe buying habit."

She stared at him. "What about your beer drinking habit. Have you cut back?"

"I only drink socially, and I stop at one."

She nodded and bit her bottom lip. "I don't have to get rid of the ones I have, do I?"

"No. The seven thousand you've already bought are yours. You're going to have to keep it down to a couple a hundred a paycheck for a while."

"I can do that, Jack." She glanced around. "I think. I hope."

"Be aware. The withdrawals will be painful."

"But you'll be with me, right? How can I lose?"

"You can't." He pushed her to the hay as his lips hovered over hers.

She laughed. "You're right, Jack. I can't."

A word about the author...

Debra was born in Waco, Texas and is a lifetime Texan, living in different areas throughout her adult life. She enjoyed creating stories growing up, though the idea of becoming an author did not occur to her until 2004. Since then, she has worked on learning to write while pursuing her Bachelor's Degree, which she earned in 2011 in Business.

She now resides in her hometown of Waco and is an active member of the Central Texas Chapter of Romance Writers of America where she is secretary of the group.

In her spare time she loves being with her son Stephen and his wife Astrid and daughter Hannah, and her husband Ryan. Besides writing she also enjoys traveling, shopping, a relaxing pedi, and a good plate of Mexican food.

You can visit her at:

DebraJupe@gmail.com

DebraJupe@wordpress.com

~*~

Also by Debra Jupe
and available from The Wild Rose Press, Inc.:

ECHOES IN THE WIND